Road Trouble

By Allie Everhart

Road Trouble
By Allie Everhart

Published by Waltham Publishing, LLC
Cover Design by Okay Creations
ISBN: 978-1-942781-10-3

CHAPTER ONE

"See you tomorrow." I hurry out of the garage, swinging my purse over my shoulder.

"Sage, wait!" Jesse races up to me, wiping the sweat off his face with a greasy rag.

"I can't." I keep walking. "I have to get home."

He holds my arm, stopping me. "Just one night. One dinner. Can't you give me that?"

I sigh. "Jesse, for the last time, I'm not interested in dating you. Or anyone. After everything I've been through, I need time to myself. And once I get everything figured out, I'm not staying here, which is another reason I'm not getting involved with you, or any other guy in town." I pull my arm back. "I really have to go."

He folds his arms over his chest. "I don't know why you won't agree to this. I'm not asking you to marry me. It's just dinner. You at least owe me that."

"Owe you?" I huff. "Are you serious?" I storm off toward my car, feeling the dust kicking up on my legs. This town is so freakin' dusty. I feel like I'm constantly covered in it.

"Sage, you know I didn't mean it that way," Jesse calls out from behind me.

I whip around and see him still standing in the same spot. His faded jeans and blue work shirt are covered in grease and for a moment I feel sorry for him. Stuck in this town forever, working at his dad's shop. But then he makes a stupid comment like he just did, and any sympathy I had for him is gone.

My purse slipped down my arm so I fling it back over my shoulder and say, "You mean you weren't implying I owe you sexual favors in exchange for this job?"

He starts to smile but then quickly shuts it down when he sees how angry I am. "I never said that, or implied it. I asked you to dinner. That's it."

"Yeah, and I said I'm not interested. I've told you that like a million times. If turning you down means I'm fired then..." I stop, wishing I hadn't said that. I need this job. It's the only place in town that would hire me and it actually pays well, or at least what's considered good for a town this size. I whip back around and start walking. "Bye, Jesse."

He doesn't respond. Shit. I hope I didn't just get myself fired. I don't think Jesse would do that but I don't know him well enough to say for sure. I've only worked there a month and so far Jesse and I have gotten along fine, except for when he asks me out. Every time he does, I tell him no, and then he avoids me for a day or so. After that, things go back to normal until he asks me out again. I'm getting tired of it and just want him to stop.

He needs to find someone else to go out with. It's not like he couldn't get a date. Jesse is a decent looking guy. He's average height with sandy blond hair that always looks messy but in a good way. He plays sports with his buddies on the weekends, usually basketball, so he stays in shape. It's not like he's all muscle or anything, but he's in better shape than a lot of the guys around here. And he has a cute face, with a side dimple and soft baby blue eyes. A lot of girls like that look but I prefer guys with more of a rugged, manly face.

As soon as I drive off I call Nina. I've only known her a little over a month but she's already my best friend.

"I need a new job," I say, speeding down the road, my anger putting me on edge. I'm not just angry at Jesse, but at my situation and what got me here.

"What'd he do now?" she asks, chomping on her gum. She's trying to quit smoking so she's been chomping gum like crazy.

"He asked me out again." I cradle the phone between my neck and shoulder as I crank down the window. My mom had to sell both her car and mine which is how I ended up with this rusted-out piece of metal that barely runs. It was a sign-on bonus for taking the job at the garage, or at least that's what Jesse called it. I shouldn't have accepted it, knowing there was a catch, but I really needed a car.

"That's it?" Nina asks. "I thought you were going to say he made a pass at you. Groped you. Tried to kiss you."

"No. None of that. He just wanted to go to dinner." My window stops halfway down, obviously broken, so I give up cranking on it and turn on the fan to get some air blowing. It's a scorching hot June day in Kansas, at least 100 degrees.

"Just dinner?" she asks. "Then why are you pissed?"

I wipe the sweat off my brow. "Because I'm tired of it. I'm tired of feeling like I owe him something other than my time on the job. In fact, he even said that today. He said I owed him. That's harassment. I could turn him in for that."

"And then you'd have even more enemies. If you shut down Kenny's Garage, people won't have a place to fix their car."

"Yeah, I know. That's why I'm so pissed. I can't do anything about it other than keep telling him no. I can't quit. I need this job." Hot dusty air blows out the vents. "I'm sweating to death in this car." I attempt to lift my leg off the vinyl seats but it feels like it's glued on so I give up.

"I could try to see if Aunt Lu could give you some hours at the coffee shop but—"

"No. Forget it. I don't want her losing business because of me."

"This isn't your fault, Sage. You weren't the one stealing from them."

"No, but my dad did enough damage for their hatred to spread to me. And my mom."

"You work at Kenny's Garage and people still go there."

"Because like you said, it's the only place in town to get your car fixed. I only got the job because Jesse wants to date me. When his dad gets back, I'm sure I'll get fired."

"When's he coming back?"

"I don't know. Jesse said his dad might be gone all summer. His brother's shop isn't doing well."

Jesse's brother opened a body shop in Tulsa, Oklahoma but he didn't know how to run a business so the place was about to go under. His dad is there trying to save it.

"I wouldn't worry about it," she says. "Even if you don't go out with Jesse, he wouldn't fire you. If he did, what would he look at all day?" she says with a laugh.

"Great. So I'm getting paid to be eye candy."

"Whatever works." She pops her gum and the loud cracking sound makes me cringe.

"How much longer are you going to be chewing that gum?"

"Until I can go a week without a cigarette."

"You haven't gone a week yet?"

"Are you kidding? I haven't even made it a day. I've been smoking for ten years. You can't just give it up overnight."

Nina's been smoking since she was 12. Her mom's a smoker but she said it's her boyfriend who got her hooked. He was older than her and Nina wanted to look cool so when he offered her one of his cigarettes, she smoked one, which led to another and soon she was addicted.

"You want to go out tonight?" she asks.

"I can't. I need to study." I turn down the road that goes to my house. The road is surrounded by wheat fields with a house every mile or two. It kind of freaks me out that I live by myself in such an isolated area but it's a free place to live and right now, I need free.

"You're not in school," Nina points out.

"Yes, but I will be again soon and I need to keep up on what I've already learned."

Up until a month ago, I was a college student. I was supposed to graduate next December, but then my dad decided to skip town with my college fund, along with all the money I'd added to it over the years. Now I'm broke, completely broke, so college is on hold until I save up enough to go back. I was so close, just a few more classes and I would've been done.

"Why is it so freakin' hot out today?" I yank on the window handle. It won't budge.

"We need to go out tonight. Why don't we—"

"Shit!" I swerve into the other lane and hit the brakes, my body lurching forward before the seatbelt finally catches me and pulls me back.

"What is it?" Nina asks. "What happened?"

I check my rearview mirror and see a guy walking his motorcycle on the side of the road. His head is down, like he didn't even realize I almost ran him over.

"Sage, say something," Nina's voice is urgent. "Are you okay?"

"Yeah. Just a little freaked out. I didn't see this guy."

"What guy?"

"There's some guy in the road. His motorcycle must've broke down. He's walking it somewhere."

"Where would he be taking it? There's nothing out there."

"I don't know."

"Are you home now?"

"No. I'm stopped on the road." My eyes haven't left the rearview mirror as I continue to look at the guy with the motorcycle. He's tall, with dark hair, wearing a white button-up shirt and light-colored pants. People around here wear worn jeans and faded t-shirts, or flannel shirts if the weather's cold. This guy looks like he just walked out of a frat house at some Ivy League college.

"Get out of there," Nina says. "Go home."

"What about the guy? Maybe he needs help."

"Or maybe he's a psychopathic serial killer on the run. Or maybe he just escaped from prison with a stolen motorcycle and now he—"

"He doesn't look like a serial killer," I say, as I watch him get closer. He's still a ways from my car but he has to know I'm here, so why isn't he looking up?

"And what exactly does a serial killer look like?" Nina asks.

"I don't know, but this guy doesn't even seem interested that I've stopped so I doubt he plans to kill me."

"Not yet. But wait until—"

"I'm gonna go ask him what he's doing."

"What?" Nina yells through the phone. "Sage, no! You don't even know this guy and you're on a deserted road."

"With my friend on the phone." I slowly back up the car. "If you hear me screaming for my life, call the cops."

"Would you please just go to your house and forget this guy? I don't want to listen to him kill you."

"He's not going to kill me." I back up until I'm just in front of him, then put the car in park. I undo my seatbelt and reach over to the passenger's side door. I check that it's locked as I roll the window down. "Hey!" I yell out the window as the guy walks up beside the car.

He says nothing, his head still down. Is he deaf? Even a deaf person would look up when a car stopped beside him.

"Hey!" I yell again.

He continues to ignore me and keeps walking. As he passes by the front of my car, I see his shirt is soaked with sweat. He must be dying in this heat, pushing that heavy motorcycle. There's a large green duffle bag strapped to the seat, which also looks heavy.

"Hey, wait!" I say, getting out of the car. I go around it and meet up with him as he walks. "You need some help?"

He ignores me. What is *with* this guy? Maybe he IS a serial killer, in which case I shouldn't have gotten out of my car. And left my cell phone in it. Shit.

I'm about to go get it but then the guy finally speaks.

"I'm fine," he mutters, his head still down.

"Your motorcycle broke down?" I ask.

He says nothing and keeps walking.

I look back at my car, which is now several feet away. Part of me wants to keep following this guy to figure out what his story is, but the other part of me wants to get the hell out of here. I don't see any weapons on him but he could be hiding one in his duffle bag.

I run back to my car and grab my phone from the seat.

"Sage?" I hear Nina say. "Are you there?"

"Yeah, I'm here."

"What happened?"

"He won't talk to me."

"So you're going home?"

"Not yet." I rush to catch up with the guy.

"Sage, stop following that guy and get your ass home!" I hear Nina yell. I hold the phone down at my side as I approach the guy.

"You need a ride?" I ask, but then regret asking. I can't give a strange guy a ride in my car! What was I thinking?

Luckily, he doesn't take me up on the offer. He says nothing and starts walking faster, like he's trying to get away from me. Maybe he thinks *I'm* the serial killer.

"So where exactly are you going?" I ask, glancing back at my car. I'm getting more and more nervous the farther I get away from it. I hear the faint sound of Nina's voice coming from my phone, which I'm holding at my side, pressed against my shorts to muffle her words. I don't want the guy to hear her yelling at me.

"Do you talk?" I ask with a nervous laugh. "Or why are you so—"

"Stop," he says in a harsh tone as he finally stops walking. "Just stop talking. Stop following me. And stop asking me questions."

Now that he's looking at me, I'm finally able to see his face, and damn, he's hot. Manly-hot, not boyish-hot like Jesse. He looks about the same age as Jesse, maybe 24 or 25, but this guy has a maturity about him that makes him seem much older than that. It's the way he carries himself; the formality of his stance, the stiff upright positioning of his head, the intense look in his eyes as he stares at me.

I'm staring right back, at those deep brown eyes, those full lips, that sharp jaw.

"Now who's the one not listening?" he scolds.

I take a step back, flustered. "Um, yeah, sorry. I heard you. I'm just surprised."

His brows draw together. "Surprised by what?"

My nerves relax slightly and I stand up straighter. "I'm surprised you won't accept my offer to help. You're clearly struggling to get this bike to wherever it is you're going. It's like a hundred degrees out here. Your shirt is soaked."

He keeps his eyes on mine as he rips open his shirt, buttons flying everywhere. He yanks it down each arm and tosses it on the ground.

"Happy now?" he asks with not even a hint of a smile.

I don't answer, my gaze now stuck on the muscles that outline his chest. He's not overly muscular. His arms aren't bulging biceps. Just lean sculpted muscle. The same goes for his chest, and his well-defined abs. I do a quick count. Yep, it's a six pack.

"Are we done here?" he asks.

My eyes meet up with his. "Yes. I mean, no. You still haven't answered my question. Do you need help? Do you want me to call someone? Well, I assume you have a cell phone but—"

"I don't need help." His eyes narrow. "Unless you know of someone who could get rid of the annoying girl who won't leave me alone."

I take a moment to process what he meant, then say, "You're kind of an ass, you know that?"

He smirks. "Not kind of. I AM an ass. Now leave me alone." He turns and starts walking again.

This time I don't follow him. I bring my phone to my ear. "Did you hear that?"

"I didn't hear *anything*! Did you stuff your phone in your pocket? What's going on? Are you okay?"

"I'm fine," I say as I watch the guy walk away.

"What happened with the guy?"

"He's a self-inflated, egotistical asshole," I say loud enough for him to hear, "who doesn't deserve my help."

"Damn, girl, you're pissed. What'd he say to you?"

"That he's an asshole," I call out, still loud enough for him to hear. "As if I couldn't tell."

"Sage, stop provoking him and get out of there."

"I'm not provoking him. He's walking away. He wants to be left alone."

"Then why are you still standing there? Get in your car and drive the hell away."

She has a good point. Why am I still standing here? Watching the asshole walk away?

I should leave, but I can't seem to look away from him. He's mysterious. And hot. Damn, he's hot. Not just his looks, but his demeanor. His smooth deep voice. The way he carries himself. He seems sophisticated.

That's why I'm still standing here. Because I'm trying to figure this out. It doesn't make sense. Why would a hot, sophisticated guy be walking a motorcycle along a country road in rural Kansas?

CHAPTER TWO

"Sage, are you in that damn car yet?" I hear Nina yell from my phone.

"I'm going," I say, my eyes still on the mystery man.

"I want you to stay on this phone until you're in your house, safely locked inside."

"Yeah, got it," I tell her, getting in the car. I set the phone down and start the engine, then slowly drive down the road. As I approach the guy, I stop and yell out the window in a sarcastic tone, "Nice meeting you! My name's Sage, by the way!"

He ignores me so I drive off, my car kicking up dust at him.

Nina's voice bellows from my phone. "Why the hell did you tell him your name?"

I put the phone to my ear. "I'm not worried about him. He's not a psychopath."

"And you know that based on what? A five second encounter with the guy? He wouldn't even talk to you. He's probably bat-shit crazy!"

"He's a little odd but he's not crazy. Besides, he's not sticking around. He's heading away from town. I doubt I'll ever see him again."

"You need to be more careful. Being in a small town doesn't mean you're safe. You can know someone for years and then find out—" She stops suddenly, then mutters, "Sorry."

"It's fine."

"I wasn't talking about your dad," she says, rushing her words. "I was just talking in general. I mean, like when—"

"Nina, it's fine. You don't have to explain. I know what you meant."

She's quiet for the rest of the drive. I am too, my mind now on my dad. I'm trying to forget what he did, but unfortunately, living here is a constant reminder.

My dad took off when I was six, right after my parents' divorce. I didn't see or hear from him again until my junior year of college when he showed up at my dorm, begging me to let him back into my life.

He looked different than I remembered. He was wearing a shirt and tie and a tailored suit. His dark hair had speckles of gray and was cut shorter than I'd ever seen it. His hair had always been on the long side and kind of messy. And I'd never seen him wear a suit. When I was a kid, he worked a variety of odd jobs, none of which required wearing a suit.

When he showed up I was tempted to tell him to leave, thinking he didn't deserve a second chance after taking off the way he did. But I desperately wanted him back in my life so I went to dinner with him and listened to him tell me his reasons for leaving. He gave me a sob story about how he was lost and confused and needed to go find himself before he could be a father again. His words were all bullshit but at the time I believed him. I also believed his story about owning a successful investment firm. Turns out it was only successful for him, not the people who invested with him. They all ended up broke, including me.

My own father stole from me. He convinced me he could take my college fund and double it. At first I didn't trust him, but over the course of that year, he not only gained my trust, but also my mom's. In fact, she and my dad started dating again, and just last April, he asked her to marry him for the second time. They set a wedding date for the fall and my dad moved into my mom's house, a small but nice house just outside Kansas City.

Soon after their engagement, my dad convinced me to give him access to my savings account so he could invest the money. By then, I had no hesitations. He'd been back in my life for almost two years and I figured if my mom trusted him and forgave him, I should too. My mom, who has always been frugal and managed to save a lot over the years, also handed over her money to my dad. The fact that he could convince both of us to trust him that much after he disappeared for all those years just shows what a great liar he is and how skilled he is at the art of persuasion.

Everything came crashing down in May, my last day of finals. I was thrilled to be done and was getting ready to go out and celebrate with friends at a club near campus. As I was picking out what to wear, my mom called and asked if I'd talked to my dad. I told her I hadn't heard from him for a few days. She said she hadn't either and that he'd taken off on a business trip to Miami and hadn't checked in with her or returned any of her calls. Worried something happened to him, she called all the hospitals in Miami but none had any records of him being there. She was about to go to the police station to report him missing but then the police showed up at her house.

My college is only a couple hours away so I raced home to be with my mom. An investigator from the police department was there when I arrived. I sat beside my mom on the couch as we listened to the investigator tell us that everything my dad had told us was a lie. His investment firm was all a scam. He convinced people to give him their money, promising them a big return on their investments but instead, he stole it all, including all the money my mom and I had given him.

We were both stunned. We didn't have a clue he'd been conning us. Nobody did, until people started calling and asking for their money. Eventually the police got involved and that's how they ended up at our door.

"You there yet?" Nina asks as I pull into the garage.

"Yeah. You can hang up now." I get out of the car.

"Did you close the garage door?"

"I'm doing it now." I push the button and go in the house. "Why are you being so paranoid?"

"Because I don't like the fact that some strange guy is just walking down the road not heading anywhere."

"He's heading somewhere. We just don't know where."

"There's nothing out that way but farm fields and a few houses, one of which is yours. What if he shows up there?"

"Then I'll tell him to go away. He made it clear he didn't want my help." I set my purse on the kitchen counter and open the fridge. "Damn. I forgot to stop at the store. I have nothing for dinner."

"Let's go out."

"I don't feel like it. I think I'm just going to stay in." I shut the fridge and go in the living room to sit down.

The house I'm staying at belongs to my mom's friend, Lorraine Driscoll. She's a realtor and sold us our house years ago. It was the house I grew up in and I loved it. Last winter my dad convinced my mom to sell the house and invest the profits with him, which she did. She moved into a rental house that was a lot smaller and not as nice. After a few months, she was tired of renting and told my dad she wanted her money back to buy a new house. A few days later he disappeared. So he not only took her money. He also took her house.

Around that same time, Lorraine's aunt died and left her this house. It's in a small town, about an hour from Kansas City. She offered to let my mom and me stay here for free until we figured out what to do next. We took her up on the offer and decided to live here for the summer, but just as we were about to move, my mom got a call from a friend of hers in New York who knew about her situation and offered her an opportunity she couldn't pass up.

My mom is a high school art teacher, but when she was younger, she was an up-and-coming artist. She was selling her paintings and starting to become known. A gallery owner in New York told her she had real potential and that if she moved there, he would introduce her to the right people who could further her career. But she turned him down because by then, she was married and pregnant with me. She wanted me to grow up in a house with a yard, not a high rise condo in Manhattan.

She gave up her dream, so when her friend called, offering to let her create some pieces for her gallery, I told her to go. She has the summer off from teaching so now is a great time to do this, and hopefully it'll get her mind off what my dad did to us. Plus, she's staying for free with her friend and if she sells a painting or two, she could get a lot of money. Her friend's gallery caters to the super rich who are always looking for the next great artist.

She was reluctant to leave me here for the summer but I convinced her I'd be fine. But then I actually moved here and found out some of the families in town had invested with my dad. Turns out, he'd been selling his fake investments to people in small farm towns throughout the state. He's originally from a small town so he used that to his advantage, telling people he was no different than them, which is why they could trust him.

Now I'm paying for what he did. Living in a town where people hate me because my dad stole from them. My mom doesn't know that. If I told her, she'd worry and move back here in her mom-driven need to protect me, even though I'm an adult who is fully capable of handling all the rude comments and dirty looks.

When my mom asks about the town, I tell her the people here are nice and that I've made friends. At least the friends part is true, even though it's only one.

"C'mon, Sage. It's my night off and I'm bored. And when I'm bored I smoke. You'll be supporting my health if you agree to go out with me."

"Nice try." I yawn, tired from a day of filing invoices. Jesse is the worst when it comes to keeping track of stuff. He has no idea which customers have paid and which haven't, or what bills are due and when. He just fixes cars. If it weren't for Helen, the old lady bookkeeper who works there, and me, who replaced the receptionist who quit when she had her baby last spring, Kenny's Garage would be out of business by the time Kenny gets back. Kenny has the business brains, his sons don't.

"What's that supposed to mean?" Nina asks.

"It means there's a good chance you'll smoke even if we go out. You're just using the boredom excuse to get me to go out tonight."

"Is it working?"

I take a moment to consider it. Going out would be better than being here. This house is really depressing. It still has all the stuff from Lorraine's elderly Aunt Mabel, including the furniture, which she must've bought when she moved in sixty years ago. The upholstery is covered in layers of dust that can't be vacuumed away, making the whole house smell dusty and old. Or maybe it's death I'm smelling. Mabel died on the couch, which is why I never sit on it. Instead I sit on one of the chairs but both are tearing apart at the seams and have sunken seat cushions. At least the TV is fairly new but I can't afford cable so there isn't much to watch.

"Okay, I'll go," I tell Nina. "I'm tired but I don't want to be here right now. This place is depressing."

"Hell, yeah, it is. The old lady died there. I don't know how you sleep there. If Butthead ever moves out, you can come live with me."

Butthead is her younger brother. He's 19 but acts more like 13. He's a busboy at one of the restaurants in town and keeps telling Nina he's getting his own place, but then he never does.

"I have a feeling Jeremy's going to live with you forever."

"Then I'm moving out and he'll have to find another roommate."

"So where do you want to go?"

"Skeeter's. It's two for one night."

"I'm not really up for drinking tonight." Truthfully, I could use a drink but I don't have money for drinks. Every dime I make has to go for essentials, like food, or into my college fund.

"It's two for one burgers. The drinks are regular price."

"Sounds perfect. I'll meet you there. I just need to take a quick shower."

"I'll head over there now and have a beer. Don't bail on me or I'll show up at your door."

"I'll be there. I promise."

After a quick shower, I put on a denim mini skirt and black tank. Skeeter's isn't a place you dress up for. Even though it serves food, it's more of a bar than a restaurant. A lot of the locals hang out there so it's possible someone will harass me because of my dad, but if so, Nina will kick their ass. She's lived here her whole life and knows most everyone's deepest, darkest secrets so she's not someone you want on your bad side. As long as she's with me, people will leave me alone.

At seven I text her I'm on my way. As I'm grabbing my keys off the kitchen counter, an image of that guy pops in my head. What if he's still walking? He's got to be dying of thirst. I grab a bottle of water from the fridge, then go out to my car.

It's still light out, and as I'm driving I try to calculate where he might be right now. When I saw him, he was probably five miles from my house. I'm sure he's walked at least a mile or two since then.

Driving past Old Man Miller's house, I stop suddenly because I swear I just saw that guy in Miller's driveway. Maybe that's his grandson. I didn't think Mr. Miller had any kids. Then again, I've only met him one time and we didn't talk long so I don't know that much about him.

Against my better judgment, I back the car up and pull into Miller's driveway. The guy has his back to me, but turns when he hears the loud rumbling engine of my car as it pulls up beside him.

"Hey," I say, putting the car in park. Since I can't get my window all the way down my view of him is partially blocked through the dusty glass.

He sighs. "Now what?"

"I was driving by and saw you here." I turn the car off and get out so I can see him without the glass obstruction. Damn, he's hot. Even sweaty and covered in dirt, he still looks good. "Are you Mr. Wilson's grandson?"

He wipes the sweat off his brow with the back of his hand and glares at me. "Is everyone in this town as nosy as you?"

"I'm not nosy. I'm just being friendly. We're neighbors so I thought I should stop by and say hello."

His brows rise. "We're neighbors?"

Shit. I probably shouldn't have said that. If he's some crazy drifter with no relation to Miller, I don't want him knowing where I live.

I catch his eyes lowering to my body, just a quick glance, first at my tight tank then down at my short skirt.

His eyes dart back up at my face. "Which house?"

"It's a few miles down the road," I say, trying to be vague, but there are so few houses out here that he could easily figure it out. "Mr. Miller didn't mention his grandson was coming to town."

"I'm not his grandson, not that it's any of your business." He looks to the side, and I'm pretty sure I saw an eye roll.

"It's my business if you're here without Mr. Miller's permission. He's a friend and friends look out for each other."

The guy stares at me, that intense stare like he gave me earlier. "If he's such a good friend, where is he right now?"

"In his house." I point to it, having no idea if Mr. Miller is actually in there. "Which you would know if you were really here to see him."

"I'm not here to see him. And he's not in his house."

"Then where is he?" I ask, feeling more and more nervous as the guy stares at me with those deep brown eyes. It makes me want to look away, but I don't. I hold his gaze, and for some unexplained reason, feel something stirring inside me. I've heard the body can confuse danger with arousal so maybe that's why I'm feeling this way, although if that's true, it means he's dangerous. But I don't think he is, which means the arousal I'm feeling is because I'm attracted to him. Why would I be attracted to a guy who's has been nothing but rude to me?

"He's in Florida," the guy says. "At a condo on the beach."

"Florida?" I ask confused. "Are you sure? Because Mr. Miller isn't the type of person who travels. In fact, I doubt he's ever left Kansas."

The guy glances over at the deserted road. "He came into some money. Thought he'd take a trip. An extended vacation." He looks back at me. "While he's gone, I'm renting his house."

Now I'm even more confused. "Why would you rent his house? There's nothing to do in this town and there aren't any jobs. Why would you move here?"

"I have to go." He walks off.

"Wait." I run up to him. "What's your name?"

He pauses, his eyes darting to the side. "Kyle."

"Kyle *what*?"

He glares at me. "Kyle. That's it."

He wipes the sweat from his forehead and as he does, I notice a long red line along his left temple and a bump on the side of his head. The red line is dried blood but it looks like the cut is starting to break open, blood bubbling along the seam.

"Did you get in a fight?"

"Seriously, do the questions ever end? Are you the town gossip or what?"

"Your head. It looks like it hurts. I just..." I reach my hand up to touch his temple and he grabs my wrist.

"Stop." His tone is softer now, and unexpected. When he grabbed my wrist, I thought he'd yell at me to go away. But instead he shuts his eyes a moment and takes a breath. He's still holding my wrist but his grip is gentler.

"Please." He opens his eyes and looks at me, but instead of that intense stare he gave me before, his gaze is softer, kinder, and suddenly, any fear I had of him is gone. He's not a killer. Or a criminal. I know because my gut is telling me so. And after what I've been through with my dad, I trust my gut more than my head.

From the moment my dad showed up at my dorm room, I knew there was something not right with him. All those months when he was trying to reestablish a relationship with my mom and me, he smiled a lot and said the right things, but his words never felt sincere and he never looked us in the eye. Those should've been clues he was lying to us, along with the gut feeling I always had that told me something was up with him. But my head convinced me I could trust him. I guess because I so desperately wanted to.

But this guy? Kyle? He's not bad. He may be angry and have bad manners and act like a complete ass, but he's not bad. I know he's not. I can feel it.

CHAPTER THREE

"You need to go." Kyle releases my wrist and his arm drops to his side.

"I have a first aid kit in my car." I point to his temple. "Would you consider letting me bandage that up?"

He hesitates. "I don't think that's a good idea."

"I'll be quick. I promise." I look around the yard. "We don't even have to go inside. We can do it out here." Before he can answer I point to a tree stump. "Go sit over there. I'll be right back."

Surprisingly, he does as I told him and walks over to the stump.

I hurry to my car and grab the kit from the floor of the back seat. Then I grab the water bottle I brought him.

When I reach the tree stump, he's sitting down, looking exhausted, leaning forward with his forearms resting on his knees.

"Here." I hold out the water bottle.

He takes it. "Why did you bring me this? How'd you know you'd even see me again?"

"I didn't. But just in case, I wanted to bring you water. It's too hot to be out here walking for miles without water."

I sit beside him and open the first aid kit, feeling Kyle's eyes on me the entire time.

"I thought you were afraid of me," he says.

"Why would I be afraid of you?" I rummage through the box, searching for the antibiotic cream.

"Guy walking along a deserted road. Covered in dirt. Hasn't shaved in days. Looks like he's just been in fight. You weren't afraid of that?" His tone lightens, like he's teasing me.

I smile slightly. "Okay, yes, I was a little afraid, but I'm not now."

"Why not?" He turns to me. "Why are you doing this? Why are you helping me? A guy you don't even know who could easily hurt you."

My muscles stiffen at his words, but then relax. "You won't hurt me."

"You're right. I won't. But you didn't know that when you stopped. So why'd you do it? Why are you helping me?"

"Because you need it." I take a bandage out of my box along with the antibiotic cream. "Plus, you're kinda cute."

He laughs. I like his laugh. It's deep and real and makes me smile.

"Because I'm cute? Seriously?"

I shrug. "I didn't say it was the only reason."

When I look up, I see a smile on his face. A wide, friendly smile that shows off his sparkling white teeth and lights up his formerly serious face.

"Are you blind?" He points to himself. "Have you seen me?"

I laugh. "I'm not blind. Never mind. I shouldn't have said it."

"I'm a filthy mess and I'm sure I smell. If this is what you consider cute, I'd hate to see ugly."

"Well, consider this. We're in a very small town where there isn't much selection when it comes to men so your pool of competition is small."

"Ah." He nods in understanding. "Now it makes sense. New guy in town? Something new to look at?"

"Exactly. And I get the feeling you clean up okay."

"Trust me, this is the worst I've ever looked."

It makes me wonder what led to him looking this way. Why he ended up along the side of the road. Why he's renting this house in the middle of nowhere. I want to ask him about all those things, but it's not the time. He's finally talking to me, letting his guard down a little. If I ask him anything too personal, I'm afraid he'll shut down again.

I grab a wet wipe. "Let's get this cut fixed before you have blood running down your face."

He turns toward me, leaning his head down slightly so I can reach.

"Can I touch you without you throwing a fit like you did before?"

He smiles. "I didn't throw a fit, but yes, go ahead."

I gently move his hair aside and blot at the bloody cut.

He cringes slightly.

"Does it hurt?" I ask.

"Just stings. I'll be fine."

I continue to blot the blood, and when it's all wiped away, I see it's more of a gash than a cut, which is probably why it keeps bleeding.

"You should see a doctor," I tell him. "You need stitches."

He backs away. "I don't need stitches."

"Hey, I'm not done yet." I set the wet wipe down and grab the antibiotic cream. "Get back here."

He leans forward again. "Can you hurry this up?"

"Why? You have someplace you need to be?"

"No, but I'm tired. And I'm covered in dirt. I want to shower and go to bed."

The terse tone he used earlier is back. His guard is going up again. I can feel it.

"Sorry," I mutter as I dab the ointment on. "I'll try to go faster."

"No." His hand wraps gently around my wrist. "I don't want to rush you. Take your time."

"But you just said—"

"I know. I shouldn't have said it. I'm sorry. I'm just...uncomfortable." His eyes drop to the ground.

"With me?"

He releases my wrist. "With this."

"With what?"

"You doing this. Helping me. Without..."

"Without what?"

His eyes lift back to mine. "Without wanting something."

"What would I want?"

He shakes his head. "I don't know. Never mind." He stands up. "Anyway, thanks for your help."

"I'm not finished." I take the bandage and stand up, facing him. "Hold still." I peel the strip off the bandage and slowly and carefully apply it over his cut, which has started to bleed again. "I really think you need stitches."

He grabs my wrists.

"What are you—"

"I don't need stitches," he says as he takes my hands from his face and lowers them to my side.

"I think you do."

"Are you a doctor?"

"No, but you shouldn't still be bleeding like that. That cut's at least a few days old."

He slowly releases my wrists. "I'll be fine."

"And what if you're not?"

"Then I'll go find my nosy new neighbor and see if she'll help me again."

I stifle a laugh. "I'm not nosy. Just wait until you meet the other people in town. Talk about nosy. Except they don't directly ask you anything. Instead they make up their own stories based on rumors and gossip." I roll my eyes. "It's what I hate most about living here."

"So why do you live here?"

"Long story."

"How long have you been here?"

"Now who's the nosy one?" I ask kiddingly.

"How long?"

"A few weeks."

He nods. "Earlier you acted like I was crazy for moving here, and yet you did the same thing."

"Only because I had to," I mumble.

"The reason being..." He waits for me to answer. When I don't, he says, "Part of that long story?"

"Yeah. I'll tell you later. Actually, I'm sure someone in town will tell you before I do."

"People in town know?"

My phone dings. It's a text from Nina, asking where I am. "I have to go."

"Hot date?" he asks with a smile.

I smile back. "You ask too many questions."

As we've been talking, we've somehow managed to get closer, standing just a few inches apart.

"So you have to go," he says, his eyes locking on mine.

I stare back at him, my heart racing at record speed, my breath struggling to catch up. There's an undeniable attraction between us, but it's more than that I'm feeling. There's this spark, like the spark of electricity you feel in the air right before a storm. I felt it when we met and I feel it again now.

If he wasn't so sweaty and dirty, I think he might kiss me right now. It'd be completely inappropriate and extremely bold, but Kyle seems like someone who takes risks and doesn't hold back.

"I have to go meet someone," I tell him. "Besides, you don't want me to stay. Just a few minutes ago you were telling me to go away."

"True." He pauses, leaning even closer to me. "So go."

"I will." I'm breathing hard, staring into his eyes, feeling the heat from his body.

This sounds completely crazy, but I really want to kiss him. I know I shouldn't, but I'm clearly not thinking straight because I lean over to do it, then stop suddenly when my phone dings. I look down at it and see another text from Nina. I can't read all the words but I see lots of exclamation points.

"Shit." I quickly text, *Be there soon!* Then I gather up my first aid supplies and stuff them in the box.

"See you later." I turn and walk back to my car.

Kyle catches up to me. "Hey, where do you live?"

"Down the street." I toss the box in the back seat.

"I mean, which house? What's your address?"

I shut the door and lean against the car. "Why do you want to know?"

He shrugs. "In case I want to borrow a cup of sugar."

"You bake?" I ask, trying to suppress a laugh.

"No. But maybe I'll start."

"Then I'd suggest getting your supplies at Vindervott's."

He gives me a funny look. "What the hell is that?"

"The grocery store in town. It's small but has everything you need."

"Including magic wands?"

I pause to figure out what he means, then laugh. "Not Voldemort's. Vindervott's. It's named after the guy who opened it like a hundred years ago. Some other guy owns it now." I smile. "But I liked your Harry Potter reference."

"You read the books, I assume?"

"A long time ago. I'm a little surprised that *you* did."

"You don't think I read?"

"It's not that. I just didn't think you'd read Harry Potter. It doesn't seem like your genre, not that I know you well enough to tell. It's more of a guess."

"You're right. It's not what I'd typically read. But I read them to my—" He stops suddenly.

"Your what?"

He pauses, then says, "Never mind. You should get going." He opens the car door for me.

"Thanks," I say as I get in.

"Have fun on your date." He gives me a wink. "Hope he's as cute as *I* am."

"I can't make that judgment until you're cleaned up and I can actually see you from behind all the dirt."

"I'll work on that." He backs away as I start the engine.

"Bye, Kyle," I say as I pull out of the driveway.

He gives me a wave, then turns and walks back to the house.

After talking to him, I now have even more questions about who he is and why he's here. But I have a feeling I may never find out. He seems like a very private person.

When I get to Skeeter's I see Nina sitting in a booth, looking at her phone. There's a bottle of beer in front of her and a basket of peanuts.

I go over and sit across from her. "Hey."

"What the hell took you so long?"

"I made a quick stop." I grab a menu from the holder on the table.

"Where?"

"What?" I pretend to be engrossed in my menu. I was hoping she wouldn't ask where I went.

"Where'd you stop?" She sets her phone down on the table.

"Mr. Wilson's house."

"Wilson isn't there. He went to Florida for the summer."

I look at her. "How'd you know that?"

"Everyone knows. Patty was there when Wilson was telling Ralph about it at the barber last week."

Patty is Ralph's wife. Ralph owns the barber shop and Patty sometimes works there, cleaning up or answering the phone. She's the biggest gossiper in town.

"How come I didn't hear about it?"

"You never come into town."

"That's not true. I'm here all the time. I work in town. I go to the grocery store. I hang out with you."

"Whatever. So anyway, why were you at Wilson's house?"

"Because the new guy was there."

"What new guy?"

"The one who was walking on the road."

"The serial killer?"

"He's not a serial killer. I stopped and talked to him and he seems like a nice guy."

"Just a few hours ago you called him an asshole."

"Yeah, well, he didn't make the greatest first impression, but in his defense, he was hot and tired and dying of thirst."

"Wait." She grabs my menu and sets it down. "You like this guy?"

I laugh. "No. I mean, not like you're implying."

"You're lying." She points to me. "You should see your face right now. You're blushing."

"I'm not blushing. I'm flushed from the heat. It's like a thousand degrees outside and my car doesn't have air. I can't even get the windows down all the way."

She sits back in the booth. "I can't believe you stopped and talked to him. By yourself. Are you trying to get yourself killed?"

"I'm telling you, he's not a killer."

"You don't know that. It's not like killers come out and announce that they're killers. And even if he's not, it's still not safe to go up to some guy you found wandering down a deserted road."

"I know that, but I can assure you I was completely safe. I had my phone and keys with me the whole time. If I had to get away, I could have."

"Not if he held a gun on you."

"He didn't have a gun. I didn't even go in the house with him. We just stood in the driveway and talked."

"And what did the elusive stranger slash serial killer say to you?"

"He said he's renting Miller's house for the summer."

"Where's he from?"

"He didn't say."

"Why'd he move here?"

"I don't know."

"What's he do for work?"

"I'm not sure."

She sighs. "So you basically know nothing about him."

"He's not that talkative."

"Because he's hiding shit. Probably dead bodies."

I roll my eyes. "He's not a killer. And you have to stop calling him that or people in town are going to believe you."

"You should've invited him to come with you tonight so I could check him out."

"He was tired and sweaty from walking in the heat. He wouldn't have agreed to go out."

"See if he'll go out with us tomorrow. I'm sure he'll get bored sitting around that house all day."

"I can ask but I get the feeling he wants to be left alone."

"So he's a loner. A lot of psychopaths are loners."

I just shake my head as I look at the menu.

"How old is he?"

"I'd guess around 24 or 25. Can we stop talking about Kyle and order some food? I'm starving."

"Kyle? That's his name?"

"Yes. And if you say that's the name of a killer I'll—"

"Ha! You're wrong! I wasn't going to say that." She takes a peanut from the basket and cracks open the shell. "What's his last name?"

"Why? So you can search for him on the internet?"

"Obviously." She pops a peanut in her mouth. "So what is it?"

"He didn't say. But I'm telling you, the guy seems completely harmless. He was a total asshole at first, but as I was talking to him I found he has this whole other side of him. This sweet, vulnerable side."

"It's an act," she says, grabbing another peanut. She shoves the basket at me. "Have some. Lacey said the kitchen is slow tonight. May take an hour to get our burgers."

"Then we should order." I search for a waitress.

"I already did," Nina says. "You're getting a bacon cheeseburger."

I smile. "That's perfect. Exactly what I was going to get."

"And it's on me since I made you come out tonight."

"You didn't make me. And you don't have to pay for my meal."

"It's two for one. I'm only paying for mine. Yours is free." She pops another peanut in her mouth. "Tomorrow you can buy me a drink at the bar." She grins. "It's two for one at Healy's."

"Deal." I crack open a peanut.

"Shit, look who's here." Her eyes shift to the left.

"Who?" I follow her eyes.

"Don't look!" I feel a sharp kick to my foot under the table.

"Nina! That hurt." I tuck my foot under me.

"That's what you get for looking!"

"I don't even know what we're talking about."

She leans forward and lowers her voice. "Josh is here."

"Josh who?"

"Josh!" she whisper screams. "The guy I went out with last year."

"I have no idea who that is. You never told me about anyone named Josh."

"He's the guy I met when I tried online dating."

"Oh." I nod. "Now I remember. The cop, right?"

"Yeah. He lives in Kansas City."

"What's he doing here?"

"Probably wanted a burger. When we were dating, he said these were the best burgers he'd ever had."

"He'd seriously drive all that way for a burger?"

She looks at me. "Food and sex. That's all that matters to guys. I had a friend who dated this idiot who drove all the way to Chicago for pizza."

"Maybe Josh is here to see *you*." I smile, because out of the side of my eye, I see a guy approaching our table, who I'm guessing is Josh.

"Believe me," she laughs, "he's not here to see me. Not after I dumped him the way I did."

"It *was* pretty harsh," he says, now standing beside our booth. He's average height but in good shape; lean and muscular. He's wearing a black t-shirt and jeans and his hair is really short, like a military cut.

Nina freezes, her eyes on mine, looking at me like she wants me to say something.

I turn to Josh. "Hi, I'm Sage. Nina's friend."

"Good to meet you." He shakes my hand. "You here visiting?"

"No. I live here. I moved here a few weeks ago."

"You moved here?"

"It's a long story."

He nods and looks at Nina, who's turned her back to him, pretending he isn't there.

"Did you order yet?" I ask Josh.

"No. I just got here. Haven't even got a table yet."

"Well, in that case, have a seat." I almost laugh when I hear Nina groan. After all the crap she gave me for talking to Kyle, she deserves a little teasing.

"Thanks." Josh sits down next to Nina.

She mouths the word 'bitch' at me but she's holding back a smile.

"So how long did you and Nina go out?" I ask, deciding to continue to act like Nina's not here.

Josh plays along. "Six months. And then she broke up with me. In a text."

"Ouch." I cringe. "That IS harsh."

"I know, right?" He leans forward, putting his elbows on the table, the movement causing his body to brush against Nina's back. "And she never explained why. I called her, texted her, but heard nothing back. And to make matters worse, she dumped me two days before my birthday."

She whips around to face him. "You said your birthday was in October!"

"It is." He smiles. "I just wanted you to join in the conversation."

She narrows her eyes at him. "I'm not joining in because you shouldn't be here."

"I wanted a burger."

"See?" she says to me. "I told you he came here for the food."

"And lucky me, I just happened to run into a girl I used to date."

She huffs and turns her back to him again.

His focus returns to me. "So is Nina still working at the grocery store?"

"Yeah. She's the best cashier there. Way faster than anyone else."

I glance at her and see her mouthing *'I hate you'* to me. But I know she doesn't. And I know she doesn't mind having Josh there, as evidenced by the fact she hasn't moved farther over in the booth, despite his arm brushing against her back whenever he moves it.

"So you really came here for the burgers?" I ask. "You must really like them."

"I do, but that's not the only reason. I'm also here on business."

"This is way outside your jurisdiction."

"This is a side job. I'm doing some investigation for a friend."

I tense up, assuming this has to do with my dad.

"Don't worry," he says. "It's nothing about you. And yes, I know who you are. I didn't at first but the more we talked, the more you looked familiar. I recognize you from the pictures."

There were photos of my dad with my mom and me all over the news when the scandal broke. It was horrible. I got recognized wherever I went. People were constantly giving me nasty looks or making mean comments. That was another reason I wanted to escape to a small town, but moving here didn't help.

"There wasn't anything you could do," Josh says. "I hope you know that."

I shrug. "I guess."

"Guys like that will do anything to get what they want, even if it means hurting those they love. They're expert liars. Sometimes they can even lie their way through a lie detector test."

"I'd rather not talk about it."

"I understand."

"So you said you're here on business?"

He chuckles. "It's nothing serious. Gladys Mayfield thinks someone broke into her house today and stole one of her pies, along with some cold fried chicken."

Gladys Mayfield is an elderly woman who works the morning shift at the bakery, running the register. She always thinks someone's trying to steal from her.

"I think she just forgot that she ate it," he says, "but I told her I'd come check it out. Look for any signs of unlawful entry. It'll make her feel better and I'll probably get a pie out it."

"How does Gladys know you?"

"When I was dating this girl," he glances at Nina, "we used to go to the bakery in the morning and get pastries. Nina insisted on getting donuts, which she thought was hilarious because of the whole donut-cop thing. While we were there, I'd always get a pie to take home for later. Gladys would ring us up at the register and," he grins, "she kinda had a thing for me."

"You cheated on Nina with Gladys?" I pretend to be shocked. "No wonder Nina broke up with you."

"I hadn't thought about that, but that's probably the reason. Although Gladys and I never shared anything more than a handshake. But I could see how Nina might've thought otherwise."

I laugh. I like this guy. He's funny. I wonder why Nina dumped him.

Lacey, the waitress, stops by. "Two bacon double cheeseburgers." She sets one in front of me and the other in front of Nina. "And for you?" she asks Josh.

"I need a minute." He grabs a menu. "For now I'll take a beer."

Lacey leaves. Nina finally faces forward, but instead of eating, she checks her phone.

Mine dings and I see a text from Nina. *Get rid of him!*

Who? I text back. *The hot police officer who you obviously still like?*

I do NOT like him!! Stop talking to him or he'll never leave.

"What's she saying about me?" Josh asks from behind his menu. He's good. He picks up on the little things. I didn't even think he was paying attention.

"Something about how much she still likes you."

I feel a hard kick to my foot. "Nina!" I scold.

"She used to kick me too," Josh says, setting his menu down. "After awhile you get used to it." He picks up a fry from her plate and eats it. "Your burger's getting cold," he tells her.

"I'm busy," she mutters, swiping through her phone.

"Whatcha looking up there?" He leans over so he can see her screen.

She moves back, hiding her screen from his view. "If you must know, I'm looking up ways to get rid of crazy ex-boyfriends who are stalking me."

"Tell me his name and I'll take care of it."

I laugh, but Nina just rolls her eyes.

"Well, if you're not going to eat this." He picks up her burger and takes a big bite.

"Hey!" She swats at him. "That's mine!"

"Go ahead." He holds the burger out to her. "Have some."

She snatches it from him. "Get your own."

Lacey returns with Josh's beer. "You decide yet?"

"Yeah. I'll have what she's having." He points to Nina.

"It's two for one burger night," Lacey says.

"All the better. Give me two."

She smiles at him. "I like a man with a big appetite." She gives him a wink and walks off.

"Looks like Gladys may have some competition," he says, then takes a drink of his beer.

I laugh, but Nina continues to ignore him.

"So..." Josh sets his beer down. "Anything new in town?"

"There's a—" I stop before telling him about Kyle. I'm not sure why. Is it because I think he's running from the law? If so, why would I be protecting him?

"What were you saying?" he asks.

"Um, I was just going to say that it's been really busy at Kenny's Garage. That's where I work. It seems like everyone's been taking their car in to be worked on this month."

"Summer vacations," he says. "Nobody wants their car breaking down during a long road trip."

"Yeah, that's probably true."

"Speaking of vacations, Gladys said Mr. Miller left for the summer. She said he's never left Kansas and now he's living in Florida all summer."

"Yeah. I guess he decided it was finally time to take a trip."

"Anyone watching his house while he's away?"

"I'm sure someone is." I glance at Nina, who's giving me a questioning look, like she's wondering why I'm not telling Josh about Kyle.

I'm wondering that too.

CHAPTER FOUR

"Tell him about the new guy," Nina says to me.

She just couldn't let it go. She's been quiet this whole time but then chooses to speak when I don't want her to.

"What new guy?" Josh asks.

"Some guy is renting Mr. Miller's house while he's gone." I pick up my burger. "These really *are* good. I get why you make the drive just to come here. I wonder what kind of seasoning they use. Because there's definitely—"

"Why didn't you tell me that before?" Josh asks.

"Because I hadn't realized how good they are until I really paid attention." I take another bite.

"I'm not talking about the food." He leans back and crosses his arms. He's in cop mode now. "Why didn't you mention this guy before, when I was asking if anyone was watching Miller's place?"

I shrug. "I didn't think about it."

"What do you know about this guy?"

"Not much. Why does it matter? Who cares who's renting out Miller's place?"

"He's a drifter," Nina says, looking up at me from her phone. She thinks she's helping me but she's not. Kyle is not dangerous. I don't need Nina's cop ex-boyfriend going to check him out.

"He's not a drifter," I say. "His motorcycle broke down so he had to walk it to Miller's house."

"And you talked to him?" Josh asks.

Nina answers. "She stopped on the road and got out of her car and went up to him."

"That's dangerous," Josh says. "You should've at least stayed in your car."

I sigh. "I don't need a lecture on safety. I know how to be careful, and I was. I kept my distance from the guy and just talked to him, asked if he needed help. He said he didn't so I got in my car and left."

"But then she saw him at Miller's house and went up to him again," Nina says.

I glare at her. "Why are you so talkative all of a sudden?"

"As long as we have a cop here, might as well ask for his opinion. You obviously don't believe me when I tell you this guy is dangerous so let's get another opinion."

"Knowing Mr. Wilson, I doubt he'd rent to someone he didn't trust," Josh says. "I only met him a couple times but he seemed pretty cautious when we talked."

"Exactly." I look at Nina. "So you can stop worrying and leave Kyle alone."

"If you want, I could stop over there," Josh says. "Just say hello to the guy. See if I notice anything unusual."

"No, don't," I say. "The guy just moved here. He doesn't need the cops banging on his door, accusing him of things he didn't do. There's nothing wrong with him. He's not dangerous. Nina's just being paranoid."

"I'm looking out for you, because apparently you can't stay away from the guy."

"He's my neighbor. I was getting to know him. It's good to know your neighbors."

"You live next to him?" Josh asks.

"A couple miles down."

"In the house Mabel used to live in," Nina says. "She died last spring. On her couch." Nina shudders. "I'm never sitting on that couch."

"After Mabel died, her niece inherited the house," I tell Josh. "She's friends with my mom and offered to let me stay there until I can save up some money."

Josh nods. "It's too bad they can't recover any of it."

He's referring to the money my dad stole. The investigators haven't been able to find any of it. They also can't find my dad. My guess is that he fled the country and is now living it up on some tropical island.

"Have you heard any updates about the case?" he asks.

"No." I'm glad to be off the topic of Kyle but this topic isn't any better. "The police don't bother me anymore. My mom checks in with them but only because she's afraid he might try to contact her again."

"Why would he do that? He'd risk getting caught."

"I know, which is why he never would. I'm not sure why she thinks he might. I don't ask her about him. She's still hurting over what he did to her."

"That's too bad."

"Yeah," I mutter, wishing he'd stop talking about this.

Nina turns to Josh. "So going back to Kyle, I think you should go over there."

"Now you're talking to me?" He grins. "Now that you want something?"

"It's not for me. It's for Sage. She can't have some psychopath living next door. He could sneak in her house at night and kill her."

"Josh, don't," I say. "I mean it. Going over there would be harassing him. He didn't do anything wrong."

"Fine. I'll leave him alone, but if you have any trouble with him or want me to come back and pay him a visit, just let me know." He takes out his wallet and pulls out a business card. "Here's my number, since Nina probably got rid of it."

"It's still in my phone." She picks up a wad of fries. "But only because I didn't get around to deleting it."

"You ever gonna explain what I did to make you hate me so much?"

"I don't hate you," she says defensively. "Why would you think that?"

"Because you dumped me on a text and never talked to me again." He grabs some of her fries and shoves them in his mouth.

"It was just easier that way. A clean break."

"I think you at least owe him a reason," I say, taking a drink of my soda.

Josh smiles at me. "I agree."

"Fine." She shoves her plate aside. "I broke up with you because it would never work. You live too far away. I need to be with a guy I can see every day."

"So move to Kansas City."

She huffs. "*I* have to move? Why don't *you* move?"

Her use of the present tense makes Josh smile. It implies she'd consider dating him again.

"You always said you wanted out of this town," he points out.

"Yeah, but I can't afford a big city. The rent's too high."

"So get a roommate. I know a cop who's looking for one."

"Who?"

He just smiles at her.

She whacks him. "I'm not living with you. We broke up."

"We lived together every weekend when we were dating."

"It's not the same. And we're not dating. Can we end this conversation now?" She brings her plate back in front of her.

"If you only dumped me because I don't live here, we can work around that. That's not a reason to break up."

"It sure as hell is, which I proved by breaking up with you."

"She's impossible," I say to Josh. "Arguing with her gives me a headache, which is why I try to avoid it."

He chuckles. "She's definitely a challenge."

"I'm right here!" She points to herself. "Stop talking about me."

Josh ignores her and says to me, "Who's she dating now?"

"No one. In fact, I don't think she's dated anyone since you."

"Because I've already dated all the eligible men in town," she mutters.

"So if she refuses to date guys outside of town, I guess she'll spend the rest of her life being single."

"Guess so." I pour more ketchup on my plate.

Lacey appears again. "Two bacon cheeseburgers." She sets them in front of Josh.

"Thanks! Looks great!"

She stands there, staring at him.

"I'm good," he says to her. "I don't need anything else."

"Oh, um, I was just wondering if I knew you from somewhere. You look familiar."

"I live in Kansas City but I used to come here now and then." He glances at Nina. "To visit a friend."

"Police officer, right?"

"That's me."

"So um..." She clears her throat. "Are you seeing anyone?"

He smiles. "No. Why do you ask?"

"There's a fundraiser for the fire department this weekend. There'll be a cookout and a band. There's dancing but we don't have to dance." She chews on her lip.

"Are you asking if I'd like to go with you?"

She shrugs. "If you want, then yeah."

"Sounds like a plan." He gets his wallet out and hands her a card. "There's my number. Give me a call later with all the details."

"I will." She hurries off, grinning from ear to ear. I don't know Lacey that well, but she seems nice. She went to high school with Nina but they weren't friends. Lacey played volleyball and basketball so she hung out with the athletes. Nina has no athletic abilities and hates sports so she has nothing in common with Lacey.

Josh picks up his burger. "Guess I have a date for this weekend."

Nina huffs. "Yeah, after just asking me to live with you."

"You turned me down. I had to move on."

"Which took all of two minutes."

"Can't waste time. I'm not getting any younger." He bites into his burger.

I can't stop laughing, watching these two. I love how he gives her shit. Most guys are afraid to, but not Josh.

"Let me out." Nina pushes on his arm.

"Why? What do you need?"

"It's none of your business. Now let me out." She pushes harder on him but he doesn't budge. He's strong and a lot bigger than her. She's tall but really thin, with scrawny arms that can barely lift anything. She could put all her weight into pushing on Josh and he still wouldn't move.

"Are you going outside for a smoke?" I ask.

"No," she answers in a defensive tone, gripping her purse. I see a pack of cigarettes peeking out the side.

"You're still smoking?" Josh asks. "Then I'm definitely not letting you out."

"I've been trying to quit." She jabs him. "But then certain people stress me out and I crave a cigarette."

"Those things aren't good for you."

"No shit?" She rolls her eyes. "Never heard that before."

He looks at me. "Amazing I'd still go out with her, isn't it?"

I burst out laughing, almost choking on my burger. Josh has a great sense of humor. If Nina doesn't want him, maybe I should go out with him. The only problem is, I can't stop thinking about Kyle. Why does my head keep going back to him? I know almost nothing about the guy. Just because there's a spark between us doesn't mean he's right for me.

As we're finishing dinner, Lacey drops off our checks. Josh takes them both.

"Dinner's on me." He drops some money on the table.

"Paying the bill won't make me go out with you," Nina says.

"I'm paying because I enjoyed having dinner with two beautiful women. If Sage hadn't invited me to sit down, I would've had to eat by myself." He turns to Nina. "And in case you forgot, I was asked out earlier so I can't go out with you even if you wanted me to. I won't date two women at once."

"That's very gentlemanly of you," I say. "Isn't it, Nina?"

"I need a smoke," she mutters, pulling a cigarette from her purse.

Josh gets out of the booth. "I need to go over to Gladys' house, then head back to the city."

"Have a safe trip," I tell him.

"I will. See you guys later."

"Bye." I'm the only one who says it. Nina is too busy searching around in her purse.

"I think I left my lighter in the car." She takes handfuls of stuff from her purse and drops it on the table.

"What's the deal with you and Josh?"

"There IS no deal. I'm not interested in him anymore."

"You sure about that? Because from over here, it looked like you two were a couple."

"Why do you say that?" She holds up a tube of lipstick. "This color doesn't work on me. You want it? It's brand new. Only used it once."

"Okay." I take it from her. My tight budget doesn't allow me to buy makeup so I'm happy to take a freebie. "Going back to you and Josh, you two have real chemistry. And no matter what you say, I can tell you still like him."

"We USED to have chemistry. We don't now."

"Yeah, you do. I just witnessed it. And Josh is right. The fact that he doesn't live here isn't a good excuse to break up with him. It's not like he lives in Alaska. He's only an hour away."

"I'm going for a smoke." She scoots out of the booth. "You want to come?"

"I'll walk out with you but I need to head home. I have to be at work at seven."

"I have tomorrow off. I'm going to sleep all day then maybe go shopping. You want to come with?"

We walk outside and she lights up her cigarette.

"I'd love to go but it's not really fun when you can't buy anything."

"I get it. I've been there. I'm STILL there, but I want to get a new skirt for the firehouse fundraiser on Saturday."

"I thought you weren't going."

"Talking about it made me change my mind."

"Are you going so you can keep an eye on Josh?"

"No!" She blows out a puff of smoke. "It has nothing to do with Josh. It's about going out and doing something. It's not that often this town has a party. You're going with me, by the way."

"I don't know about that. The angry townsfolk may come at me with pitchforks."

"You'll be fine. If anyone says anything to you, I'll smack them upside the head, or kick them in the groin, depending on what type of mood I'm in that night."

"What if I want to bring a date?"

"A date? Like who?"

"I don't know. Maybe the new guy."

"You're going to ask the serial killer to go on a date with you?"

"Okay, seriously, you have to stop calling him that. And it doesn't have to be a date. He could just come with us. Like you said, he's going to get bored sitting in his house all day."

"He'll probably say no, but if you really want to ask him, then go ahead."

A red truck pulls in across the street at the hardware store.

"Isn't that Mr. Wilson's truck?" I ask.

"Yeah. And that's not Mr. Wilson."

We watch as Kyle gets out of the truck.

"That's him," I say. "That's the new guy."

She squints to see him. "He's too far away to get a good look, but from here, he *does* look kinda hot. He's got a nice ass, at least."

I agree. I checked out his ass when he was walking away from me earlier today.

"Wilson must be letting him use his truck," I say.

"Wilson doesn't let anyone drive his truck except family. Or Kenny, when Wilson has to bring it in for service."

"Well, he's letting Kyle drive it."

"He probably stole the keys and is driving it without permission."

I ignore her comment and watch as Kyle checks the door on the hardware store. It's locked so he turns and goes back to the truck. He starts it up and drives off.

Nina laughs. "Must be a city boy. Doesn't seem to know how early stuff shuts down in a small town."

"He almost made it. They close at nine and it's just after nine." I take out my keys. "I need to go. I'll call you tomorrow, okay?"

"Yeah, see ya."

I get in my car and head home, expecting to see Kyle in front of me, but he's not there. And when I pass Wilson's house, I don't see the pickup out front. It's always parked outside. Wilson has so much junk in his garage that he can't park his truck in there.

Where would Kyle be going this time of night? He doesn't know his way around town and bars are the only thing open. Maybe that's where he went. But he said he was tired and going to bed.

Okay, this isn't good. I'm starting to sound like one of the locals. Getting in other people's business? I don't like it when people do that to me so I shouldn't be doing it to Kyle. But I still can't stop myself from thinking about him.

CHAPTER FIVE

"Hey, Sage." Jesse walks into the office, already covered in grease and it's only eight in the morning.

"Hey." I keep typing, my eyes on the computer monitor.

"Can we talk a minute?"

I check the clock. "It's almost my break. Can we talk later? I shouldn't have to work on my break."

"It's not work-related. This won't take long, but if you want, you can take a longer break. I don't care."

I stop typing and turn to face him. "Go ahead."

"The firehouse fundraiser is Saturday and I thought we could go together."

"No." I turn back to the computer. "Was that all?"

"Why won't you go with me? We could just go as friends."

"People would see us there and think we're more than that, which is completely unprofessional given that you're my boss. In fact, just you asking me out could be considered harassment."

"Don't give me that harassment bullshit. I'm not grabbing your ass. I just invited you to something. And I don't care what people think. I know everyone in the whole damn town. They don't care what I do."

I sigh and look back at him. "Jesse, I told you I'm not interested in you. Even if I didn't work for you, I'd still say no. I think of you more as a brother than someone I'd go out with. And besides, I already told Nina I'd go with her."

He scratches the stubble along his chin. "I don't know why you have to be this way. There aren't many guys your age in this town, and compared to them, I'm a success. I run this garage and I've got my own place." He takes a step closer to me. "If you were mine, I promise I'd treat you right. I'd buy you flowers and shit."

"The answer is still no. I'm sorry, but you'll have to find someone else."

There's a knock on the office door. It has a glass partition and is partially open but I can't see who's there because Jesse's blocking my view.

"Come in," I say, desperately wanting someone to barge in and end this awkward conversation.

"Hi, I'm looking for Jesse," a guy says.

Jesse turns around and behind him I see Kyle. My heart suddenly picks up its pace and I quickly stand up.

"I'm Jesse," he says. "What do you need?"

Kyle sees me behind Jessie and says, "You work here?"

"Yeah. I do the office work."

Kyle is all cleaned up today, wearing dark jeans and a white t-shirt. He hasn't shaved, but his hair isn't the sweaty mess it was yesterday. It's been styled neatly in place with some kind of product.

He's really hot. And not farm-boy hot, which is all you really see around here. This guy is sophisticated hot. Even in jeans and a t-shirt, he looks sophisticated. Then again, anyone would look sophisticated standing next to Jesse, who always looks like a mess, even when he's not at work. His clothes are always wrinkled. His shirt is always half tucked in, half hanging loose. He lets his jeans hang so low you can see his boxers.

"You two know each other?" Jesse asks.

"He's my neighbor," I explain. "He's renting out Old Man Miller's place."

"Oh, yeah?" Jesse says. "You his nephew or something?"

"No." Kyle looks at Jesse. "I'm here to see if you can fix a motorcycle."

"Probably. What's wrong with it?"

"I don't know. It won't start. You'll have to take a look at it."

Jesse meets him at the door, then turns back to me. "Think about it."

I shake my head as the two of them leave. Jesse is so annoying. He refuses to take no for an answer.

Five minutes later, Jesse comes in again. "Can you get him in the computer?"

"Who?"

"The guy with the motorcycle. He's pulling it in the garage. I told him to come in here when he's done."

"Okay, I'll take care of it." I set my phone down.

He goes to leave, then stops. "Shit, it's your break, isn't it?"

"Yeah, but I don't mind." I would if it were anyone else, but I don't mind missing my break for Kyle. I thought about him all last night until I finally fell asleep.

Kyle appears in the doorway.

"Bike should be ready in a few days," Jesse says to him. "Sage will give you a call when you can pick it up."

"Great, thanks."

When Jesse is finally gone, I say, "You can close the door, unless you want the waiting area to hear all your personal details."

He closes it and comes over to sit down across from my desk. "What kind of details do you need?"

"Name, address, phone number. I'll also need a payment method on file. Whatever credit card you want to use."

"I'll pay in cash," he says.

"That's fine but we still need to have a card on file to cover our costs in case you don't show up to get your motorcycle."

"If I don't pick up my motorcycle, then you could sell it and recoup whatever costs were incurred."

He's definitely not from around here. The people here don't use words like 'recoup' and 'incur'. In fact, they'd think you're a snob if you used words like that.

"I'm not saying it makes sense. Kenny, the owner, made that rule years ago after some guy didn't pay him. I don't know the whole story. All I know is that from then on, he required a credit card be on file for every customer."

"Well, I don't have one."

"You don't have a credit card? Not even one?"

"No. And I don't plan to get one. So I guess my only option is to prepay whatever this Kenny guy feels is enough to cover his losses if I fail to show up, which isn't going to happen because I need the motorcycle."

"Kenny isn't here so I can't check with him but I could ask Jesse. He's running the place for his dad for a few months."

Kyle's brows rise. "That guy's running the place?"

"Yeah." I laugh a little. "He doesn't handle the business side of things. He just works on the cars. He's actually a really good mechanic. I'm sure he can fix your motorcycle." I get up from the chair. "Let me ask how much he wants. I'll be right back."

I go explain the situation to Jesse, then return to the office. I catch Kyle watching me walk in. I'm wearing a blue cotton sundress that hits just above the knee. It's sleeveless so shows off my tan. When I'm not at work, I spend a lot of time outside. I hang out on the back patio of the house and read or listen to music. The less time I have to spend in that old stinky house the better.

"He said $500 should be enough. If not, you can pay the rest when you pick it up."

"Five hundred? That's it?" Kyle gets his wallet out, a sleek black leather wallet that looks expensive. His t-shirt looks expensive too. It's just a basic white t-shirt but the fabric looks soft and smooth, like it's a high quality cotton or some kind of cotton blend.

"Things are cheaper in a small town."

"Guess so." He places five crisp hundred dollar bills on the desk. "I'd pay at least twice that in—" He coughs.

"In where? Where are you from?"

"California. The Los Angeles area."

"Really? You don't look like a California guy."

"Why?"

"I don't know. I guess I just always pictured California guys having blond hair and blue eyes. Like those surfer guys in the movies."

"I'm not originally from there."

"Where'd you grow up?"

He motions to my computer. "Could we finish this up? I'd like to get going."

"Yeah, sure." I turn and face my monitor and type his first name into the form. "Last name?"

He pauses, then flips open his wallet. "Shadwick. Kyle Shadwick."

I laugh. "Did you forget your name for a minute?"

"No." He puts his wallet away. "I was just checking how much cash I had left."

"Hey, you didn't notice any nausea or dizziness from that bump on your head, did you?"

"No. I'm fine."

Leaning toward him, I check out his bandage. It's tinged with blood.

"You need a new bandage. When we're done here, I'll get one from my car and put a new one on." I sit back. "Since you refuse to get stitches."

"I don't need stitches."

"You do. You're just too scared to get them."

"I'm not scared. I just don't need them. It's just a small scrape to the head."

"It's a large gash and it's bleeding through the bandage. That must've been some fight you were in."

He doesn't respond.

"So what's your address?"

"Whatever Miller's address is. I can't remember. Can you look it up?"

"It should really be your permanent address, not a place you're renting for a month or two. If there's a warranty on any of the parts, having your permanent address on file will help us find you if we need to ship you a replacement."

"Just put down Miller's address."

"But—"

"Sage. I'm not arguing about this."

"Fine." I type in the address, which I know because it's so similar to mine.

"Phone number?"

"I can't remember. I'd have to check. Whatever Miller's landline number is. Do you have it on file?"

"Yes, but I need your cell number so I—I mean, *we*, can reach you when you're not at home."

"I don't have one."

"Have what?"

"A cell phone."

"You don't have a cell phone?" I smile. "Yeah, that's funny. Now what's the number?"

"I'm serious. I don't have one."

"That doesn't make sense. Everyone has one, unless they're like a hundred years old. Even Old Man Wilson has a cell phone and he hates technology."

"I used to have one but I don't now."

"Why not?"

"I don't need one. I don't like talking on the phone."

"You can use it for other things. Searching the web. Storing phone numbers. Checking the time."

"I have a laptop to search the web. And any phone numbers I need are in here." He taps his head. "As for checking the time, I have this." He holds up his arm, showing me his watch, which has a silver face and black band. I don't know much about watches, but that one looks expensive.

"Um...okay." I look up Wilson's number and put it into the form. Then I hit 'save' and wait for it to confirm that Kyle has been added to the system.

"I saw you last night," Kyle says.

"You did?" I see the computer screen return to the main page, meaning his information is saved, but I pretend to still be waiting, my hand on the keyboard. I'm not ready for him to go yet.

"You were across from the hardware store."

"Yeah, I'd just had dinner at Skeeter's. You should go there sometime. It's kind of a dive but the food's good."

"Was that your friend? The girl who was smoking?"

"Yeah. Nina. She's trying to quit but..." I let out a laugh as I remember last night, "her ex showed up and by the time he left she needed a cigarette."

"Did they get in a fight?"

"No. He sat at our table and they were flirting with each other all night, the type of flirting where you pretend to not like each other when in reality all you can think about is how much you want the person." I swallow and look away, hoping he didn't think I was implying anything. As I was saying it, I realized I just described me with him.

He must not have read anything into it because he doesn't react. Instead, he says, "How long did they go out?"

"I'm not sure. I think around six months? He doesn't live here. He lives in Kansas City. It was a long distance relationship, which is why she claims she broke up with him. But if you ask me, I think they should try again. I think they make a good couple."

"Why is that?"

"The way they act around each other. They have a lot of chemistry, but besides that, he seems to really care about her. And I could tell she cares about him, even though she tries to hide it. Nina pretends to be tough as nails, and part of her is, but she also has a soft side that she doesn't let many people see. I think Josh was one of the few guys who was able to get her to show that side of herself when they were dating. I just got that feeling last night when I saw them together."

"Maybe that's why they're not together. Maybe she doesn't like feeling vulnerable, if that's how he made her feel."

"Maybe. I don't know. If I asked her, I doubt she'd tell me. She probably wouldn't even admit it to herself."

"So why was this guy in town? To try to get her back?"

"No. He was helping out Gladys, this old lady who always thinks people are trying to steal from her. The truth is she's just forgetful and loses stuff and then accuses people of stealing it. So she called up Josh."

"What did she want him to do?"

"Check her door. See if anyone tried to break in. He was her only option. The cops here don't believe her anymore. They've stopped looking into her fake robbery stories."

"So he's a cop?"

"Josh? Yeah. In Kansas City. Gladys knew him because he used to be here a lot when he was dating Nina."

"And this lady thought she was robbed?"

"She said someone stole a—" I stop as the door opens.

Jesse pokes his head in the room. He sees Kyle across from me and says, "You're not done yet?"

"No." I glance back at the computer. "But we're almost finished."

His gaze pauses on Kyle and then he says, "Come see me after your break."

I nod, and wait for him to leave.

"He's so annoying," I mutter under my breath.

"Are you having problems with him?"

"He hits on me almost every day. Right before you got here, he asked me out for like the millionth time."

"That's harassment. Why don't you report him?"

"In a town this small? Where Jesse was born and raised? I'd be the one getting in trouble, not him. I'm the outsider, and most of the town hates me."

"Why do they hate you?"

"Because my—" I take a breath. "I'd rather not talk about it."

"Why do you live in a town you're not from where the people don't like you?"

"Because I have a free place to stay. I'm a little short on cash right now. Actually, I'm broke, which is why I won't be going back to college in the fall. But eventually I'll save enough to go back. I only have a semester left before graduating."

"Why don't you get a loan?"

I let out a laugh. "Yeah. Banks would never give me a loan."

I tried getting a loan but banks wouldn't even talk to me. Every financial institution had a fraud alert out for my dad, and since I'm his daughter, banks assumed I was a scammer like him. A lot of people think that. They think my mom and I were part of my dad's scam, assuming we had to have known what he was up to. But we didn't. We had no idea, and it hurts to have people treat you like a criminal when you didn't do anything wrong.

"I get the feeling there's a story there."

"There is, but not one I can tell you when I'm at work. Maybe we can get together some night and I can tell you how I ended up here."

"Maybe." His lips turn up. "I'll have to check my schedule."

So he's open to it? Given how guarded he's been up until now, always wanting to be alone, I thought for sure he'd tell me no.

I need to seize this opportunity before he changes his mind. "How about tonight? Could you clear your schedule for an hour or two?"

"It'll take you that long to tell me your story?" He smiles a little more.

"Probably not, but you might end up enjoying my company and want to stay."

"I have a feeling that might happen."

He's flirting. And it's making my heart spring to life, along with other parts of me.

When Jesse flirts with me, I feel nothing. Except maybe dread with a touch of nausea.

"So what time should I come over?"

"Six? Or seven, if that works better."

"Six is fine. But I'll need your address."

"Just take a right out of your driveway and drive until you see another house. That's me. Yellow house. White shutters."

"You're the only house out there?"

"There are others farther down but I'm the one closest to you, if you call a couple miles close."

He chuckles. "There's really nothing out here, is there?"

"The town is actually big for a farm town. At least it has stores and restaurants and a few bars. But outside of town? Where *we* live? There's nothing out there but wheat fields and some cows."

He checks his watch. "I should let you get back to work. I'll plan on coming over at six."

"I'd offer to make you dinner but given my cash situation right now, I don't have much food at my place. I pretty much live on grilled cheese sandwiches or peanut butter and jelly."

"I like grilled cheese sandwiches."

His face is serious but I'm sure he's kidding.

"I wish I could offer you some real food but since I can't, I suggest having dinner before you come over."

"Grilled cheese isn't real food?"

"It is, but it's not something you make for guests."

"I disagree, but I don't expect you to make dinner so don't worry about it."

I cock my head. "You really want grilled cheese?"

"If it's not too much trouble. I used to love grilled cheese sandwiches when I was a kid. My mom used to make them but then—" He picks at something on his jeans, looking down. "My dad didn't like them so she stopped making them."

"She could've made them just for you. He didn't have to eat them."

"Yeah." He looks up again, forcing out a smile. "I suppose she could have. Anyway, it's been a while."

"Then I'll make you one. Or two, depending on how hungry you are. I'll need to stop at the store after work. I'm totally out of groceries. So if you have any requests for a certain type of bread or cheese, let me know. Not that there's much of a selection at Vindervott's, but they do have a few varieties."

"Let me get the groceries. I'm going over there now anyway."

"Really? Because if you could just pick up a few things, that'd be great." I open the drawer and take out my wallet.

"I don't need money," he says as I pull out a twenty. "Just tell me what you need."

"I have to pay you for it." I hand him the twenty.

"You're not paying me. Now make a list." He picks a pen off my desk and hands it to me. As I'm writing out the list, he says, "And don't just put down what you need for dinner. Add anything else you want. Steak. Chicken. Those little cookies shaped like peanuts."

I laugh. "Nutter Butters?"

"I think that's what they're called. They have like a peanut butter filling."

"Yeah, I've had them. They're good, but it's kind of an odd thing to bring up. What made you think of those?"

"I don't know. Maybe the grilled cheese. It was another one of those foods I used to eat when I was younger. I'll get some, just in case you want them for dessert."

Handing him my list, I say, "Thanks for doing this. You might be a good neighbor after all."

"You didn't think I would be?"

"Not at first. I was starting to think you'd be even crankier than Old Man Wilson. He used to complain that my car was too loud and would wake him up when I'd drive to work in the morning."

"Your car IS too loud. It woke me up at the crack of dawn."

"Sorry. I'd ask Jesse to fix it but he gave me the car so I don't want to complain. And I don't have the money to pay him to fix it."

"He gave you the car?"

"Some old guy was getting rid of it so he left it here. It was always breaking down. Kenny was going to sell it for scrap metal but Jesse asked if he could keep it and try to get it working again. That was around the time I moved here. When I applied for this job I told him I'd have to work my schedule around the bus times because I didn't have a car. He told me the town didn't have a bus and then he offered me the car."

"By accepting it, you know he thinks you owe him, right? He was trying to guilt you into going out with him."

"I know, but it's not going to work. He can ask me out all he wants but I'm not going out with him. And until I can afford a better car, I have to keep driving that boat around."

He chuckles. "It IS a boat. That thing is huge. And that motor could wake the dead."

"Sorry." I laugh. "I'd like to say I'll try to be quieter but I really can't do anything about it."

"It's fine." He reads over my list. "There's not enough on here. Going to the store is my big activity for the day. I've gotta make it last. Add some more stuff. Fill up the whole page."

"I don't need that much."

"You said you were out of groceries."

"I'll go shopping later. For now I just need stuff for tonight."

"Maybe I'll stop by your house tomorrow too, in which case you might want to have some food on hand."

I smile. "Then just buy whatever you want and I'll keep it at my place for random visits from my evasive new neighbor."

He was smiling but got serious when I said 'evasive'. I didn't mean it as an insult. It was more of a comment about our interactions, because every time I ask him a question about himself he changes the subject. Maybe he took offense to the term, but evasive is the best way to describe him.

CHAPTER SIX

Kyle stands up. "I should go. The grocery store is just down the street?"

"Down the street and to the left. The sign is really faded and hard to read. Just look for a building that looks like a warehouse. Oh, and make sure you check out at Nina's register. She's a cashier there."

"Got it." He shoves the list in his pocket.

"No, wait. Nina's not working today. Go to Val's lane. She's the second fastest. Whatever you do, avoid Opal. She's the slowest cashier ever and she'll ask you about every item you buy. She's like 90 and has blue hair."

"I'll be sure to avoid her." He grins. "Can I go now?"

"Yeah." I walk him to the door and notice the bloody bandage. "Wait. I forgot to change your bandage. Follow me out to my car. It won't take long."

We go to the back lot where the employees park and I get my first aid kit. Yesterday was the first time I ever used it. I keep it in my car for emergencies. I have one in the house too. Living out in the middle of nowhere, I have to be prepared. If I ever get hurt it'll be a long time before an ambulance reaches me.

As I'm changing the bandage, Jesse walks out with a bag of garbage in his hand. On his way to the dumpster, he stops and yells out, "Everything okay out here?"

"Everything's fine," I tell him. "I'm still on break, by the way. I have another five minutes."

He keeps his eyes on Kyle and me as he brings the bag to the dumpster. He mutters something to himself as he goes back inside.

"I get the feeling he doesn't like me," Kyle says.

"You're competition. The new guy? Single? All the girls in town will be after you. Which means all the guys your age will hate you."

"I'm not looking to date anyone."

"You're not?" I hear a hint of disappointment in my voice. I hope he didn't notice.

"I'm not going to be here long enough. It wouldn't be right to start something with someone and then have to end it."

"Did you leave someone back home?"

"I had a girlfriend a few months ago but that's over. Haven't dated anyone since." He touches the bandage I just put on. "Is this good?"

"Yeah. You're all set."

"Then I'll see you tonight."

"Yeah. Bye."

He walks around the building to the front, where his truck is parked. I remain outside and lean against the car as I check my phone.

I call Nina. "Hey, are you up?" I ask, because sometimes she sleeps late on her day off.

"Yeah, I'm up. I had to drive Butthead to work. He had a flat tire."

"Why didn't his girlfriend take him?"

"She was already at work and couldn't leave. Anyway, what's up with you?"

"I'm on break. Thought I'd check in and see what you're doing."

I hear her yawn. "I was just about to eat something and then I'm going shopping. What time do you want to meet up tonight?"

"What's tonight?"

"Drinks at Healy's. It's two for one, remember? First round's on you."

"Shit, I forgot about that. Can I get a raincheck?"

"Why? What happened?"

"I made plans. I'm really sorry. I totally forgot we were going out."

"Plans with who?"

"Um..." She's going to be mad, but to be fair, she's ditched me more than once to go out with a guy. And unlike her, I didn't do this intentionally. I honestly did forget we'd made plans. "Kyle's coming over."

"Kyle, the serial killer?"

"No. Kyle, the guy who just moved here." I swear I'm going to stop talking to her if she keeps calling him that. She knows how much I hate it when people in town mutter things like 'criminal' or 'thief' when I walk by, so she should know I don't like that type of stuff being done to someone else either. She doesn't even know the guy and she's already making assumptions about him.

"You're having him over to your house? Are you crazy?"

"We're just talking. Getting to know each other. He was just here, dropping off his motorcycle. As I was taking his information down, we were talking and I invited him over. It was a spur-of-the-moment thing. And I don't want to cancel on him now because he's already at the store buying stuff for dinner."

"You're making him dinner?"

"Just grilled cheese. It's all I can afford but he was fine with it. And then he offered to go to the store for me, which was really nice of him. He wouldn't even let me give him money."

"Because he wants to sleep with you. Buying you groceries is code for 'I want sex later'. So unless you're ready for that, you might want to cancel your dinner plans for tonight."

"He's just being nice. It's not about sex."

"I'm not making this up. I'm a cashier. I know this shit."

"You've seen guys buying girls groceries in exchange for sex?"

"All the time." She must've put some gum in her mouth because I can hear her chomping on it.

"How do you know that's what they're doing?"

"I *see* all. I *know* all. Have you not figured this out by now?" She pops a bubble, which makes me cringe.

"That was really loud. Could you not do that in the phone?"

"Sorry. My cravings are bad this morning. I've already been through two packs of gum. I accidentally swallowed a piece. Is that shit about gum sitting in your stomach for seven years really true?"

"Shouldn't you already know that? You just said you know everything."

"About the people in town, smart-ass. Not facts about gum. So what are you going to do?"

"About what?"

"Kyle. You're really going to have him over to eat grilled cheese and make out on the dead lady's couch?"

"We're not going to make out. He told me he's not looking for a girlfriend."

"Which is code for 'I'm just looking for sex'. That's why he bought you the groceries. How are you not seeing this, Sage? He's giving you all the signs." She pops another bubble. "Oops. Shit. Sorry."

"He's not giving me any signs. And if he tries anything tonight, I'll..." I pause to imagine what I would do if he kissed me. How I'd react.

"You'd what? Have sex with him?"

"No, but...I don't know. Maybe I would. It's been over a year since...well, let's just say I might not turn him down."

"Huh. You're not as prudish as I thought."

"You thought I was a prude?"

"It's better than thinking you're a slut."

"I'm neither a slut nor a prude. I just haven't been with anyone for a while. I haven't met anyone I was interested in until now."

"Why do you like this guy so much? Is it the motorcycle?"

"No. I haven't even seen him ride it."

"So you just think he's hot. Is that it?"

"I guess, but I feel like there's something else there. More than just attraction."

"Meaning what?"

"I'm not sure yet. That's why I need to get to know him. He's really guarded so I think it'll take a while for him to open up to me. He's like you that way."

"Me? What are you talking about? I'm an open book."

"No you're not. You act all badass at first, just like Kyle did when I first met him. Then over time, you soften up a little and show off your sweet side."

"Uh...sweet side? I don't have a sweet side. I have a nice side, but definitely not sweet. Seriously, have you met me?"

I laugh. I knew she'd react that way. "I think Kyle is the same way. I think he puts on a tough act, but underneath it all he can be sweet. Maybe that's why I like him. He's just like my best friend."

"I'm your best friend? Aww, that's so sweet. See? You're the sweet one, not me."

"I mean it, Nina," I say, being serious. "You're the only friend I have right now."

She sighs. "Don't get like this, Sage. You know I hate all that sappy stuff."

But it's true. After the scandal broke, the people I thought were my friends disappeared. They wouldn't respond to my texts or return my calls. I have a feeling if I went back to campus in the fall, none of them would even talk to me. They'd pretend they don't know me or they'd find excuses not to hang out with me. So as of now, Nina is my only friend.

"I'm stopping by tonight," she says.

"What?"

"I'm stopping by your house tonight. I want to meet this guy."

"I don't think that's a good idea. I told him it'd just be him and me."

"I'm sure he wouldn't mind if I came over. If it's not a date, then what's the big deal? It's just three people hanging out."

"Can we do it some other time? I'm really trying to get to know him and I've finally got him starting to talk more. If you're there, he'll get quiet again."

"I can get him to talk. It's one of my many skills. How do you think I get all the town gossip?"

"Could you please just let me be alone with him tonight? We can all hang out together some other night. I promise."

She doesn't answer. Maybe she's mad at me, but I really don't want her there tonight. I want to learn more about Kyle and I know that won't happen if she's there.

"So did you hear anything from Josh?"

"Yes." She chews on her gum.

"You did? I was just kidding. I didn't think he'd actually call you."

"He didn't call. He came over."

"He showed up at your apartment? When?"

"After he went to Gladys' house."

"Why? What did he want?"

"He said he wanted to make sure I got home safe but I'm guessing he wanted sex."

"Did he try anything?"

"No. He didn't even come inside."

"Then he wasn't there for sex. He was just doing like he said, making sure you got home safe. You have to stop making all these assumptions about people. Not everyone has bad intentions."

"If I'd invited him into my apartment, we would've done it."

"Only if you agreed to it."

"Did you see how hot he looked last night? Of course I would've agreed to it. That's why I didn't invite him in."

"You make no sense."

"If it could be just sex and nothing else, then I would've done it. But Mr. Sensitive has to turn it into a relationship, which doesn't work when we don't live in the same town."

"It could work. You just don't want it to, which I don't understand. Josh is a great guy. He had me laughing so hard last night I could barely finish my dinner. If you don't want him, do you care if I date him?"

There's silence and then, "Are you serious?"

"No! Nina, I know better than to date a friend's ex. But the way you reacted just now shows how much you still like him. So why'd you let Lacey ask him out?"

"Because he's not mine. He can go out with anyone he wants."

"You could've asked him to the fundraiser as a friend."

"We can't be friends. It doesn't work. And as for Josh and Lacey, I doubt it'll go anywhere. She's not his type."

Jesse appears with another bag of garbage. He looks my way as he tosses it in the dumpster.

"I have to go. My break's almost over."

"Ok. What time's he coming over tonight?"

"Six."

"What time should I call with the fake emergency?"

She's referring to the thing girls do to escape a bad date. But this isn't a date. It's just neighbors having dinner.

"I don't think I'll need it."

"You always think you won't, but you never know. I'll call around six-thirty. And you better pick up or I'll think he killed you and I'll call the cops."

I tell her goodbye as Jesse approaches, then quickly put my phone away.

"I'm not late," I tell him. "Besides, you said I could take a longer break."

"I didn't say you could spend it flirting with our customers."

"I wasn't flirting. I was taking his information down for his account."

"And playing nurse to him in the parking lot?" He folds his arms over his chest. "What the hell was that about?"

"He was bleeding, so I offered to bandage it up for him. I'd do it for anyone. It's called being a nice person."

"You wouldn't do it for me."

I sigh. "Yeah, actually I would. Now what did you want to talk to me about?"

"I need to know how long you'll be sticking around. My dad's not coming back until at least September and he wants to make sure the office staff isn't quitting anytime soon. He doesn't trust me with the office shit and finding help around here is damn near impossible."

"I don't know how long I'll be staying, but I'm sure I'll be here the whole summer. I'm trying to save money. I can't even afford to go back to school in September."

"Maybe your rich boyfriend will give you the money, and then you'll take off and I'll be shit out of luck with no employee."

"I don't know what you're talking about. I don't have a rich boyfriend."

"That guy who was here. The one you were falling all over?"

"He's not my boyfriend. I just met him. And why do you think he's rich?"

"I saw him checking his wallet while I was looking at his bike. He had a stack of hundreds. Crisp bills, like he'd just robbed a bank."

"He didn't rob a bank. He just likes paying for stuff in cash."

"So do criminals. No paper trail. Makes it harder for the cops to track him down."

Seriously, what is wrong with people? A new guy moves to town and everyone just assumes he's up to no good?

"He said he's from California," Jesse says. "So what the hell's he doing in Kansas?"

"I don't know but it's none of your business."

"I bet he's running from something. Hiding out. I'm gonna send Craig out there to check him out."

Craig is one of the local cops. He went to high school with Jesse.

"The guy didn't do anything and you're sending the cops after him?"

"If he's innocent, he has nothing to hide."

"That's completely ridiculous. Just leave the guy alone." I go around him, heading back to the garage.

"Stay away from him, Sage," I hear Jesse yell as I go back inside.

The rest of the day I avoid Jesse and he leaves me alone. He knows I'm angry and that if he keeps pushing, there's not a chance in hell I'd ever date him. He doesn't realize that even if he's nice to me, I'm still not going to date him. I could tell him that a million times and he still wouldn't accept it.

When I get home it's after five and I hurry into the shower. The first thing I do when I get home from work every day is shower to get the garage smell off of me. Even hidden away in the office, I still end up smelling like grease and exhaust fumes.

My phone rings as I'm toweling off. It's my mom. I answer while hurrying over to my closet to find something to wear. I don't know if Kyle is someone who's on time or shows up late, but if I had to guess, I'd say it's the former.

"Hi, honey, how is your week going?"

"Okay. How about yours?"

"Great! I've had this burst of energy and it's fueling my creativity. Or maybe it's the other way around. Either way, I've only been sleeping a few hours a night. The rest of the time I've been spending in the studio."

"Mom, you need to get more sleep."

"You'd think so, but I'm just not tired. I finished a painting yesterday and started another one last night. It's like I can't stop. And I have to say, I'm loving it. Completely loving it!"

I don't think I've ever heard her this excited. Moving to New York for the summer was a great idea. She's loving it there and it's been a good distraction to keep her mind off my dad.

"That's great, Mom. Send me a picture of the painting."

"I will. I took pictures of it last night because it's being delivered to the gallery today."

"They're already showing your work?"

"Yes! Isn't that wonderful? The first painting I did along with the one I just finished will be featured in the showing this weekend."

"Mom, that's amazing! Congratulations!"

"It *is* amazing. I just wish you were here with me. I miss you, honey."

"I miss you too. But there's no room in Claire's apartment and we definitely can't afford our own place in New York."

Claire, the friend my mom's staying with, has a 600 square foot apartment. It's just one room with a kitchen and living space that also serves as the bedroom. My mom is sleeping on the couch.

"We'll see each other soon," I say. "You'll be back here teaching in a few months. September isn't that far away."

"That's true." I hear the disappointment in her voice. Does that mean she doesn't want to come back? There's no way she could stay there. Apartments are way too expensive and I'm pretty sure Claire doesn't want a permanent roommate. "The time will go fast. It already has. I can't believe it's almost the middle of June."

"Have you figured out where you want to live when you get back?"

"I may end up living with you in that house and doing the commute every day."

"That's an hour each way. And you don't have a car. I thought the plan was to get an apartment on the bus line."

"Everything's up in the air until I sell a painting. And if I don't sell one, then..." she sighs, "I don't know what we'll do."

"Mom, you'll sell one. I know you will. You'll probably sell both of them. Did Claire say how much you might get?"

"She really doesn't know. She said it depends on how people react when they see my work. If a lot of people are interested, she'll price the paintings higher. If there's little to no interest, they'll be priced lower or removed from the gallery."

"They'll sell. I've seen your work and it's awesome. Everyone's going to want your paintings."

"If they do, whatever money I make is going into your college fund. Obviously I'll have to take some of it for living expenses but the rest is going to you. You're so close, Sage. Just a few more classes."

"I know. I'll graduate. I promise."

As we've been talking, I've been searching my closet for something to wear but can't seem to make a decision. I don't want to wear a dress or a skirt or Kyle might think it's a date, so do I wear shorts? Or jeans? It's hot out so if we sit outside, I'll want to be wearing shorts.

"So tell me what you've been up to," my mom says. "How's work?"

"Same as always. It's basically the same every day. Trust me, you have a way more exciting life than me right now."

"I'm sorry, honey. I really wish you could be here. I feel terrible that you're stuck living in a town where you barely know anyone."

"It's not that bad. I'm not complaining. I was just saying there's not much to do here so I don't really have anything exciting to tell you."

"How's Nina? Have you two been going out?"

"Yeah, we were out together last night. It was two for one burgers at Skeeter's." I laugh. "That's about as exciting as it gets here. Oh, and Saturday there's a fundraiser for the fire department."

"Are you going?"

"Nina's making me, so yes."

"I'm glad you have a friend there. And even though it's not that exciting, I like that you're in a safe small town. I don't have to worry so much."

I hope my mom never talks to Nina. She'll tell her I'm living next to a serial killer.

I check the clock. Shit, it's quarter to six and I'm not ready.

"Mom, I have to go. I have someone coming over soon and I haven't even dried my hair." I race into the bathroom.

"Who's coming over?"

"Just a friend." I search for the blowdryer.

"Nina's coming over?"

"No, um..." I can't find the blowdryer. Where did I put it? I go back in the bedroom.

"Then who is it?"

"It's just this guy next door." I find the blowdryer on the floor by my closet. My room's a mess. I really need to clean it.

"What guy? You mean that old man who complains that your car is too loud?"

"No, he went to Florida for the summer. He's renting his house out to this guy, Kyle. He doesn't know anyone here so I invited him over."

"How well do you know this boy?" she asks in her concerned mom voice.

"Mom, you don't have to worry. I've met him a few times now and he's not some crazy lunatic." I set my phone down and put it on speaker so I can work on my hair.

"Just be careful."

"I will. He's going to be here soon. I have to get ready. I'll call you tomorrow."

"Send me a text goodnight so I know your date went okay."

"It's not a date, but yes, I'll send you a text."

"Okay. Bye, honey."

Even my mom thinks Kyle is dangerous. But to be fair, she thinks every guy I go out with is dangerous.

But I'm not going out with Kyle. He's not looking for a girlfriend. We're just two people who are new in town, getting to know each other. That's all this is.

So why am I so nervous?

CHAPTER SEVEN

At six, Kyle arrives at my door, his arms loaded up with grocery sacks.

"Delivery," he jokes, a big smile on his face. When I first met him, he was so grouchy I didn't think he ever smiled. But the more I've been around him, the more I see that smile.

"Let me help." I take some of the sacks and walk through the tiny living room to the kitchen. It's a small house, with just two bedrooms, a living room and an eat-in kitchen.

He sets the bags down on the counter. "I'll go get the rest."

"There's more? You brought in four bags. I had like five items on my list."

"I went a little crazy at the store. Sorry." He doesn't sound sorry. I think he felt bad for me after I told him I didn't have much money for groceries. But I wasn't implying he had to buy me some.

He returns with three more plastic sacks. He sets them down and pulls out a bottle of wine. "Chardonnay. To go with the grilled cheese."

"Funny." I laugh, but he's not laughing. "Wait, are you serious? We're having wine with grilled cheese?"

"You don't have to drink it. I got it just in case you wanted it with dinner. The Chardonnay will balance well with the buttery bread and creamy cheese."

"Did you make that up?"

"No. It's true. I know my wine pairings. I'm from California. They teach wine pairings 101 in kindergarten."

I know he's joking, but I play along. "Makes sense. So what goes with peanut butter and jelly?"

"Merlot, preferably one with dark cherry undertones." He opens my fridge and puts the wine in it.

"So what else did you get?" I look in one of the bags and see packages of meat. "Are you trying to tell me you'd rather have a steak tonight?" I ask, holding up a t-bone.

"They were having a meat sale and I got some for myself so I thought I'd throw in a few for you too. They're not for tonight. You can have them later this week, or freeze them if you want."

"Thanks." I put the steak in the freezer, but then take it out and put it in the fridge. I'm going to make it tomorrow. I haven't had steak since before my dad left.

The rest of the meat I put in the freezer, along with the ice cream he bought me, three different kinds, all flavors I like.

I don't know why he did all this. Shopping for groceries AND paying for them? Just yesterday he was yelling at me to go away. But he could've just been in a bad mood from his motorcycle breaking down.

We finish putting away the groceries and I start making the sandwiches.

"This is a really lame dinner," I say. "I can't believe the first time I have someone over for dinner I'm making grilled cheese."

He finds a bowl under the counter and dumps a bag of potato chips in it. "There. Now it's not as lame. We have a side dish."

I laugh. "Fancy."

He puts the bowl on the small square dining table.

"Actually, we're eating outside," I tell him. "I don't like eating in here. I try to eat outside whenever I can."

"That's fine."

As I'm making the sandwiches, Kyle opens the wine, then finds some glasses in the cupboard. It doesn't feel awkward having him here, like I thought it would. I was nervous when he arrived, but now I'm relaxed.

Turning away from the stove, I go to get some plates and walk right into Kyle.

"Sorry," he says, but he doesn't back away. His hands are clasped around my shoulders and he looks at me, pausing, almost like he wants to kiss me.

I'm no longer relaxed, my heart beating hard and fast. I want to kiss him. I probably shouldn't, but his face is right there, like he's waiting for me to make a move. Before I can decide what to do, he slowly leans down, making the decision for me.

I close my eyes and feel his lips press against mine. My hands go to his sides and I step closer, my mouth parting as he takes the kiss deeper. His hand rises to behind my neck, his fingers threading through my hair, sending a tingle down my spine. More tingles ripple through me from the feel of his soft lips, his teasing tongue, his warm breath. It's just a simple kiss so I don't know why I'm reacting this way. It's either because it's been so long since I've been kissed or because of Kyle. I have a feeling it's because of Kyle.

When he backs me up to the counter and presses his hard body against my soft curves, a surge of heat fills me. An intense need. I haven't wanted someone this badly for a long time.

"Sage," he says, dropping his forehead against mine. "I know I should stop but..."

"But what?"

"I'm so damn attracted to you." He looks in my eyes. "From the moment I saw you..." He doesn't finish the statement, his eyes squeezing shut like he's trying to control whatever urges he feels.

I kiss him, with just my lips. Short, innocent kisses that he returns, but with tongue, teasing my mouth and working me up even more. Our kisses become faster, our breathing heavier. Then suddenly, he breaks from the kiss and takes my hand and leads me to the living room. Just as he's about to sit down, I yank on his hand and pull him back.

"Don't sit there!"

He looks at the couch, then back at me. "Why not?"

"She died on there."

"Who?"

"Mabel. The old lady who used to live here. She died on the couch."

"Then why do you still have it?"

"Because I can't afford a new one. But I'm never sitting on that thing and neither are you." I shoo him away. "Stand back. You shouldn't even be near it."

"Why?" He chuckles. "Is it going to kill me too?"

"Maybe. I wouldn't take any chances."

He gives me a half-smile. "You're funny, you know that?"

"I was being serious. You can't sit on a couch where someone died."

He steps up to me and runs his hand down my cheek.

I look up at him. "What are you doing?"

His eyes are on my face, studying it.

"God, you're beautiful."

I don't respond. Honestly, I'm too shocked to respond. Yesterday he acted like he hated me and now he's being really nice. Maybe he's just acting this way because he wants sex. If so, I'd be up for that. I'm completely turned on and it's been over a year since I've done it.

"Sage." He pauses, his eyes fixed on mine. "I didn't plan on kissing you. I told myself I needed to stay away from you and I was right."

"Why? I don't understand."

"From the moment I saw you, I haven't been able to stop thinking about you. I don't know if it's your kindness or your persistence or the fact that you're so damn beautiful...maybe it's all of that. All I know is that I felt something for you from the instant I saw you." He looks down and shakes his head. "But I can't."

"Can't what?"

"I can't do this. I can't...be with you. Not that you would want that. I mean, obviously you kissed me but I'm sure that was—"

"I wanted to." I put my hand on his chest and he looks up. "I wanted to kiss you. And I'm just as confused as you are. I know I shouldn't get involved with you knowing you won't be here long, but I haven't been able to stop thinking about you, which doesn't make sense because up until today, you've been really rude to me."

"I know. And I'm sorry. I've just..." He tightens his jaw and swallows. "I've got a lot going on. I'm not at a point right now where I can be in a relationship, so when you kept trying to help me, I had to tell you to go. I'm sorry it came out so harshly but that was the only way I could get you to leave."

"So you're saying you don't want this."

"I do, but I don't want to get involved with you and then have to leave you. That wouldn't be fair to either of us."

"Meaning you just want to be friends."

"I don't even know if I can do *that.* As you saw just now, I have trouble being just friends with you. I promised myself I wouldn't kiss you tonight and I'm barely here five minutes and already broke my promise."

"Is that a bad thing? Kissing me?"

"Yeah. It is, because it'll lead to more. It probably would have if you hadn't freaked out about the couch."

He's being so honest, so open, that I keep quiet to see what else he'll say.

"I wasn't going to come over here tonight. I was going to make up some excuse for why I couldn't. I was going to drop off the groceries and leave."

"So why didn't you?"

"Because I wanted to see you so fucking bad. You calm me, Sage. I don't know how you do it, but you do. And you make me laugh, which if you knew me, you'd know isn't easy to do. Or, it hasn't been for a really long time. Even when you're yelling at me or scolding me, I still want to be with you. Because I know you aren't doing those things to piss me off. You're doing it because you care. You cared about some strange guy walking down the side of the road. You cared that my head was bleeding and bandaged it up. You were worried I'd get dehydrated so you brought me water. You know how fucking rare that is? To do all that for someone you don't even know?"

Again, I remain silent, and wait for him to finish.

"So I made a deal. I told myself I could come over here but I had to keep my distance. I was here to have dinner. Nothing more. But then..." He cups my cheek with his hand. "Then I kissed you, like I've wanted to since the second I laid eyes on you."

I close my eyes and feel his lips over my mouth. This time the kiss is softer, his lips barely brushing over mine.

"God, I can't stop," he says, frustration in his voice. "I keep telling myself to, but then I don't. I can't." He rests his forehead on mine. "I'm sorry. I shouldn't have come over here."

I pull back and look at him. "I think we should make a deal."

"What kind of deal?"

"We're both outsiders in this small town. We're both only here for a short time. And we both can't stop thinking about each other so I say we—"

"You can't stop thinking about me?" he asks with a smile. "And why is that?"

"Because you're..." I look away, feeling embarrassed.

"I'm what?"

"You're cute. I've already told you this so I don't know why—"

"Cute?" He laughs.

"Handsome," I say, feeling even more embarrassed. "Whatever. Can you just let me finish what I was about to say?"

"Go ahead."

"In regards to kissing, and whatever happens next, I think we do what we want to do and not worry about what comes after that."

"And risk getting hurt when it ends? That's really what you want?"

"After what I've been through the past few months, I don't know what I want. So for now, I'm just taking each day as it comes. And as of today, right now, I like this. I like being with you. I like how you make me feel."

"Sage, as much as I would love to start something with you, I just wouldn't feel right doing that, knowing it wouldn't end well."

I shrug. "Then I guess we'll just go back to how things were. I'll keep bothering you and you'll keep telling me to go away."

A smile slides up his face. "You ARE very persistent."

"And you're conveniently located for frequent drop-ins so expect to see me at your house all hours of the day and night."

"I actually wouldn't mind that. And just so you know, you were never bothering me. Even that day on the road, I knew you were only trying to help. I just didn't want it, especially from some girl I'd just met who was already making my heart beat out of my damn chest."

"It did?" I smile, loving that I had that effect on him. He had that effect on me too.

"I don't think I can do this. I like you too much to risk hurting you."

My smile drops hearing his words. I really wanted this. I wanted just a few short months with a guy I really like to make this summer not so bad. To keep my mind off what happened. This was my distraction, just like my mom distracts herself with her art. But Kyle turned me down. I guess I should be happy about that. It proves he's a good guy, not just out to use me for sex, then toss me aside. But he wouldn't have been using me. I wanted this. I wanted *him*.

"Do you want me to leave?" he asks.

"No." I force out a smile. "It's fine. I understand." I sniff the air. "Oh, shit, I think dinner's burning!" I race over to the stove and flip the sandwiches. "They're ruined. I have to make new ones."

"Sorry. It's my fault."

"It's not your fault. We were both um...distracted." I take the skillet to the trash and dump the sandwiches in it.

"Distracted." He chuckles as he walks over to me. "That's a good way to put it. So what can I do to help?"

"You could butter the bread." I open the fridge to get the butter and when I turn around, Kyle is right there, our bodies almost touching.

"I was going to get it," he says, doing that thing again where his eyes move over my face, taking in all my features. Why does he do that? So he'll remember me when he leaves?

"I'll get the bread." I close the fridge and go around him, my body brushing against his. It's a really small kitchen, which is a problem when you're trying not to touch the person you really want to touch.

In an attempt to make things less awkward, I turn on the radio that's in the kitchen and start singing and dancing along to the songs, not even caring that Kyle is there. I feel comfortable around him enough to be myself.

"You want to grab some glasses?" I ask, moving to the music as I flip the sandwiches. "There's iced tea in the fridge."

He stands there, smiling as he watches me. "God, you're adorable. I've never met anyone like you."

"What does that mean?" I ask with a laugh. "You don't know anyone who dances while they cook?"

"Can't say that I do."

I point to the fridge. "Are you going to get the iced tea?"

He stays where he's at. "I'm going to have to move."

"Yeah." I walk up to him. "You're blocking the silverware drawer."

"I meant I'm going to have to move out of this town."

"And why is that?"

He puts his arms around me and pulls me against his body. "Because I can't be around you. Even two miles down the road is too close."

"Was it the dancing?" I tease. "Did it make me irresistible?"

"Everything about you is irresistible." He leans down and kisses me, soft and slow, and my knees go weak. His kisses just keep getting better, or maybe I like them more because now they're off limits.

"You said we weren't going to do that," I point out as he stands up straight again, his arms still around me.

"Last one."

I laugh. "Yeah. Okay. Now move so I can get the silverware."

We set up dinner outside and just as we start to eat, my phone rings. It's Nina.

"Sage, I'm so sorry," she says, "I got busy and forgot I was supposed to call. How's it going?"

"Great. We just sat down for dinner."

"Was that 'great' meant to be sarcastic? Is he listening? Do you need to be rescued?"

"No. Hey, I should go. The food's getting cold."

"Did you really make grilled cheese?"

"Yeah, but I burned the first batch and had to make more."

"You sure you don't need me to stop by?"

"We're good, but thanks."

"Okay, but if you need rescuing, just call and hang up. I'll take that as a signal and be over as fast as I can."

"Got it. Bye, Nina."

She's funny. She's had so many bad dates, she just assumes mine will be too. Except it's not a date. I have to keep reminding myself of that.

"Rescue call?" Kyle asks.

"What?" I pretend to have no idea what he's talking about.

"Was that your friend, trying to see if you needed an excuse to get out of having dinner with me?"

"No, of course not."

"Liar," he says as he picks up his sandwich.

I pick up mine too and start eating, not addressing his comment.

"What excuse was she going to give you? Her car was on fire? Her dog ate chocolate and needed a ride to the vet?"

"No." I laugh. "She doesn't even have a dog."

He smiles. "Are you admitting it was a rescue call?"

"Okay, yes, but I told her not to do it. I told her this wasn't a date, but she didn't believe me."

"So is this friend of yours someone in town?"

"Yeah. Nina. As of now, she's my *only* friend. All the friends I had in college kind of disappeared, and as for here, as soon as people found out who my dad is, they started avoiding me. Nina's the only one who's welcomed me."

"Are you ready to explain what happened or would you rather wait?"

"I'm ready. But before I start, I need to tell you that a lot of the stuff written online isn't true. If you look up my name on the internet, the first thing you'll see is news about my dad, but a lot of those stories are from people my dad stole from, so they're making up stuff to get revenge. You'll see a lot of bad things about my mom and me that aren't true. Not even close."

He sets his sandwich down, giving me his full attention. "I'll only believe what you tell me."

I'm glad he said that and I hope he means it. After I tell him this, I hope he doesn't turn on me and assume I was part of it. I hope he doesn't judge me, and think I'm stupid or naive for not knowing what my dad was up to. Those are the reactions I've had in the past after trying to explain what happened. Even my friends turned on me.

But I don't think Kyle will. I barely know him and yet I'm already starting to trust him more than people I've known for years.

CHAPTER EIGHT

For the next half hour I tell Kyle the story, starting from the beginning, when my dad showed up at my dorm. I end with the day I moved here, which was when I met Nina.

When I'm done, Kyle is shaking his head and I'm not sure why. Does he think I'm lying? Does he think I was part of it? It wouldn't surprise me if he did. That's what everyone in town thinks.

"What's wrong?" I ask.

"I just wasn't expecting that." He leans back on the patio chair and laces his hands behind his head.

"What did you think I'd say?"

"You said the town didn't like you so I thought maybe your dad was from here originally and people didn't like him for some reason. I didn't think you were going to tell me he stole hundreds of millions of dollars from people with some made-up investment company."

"I was completely shocked when I found out. Sometimes, I still can't believe it. He hid it so well that nobody knew, not even my mom. I think we were both just so happy he'd changed from how he was before that we just ignored anything that didn't seem right."

"What was he like before? When you were a kid?"

"He had no focus. He'd jump from job to job. He wasn't reliable. My mom would ask him to pick me up from school and he'd forget. He'd be home watching TV and she'd have to leave work to come get me. Or he'd place bets on a sports game and not tell her and then lose everything he bet. He was just really immature and didn't care about anyone but himself."

"Most people don't change."

"I know, but my mom and I believed that he could, and that he did. But it turns out he just learned how to be a better liar. And he learned how to dress well so that people would believe he was successful. He earned their trust then took their money, including ours."

"You and your mom had nothing left?"

"We had our cars but they were both old and not worth much. We sold them to get enough money to pay off whatever debts we had and were left with just enough to buy my mom's ticket to New York."

"So living here was your only option."

"Yeah, but it's not that bad. Other than that couch. I really need to get rid of that."

He stands up. "Let's do it right now."

"Do what?"

"Get rid of the couch. We'll take it out and set it by the garage, then later this week, we'll load it in Miller's truck and take it to a dump. Do you know if there's one close to here?"

"I have no clue, but Kyle, you don't have to do that."

"I want to. I know it bothers you to have it in the house and I agree. It gives off a bad aura, and that's the last thing you need right now." He walks to the door and opens it. "Come on."

We leave the patio and go inside.

"I don't think we should do this," I say. "It's not my couch. It's Lorraine's, the woman who inherited the house."

"You really think she'd want this?" He points to the couch.

Looking at it, I don't know why *anyone* would want it, even if someone *hadn't* died on it. It has a brown wooden frame that's curved at the top and sides, like a Victorian style, and it's covered in a pink velour fabric. There are brown stains, which I hope are coffee stains, on the cushions, and the seams at the very bottom of the frame are tearing, leaving threads dangling down.

"Lorraine definitely wouldn't want this," I say.

"Then let's go." He's already positioned himself on one end of the couch.

I position myself on the other and we lift it up and carry it outside. We set it down on the grass behind the garage.

"I'll look up where the closest dump is and maybe we could go tomorrow if you have time. Or if you can just help me get it in the truck, I can take it there myself."

"Thanks."

"No problem. Should we finish dinner?"

"Yeah, but first I need to wash my hands."

He agrees and we both go back inside to wash up. When I walk into the living room I notice that it does feel different having that couch gone. Kyle was right. It had a bad aura. It was making this place feel dark and sad and I'm sure it's what was making this place smell so bad. Just having it out of here a few minutes has made the place smell better.

I close my eyes and take a deep breath.

"Before you do that, let's air it out."

I open my eyes and see Kyle opening all the windows.

"You shouldn't open them. It's too dusty."

"It's not windy today. And you need the fresh air. I bet this place hasn't been aired out in years."

"Okay, but remind me to close them when you leave."

"You should just keep them open all night. Give it time to air out."

"And get murdered? No, thanks."

"Murdered?" He gives me a concerned look. "Why would you be murdered?"

"A woman all alone at night with the windows open? Have you not seen horror films?"

"Those are movies, not real life. There's nobody out here. You're safe to leave the windows open."

"I wish I could. I love sleeping with the windows open. But I can't. I'd worry too much. I'd never sleep."

He looks at me like he's about to say something, but then doesn't and continues opening windows.

When he's done, we go back outside and finish dinner.

"So tell me about yourself," I say.

"Do I have to?" he asks, kiddingly.

"You don't want to?"

"Not really. I'm not that interesting and I don't like talking about myself."

"Yeah, I kind of already figured that out."

He doesn't laugh at my joke. "I really don't, so if you ask me something and I don't give you an answer, that's why. I'm just a really private person."

"So what *can* you tell me?"

"What do you want to know?"

"Why are you here? In this town?"

"I needed to go somewhere where people couldn't find me. I needed privacy."

I feel a nervous twitch in my chest. Maybe he really *is* on the run, like Jesse said.

"Why don't you want people to find you?"

He pauses, then says, "Because I'm writing a book. A novel."

"You're a writer?" I smile. "What have you written? Anything I might know?"

"I'm not published yet, but I'm under contract with a publisher and if I don't finish the manuscript in the next few months, they might cancel the deal. I've been struggling with writer's block and thought getting away would help. Plus, my book is set in a small rural town so living here is research."

"That's really cool. I'm living next to a soon-to-be-published author."

"If I can finish the manuscript. If I can't, I'm just an out-of-work writer."

"I'm sure you'll finish it. Do they pay you to work on it?"

"They give me a little money up front, but the rest comes later."

"What's the story about?"

"I can't say." He grins slightly. "I'm sworn to secrecy."

"Well, if you need some insight into small towns, you should talk to Nina. She's lived here her whole life."

"What about you? Have you always lived in Kansas?"

"Yeah, but not in a small town. I grew up in Kansas City and I go to—or *used* to go to—college not far from there."

"You said you only have a semester left?"

"Yeah, and I'm definitely finishing. I just don't know when."

He nods. "How much do you need?"

"For what?"

"College. How much money?"

"Eight thousand, which means I need to get a better job than working at a garage. When my mom moves back to Kansas City, I'll go live with her and have more options for jobs. I'll get three if I have to. Whatever it takes to get the money I need. I want to go back to school in the spring."

"When's your mom moving back?"

"Late August, right before school starts. She's an art teacher. But when I talked to her the other day, it sounded like she's not too excited to come back."

"After living in New York? Yeah, it'll be hard, especially if she likes it there."

"She loves it. And she loves being able to paint every day instead of teach. Not that she doesn't like teaching but she's done it forever and I know she'd like a change. Her dream was always to be an artist so this summer she's living her dream, but in a few months it'll end."

"Maybe she could stay there. If the art community embraces her, she could have a big future ahead of her."

"You sound like you know about this. Are you an artist as well as a writer?"

"No." He chuckles. "I can't even draw a straight line. But I appreciate art and I go to museums and the occasional gallery opening."

"You're not going to fit in at all around here," I say, jokingly, but it's true. "Most people in this town think art is a waste of time, both creating it and going to see it."

"Are you saying I won't be making many friends?"

"Not if you bring up art or use fancy words. Do that and they'll say you're a snob. But you have me as a friend. And maybe Nina, if she approves of you."

"Are you thinking she won't?"

"She will, but she'll give you a hard time before she does. She's kind of protective of me, but that's a good thing. She keeps people from harassing me. They used to come up and say stuff to me, like call me a thief like my dad. I still overhear them talking about me sometimes but they don't say it to my face anymore, thanks to Nina. She's been a good friend."

"Those are hard to find."

"Believe me, I know. Do you have many friends back home?"

"A few, but they're not the type I could count on."

"Did you grow up in LA?"

"No." He looks out at the yard. "You need help with the lawn? Because I could help if you need it."

"Thanks, but I can handle it. So um, that's it?"

"What?" He looks back at me.

"You didn't elaborate on where else you've lived. You changed the subject."

"I told you, I don't like talking about myself."

"If we're going to be friends, we should probably know some stuff about each other."

"Where I've lived doesn't matter. I don't like looking back. I look at what's ahead and focus on that."

He's being evasive again, but why? What's the big deal about telling me where he's lived? Why wouldn't he want me to know?

"Were you in prison?" I ask.

He coughs on the wine he was drinking. "Prison? Why would you ask me that?"

"You're being so secretive about your past that I thought maybe it's because you were in prison."

I don't really think he's been to prison but I had to say something that might prompt him to tell me more.

"Boston, New York, Dallas, and L.A. That's where I've lived. Happy now?" His tone is harsh and he won't look at me.

"It was just a question. You don't have to get angry about it."

"I wasn't. I was just stating the facts."

"You seem mad. Is this just how you are? Sometimes you're nice and sometimes you're an ass?"

He shakes his head. "Sorry. I just really don't like talking about myself."

"Then maybe we can't be friends. After what I went through with my dad, I'm not comfortable being around someone who's secretive. And if you act this way with the people in town, they'll make up their own stories about you, and believe me, they're way worse than anything you could come up with. You're better off telling your own story. Keeping quiet will just make things worse for you."

"Where I'm from and what I do. That's all they need to know."

"And what about *me*? I'm not allowed to know more?"

"Maybe later. Not now." He sounds irritated so I don't push him. Maybe he really is just a private person and needs more time to open up.

"So what are you studying?" he asks.

"Human resource management."

"HR." He nods. "Tough field. You'll have to fire people."

"And hire them. I'm hoping I'll do more hiring than firing. I want to work at a company that actually wants their employees to succeed and doesn't just say that they do."

"Those companies exist?" he asks in a kidding tone.

I smile. "Believe it or not, they do. I just don't know if they'll hire me." I look down at the table. "What's funny—well, not in a haha way but in an ironic way—is that human resources is all about people. Learning how they think. What they want. What motivates them. I took all these classes on psychology and human behavior and yet I couldn't even figure out my own father and what he was up to." I pick my wine glass up and swirl it around. It's nearly empty but the motion distracts me from the feelings that bubble up whenever I think about my dad. "I should've seen the signs. They were all laid out in front of me and yet I didn't put it together. My mom was too blinded by love to see what he was up to. She needed me to tell her. I should've been the one to see through his lies. I don't know why I didn't."

"Because you wanted him to be someone else." Kyle takes my glass from me and sets it down.

"But I knew he wasn't. In my heart I knew he hadn't changed but I wouldn't let myself believe it. If I'd just trusted my instincts, I could've stopped him. I could've found out what he was doing and kept all those people from losing their money."

"It was probably too late. A scheme like he had going could take years to develop. He'd probably spent half the money he stole by the time the feds found out what he was up to."

That's exactly what investigators think happened. According to what they told my mom and me, my dad started this scam years ago and spent the money as soon as he got it. They said guys like him are impulsive and buy whatever it is they want as soon as they get the money. But then they want something else so they have to keep the scam up to get more money. It becomes an addiction. The more they spend, the more money they want, and they live off the high that comes from stealing from people without getting caught.

"You can't blame yourself." I feel Kyle's hand on my arm and look up at him. "I know, thinking back, it seems like you should've seen the signs, but when you're in the moment, sometimes that's just not possible. You want the person to be who you want them to be, so you look past any signs that go against that. You see what you want to see and make excuses for whatever doesn't seem right. Or you may not even notice it."

He's almost talking like he's experienced this himself. Maybe it was with an ex-girlfriend. Maybe she lied to him, or stole from him.

"How do you know all this?" I ask.

"Know what?"

"About people deceiving you. Are you talking from experience?"

He leans back in his chair and folds his arms over his chest. "I just know how people work. Some people will do anything to get what they want, even if that means hurting the people they're supposed to care about."

"Has it happened to you?"

"Not personally, but I *know* people it's happened to. I live in L.A. That town is full of people trying to get what they want and not caring who they take down to get it."

"Sounds like a great place to live," I kid. "Why do you live there, anyway? Don't writers usually live in New York? Isn't that where all the publishers are?"

He unfolds his arms and leans toward me, looking me in the eye. "I know you can't help but look back and think you should've known what your dad was up to, but if you keep thinking that way, you'll never get past this. What happened is over. You can't change it, and trying to relive it, wishing you'd been more aware or done something different, doesn't help anything."

He avoided my questions. He really doesn't like talking about himself. Or maybe he's just being nice, keeping the focus on me in an attempt to help me get past this. Ever since my dad took off, I've had this nonstop loop in my head, telling me what I should've done, scolding me for not paying enough attention to what was happening around me. Kyle is right. I can't change the past so why do I keep reliving it?

"I wish I could stop thinking about it," I say.

"You can. You just need to put all your energy on the future and what you're going to do to get back to the place you were at before your father came back into your life."

"I'm trying to but it still keeps me up at night."

I've never told anyone that, not even my mom. I act like everything's fine, like I no longer think about my dad and what he did, but the truth is, I think about it constantly. The guilt I feel never goes away. I let my dad back into my life, which helped him get back into my mom's life. If I'd turned him away that day he showed up at my dorm, there's a chance he would've gone away and left us alone. But instead he stuck around.

"It's not your fault," Kyle says.

"People keep saying that, but it's not true. If I'd just gone with my gut and paid more attention and asked the right questions, my dad could've been stopped. Instead, he's on the loose, living off other people's money. He's a criminal and I could've stopped him but didn't."

"You can't keep doing this, Sage. I'm telling you, you'll go crazy if you keep playing this game of what-if. You have to accept what happened and move on."

"It's not that easy."

"No. It's not. But replaying what happened is just giving your dad power over you. He's still controlling you, controlling how you think and how you feel. Is that what you want? To keep giving him power?"

"No. Of course not."

"Then don't. Stop thinking about him, and most of all, stop blaming yourself. People like him are always trying to place the blame on others. They never take responsibility for their actions. So by continuing to blame yourself, you're letting him continue to manipulate you."

I hadn't thought about it that way, but I guess in a way, I *am* letting my dad have power over me. I'm taking the blame for what he did, which is exactly what he would want. He was always blaming others for his actions. Never taking responsibility. If he were ever caught and put in prison, I'm sure he'd blame my mom and me for why he stole from people. He'd say he was trying to provide for us. To be a good father and husband. He'd never admit the truth, which is that he's a lying, manipulative, selfish person who uses people for his own personal gain.

It's time I accept that and stop making excuses for him. He may be my father, but that doesn't mean he's a good person.

CHAPTER NINE

Kyle

"Thanks," Sage says.

"For what?"

"Telling me all that. I needed to hear it."

I just nod. I've said enough. I don't want her figuring out that what I said applies to me just as much as it does to her.

If she only knew the truth. How similar our experiences are, except mine is so much worse. If my father had only stolen money....shit, I'd be doing a fucking happy dance. I'd still have my life. I'd still have a home. I'd still be able to see my little brother. But instead, I'm stuck in this shitty small town in the middle of nowhere.

"Do you want to go inside?" Sage asks. "I have some cake we could have for dessert. Nina's aunt owns the bakery in town. She's always giving me free stuff. I'm surprised I don't weigh five hundred pounds." She lets out a laugh; a soft, sweet laugh I could listen to all day.

This girl...she's driving me crazy. Not in a bad way, but in a way that gets my heart thumping harder than it should be when I'm just sitting here having dinner. She's had this effect on me since I met her and it's freaking annoying. I'm not here to meet a girl and I'm definitely not available for a relationship. In fact, that would be the worst thing I could do right now, or any time in the foreseeable future. Right now I need to be focused on getting my brother out of my father's house. That's my number one priority.

Scratch that. Saving Cain is priority number two. Priority number one is staying alive; not being found and not being killed so that I can go back and get Cain.

He's safe for now. He's too young to understand what's going on. But I still don't want him around my father. The man is surrounded by criminals—people who wouldn't think twice about hurting an innocent child.

"What do you think?" Sage asks, showing off that beautiful smile of hers. That smile had me stopping in my tracks when I saw her on the road. I was on a mission, wanting to be left alone, but then she followed me and I saw that smile and couldn't move my damn legs. There I was, standing in the road, staring at that smile like I'd never seen one before.

"Why don't we have dessert out here? Your house still smells like the dead lady's couch."

She laughs as she gets up. "You're right. I'll be right back."

"Need some help?" I ask as she goes inside.

"Nope, I'm good," she calls back through the screen door.

I'm glad she said that. I can't risk going in that house again, at least not the kitchen. Not after what happened earlier.

That kiss. Why the hell did I do that? I know she's off limits and then I fucking kiss her. I wasn't even thinking when I did it. It's like a switch shut off my brain and my feelings just took over. It was a response, a need, an uncontrollable urge. She was right there in front of me. So close. Her body almost touching mine. I tried to stop myself. I almost pulled back but then I saw her eyes. I heard her breath quicken. And I knew she wanted me to do what I was about to do. So I did it. I kissed her.

It was a kiss I'll never forget. It was one of those kisses that was good from the start. It wasn't awkward. It didn't need to be practiced a few times before it felt right. It was just right from the moment our lips touched. It told me there's something special about this girl. I already knew that from the moment I met her but the kiss just confirmed it. There's something about her—about us—that feels right.

I've been trying to come up for a reason why I feel this way. When she told me about her dad, I assumed that was the reason. We both have fucked-up fathers so that's why we feel so drawn to each other. But maybe that's not it. Maybe she just happens to be the girl for me. But that doesn't make sense. There's no way fate would put me through what I had to go through to get here just to meet a girl.

"It's chocolate with a strawberry filling," Sage says as she brings out two pieces of cake.

"Sounds great," I say as she sets the plate in front of me.

"It is. I've already had two slices." She sits across from me and refills our waters from the pitcher on the table.

I watch her, my heart thumping faster, my eyes unable to leave her beautiful face, those eyes, that smile. Fuck. What is going on with me? I can't react this way. She's off limits. All women are until I can get control of my life again and get my brother away from my dad.

"It's good," I say, taking a bite of the cake.

The last time I had cake was at my brother's birthday party last year. It was Cain's twelfth birthday so it should've been at a pizza place or arcade or some other place appropriate for kids that age. But instead, my father had the party at a fancy restaurant in Midtown. A place *he* wanted to go. My brother didn't like it but he kept quiet, knowing if he complained, he'd be scolded and told he was being ungrateful. I tried to make the night better for him by bringing along some gifts, mostly video games along with a watch he wanted that connects with his phone.

Dad gave him money, which is what he's been giving us since Mom died. She always bought us presents, but Dad just gives us money inside a generic card.

That night of Cain's birthday, Dad disappeared during dessert. The cake had just arrived at our table when he got a phone call. He went outside to answer it and was gone for a half hour. I don't know where he went or what he was doing but when he returned to the table, he was on edge, his hand shaking just slightly but enough for me to tell something was wrong. I ignored it, much like Sage ignored the warning signs about her dad. We both chose to not see what was right in front of us.

"Want another slice?" Sage asks, getting up from the table.

"No, but thank you for offering." I stand up. "I should probably be going. You have to be at work early."

"Don't worry about it. I don't sleep much."

Because of her dad. I know exactly how she feels. Despite the speech I gave her earlier, I'm unable to follow my own advice. I still lie awake every night, beating myself up for not seeing what was right in front of me. For going along with his lies and never questioning them, even when my gut told me something was up. And in those rare moments when I do fall asleep, I'm tortured by nightmares. Scenes of that night playing over and over again, then scenes of my brother meeting a similar fate.

"Would you mind staying?" she asks. "If you're busy, I understand. It just gets really boring being out here alone every night. We could just watch TV if you want."

What do I do? I can tell she really wants me to stay, but if I agree to it we might end up repeating what we did in the kitchen. But there's no couch anymore so we'll have to sit in separate chairs. Chairs that aren't even next to each other. If we're that far apart, chances are nothing will happen.

"I guess I could stay a little longer."

She smiles. "Great! Let's go inside."

This girl is far too nice, and far too trusting. I've only known her a short time and she's already trusting me enough to go in her house, which is out in the middle of nowhere. It's not surprising her father conned his way back into her life.

She needs to be more cautious, even with me. I'd never hurt her, or even consider it, but I'm still basically a stranger and she's alone with me, at night, with nobody else around.

We watch TV but she only gets a few channels so our choices are limited. She stops on an action movie, which I think she did for my sake, not hers, because after a few minutes, she's dozing off in the chair. I could leave but I'm not ready to so I continue to watch the movie but my eyes keep wandering over to her. God, she's beautiful. That long, wavy brown hair. Those soft full lips. Her long tan legs are dangling off the side of the chair, angled toward me. I want to reach over and touch them, run my hand along her smooth skin. But I can't, and so I force my eyes back to the TV.

Over the next hour, Sage remains asleep and my eyes keep going back to her. I can't make myself stop. She's so beautiful. So kind. So trusting.

My mom was trusting like that. How she ever ended up with my father I'll never understand. The two of them were complete opposites. Maybe that's what he wanted. Someone completely different than himself to remind him that good people do exist. But then why didn't he love her? I just met Sage and already feel something for her, so how could my dad be with my mom all those years and not love her?

Sage moves in her sleep and must've hit the remote because the TV suddenly blares so loud it wakes her.

She quickly sits up, searching for the remote. "What happened?"

"I got it." I get up and grab the remote, which fell on the floor when she moved. I turn the volume down on the TV.

"Was I asleep?" she asks, looking up at me. Her eyes are droopy and her hair's a mess. Damn, she's adorable.

"Yeah. Here." I hand her the remote. "I should get going."

She checks the clock on the wall. It's a wooden clock carved in the shape of a tree that has birds on the hands, pointing to the time.

"It's after ten?" She stands up. "I didn't know it was so late."

"Yeah. So I guess I'll see you around. Thanks again for dinner."

She laughs. "Sorry I couldn't give you anything better than grilled cheese."

"It was great. Best dinner I've had in a long time."

It's true. Sometimes simple is better. After my mom died, my father hired a chef to make dinner every night. The guy would only make what my dad told him to, which was always gourmet shit that looked better than it tasted. When my mom made fancy meals, they actually tasted good so I'm not sure why this chef couldn't do the same. And since he was afraid of my dad, he wouldn't make what my brother and I asked him to, like burgers or hotdogs.

"That's pretty sad," Sage says, and for a moment I panic, wondering if I just said what I was thinking out loud. I relax when I realize she was referring to my comment about dinner, not my mom. "I thought they had decent restaurants in L.A."

I make a mental note to do some research on L.A. I've been there a few times but never lived there so I really need to learn more about it in case people ask me about it.

"They have a few decent places but so many people there are on some kind of diet that it's hard to find a restaurant that serves real food. Cheese is like the devil out there."

She laughs. "I doubt that. California is a dairy state, isn't it?"

Is it? Hell, I don't know. She seems to know more about the state than I do.

"Before you go, would you mind helping me with this?" She points to the window in front of her. "I can't get it closed. It's stuck."

"Why don't you leave it open? Let the place air out all night."

"I would, but I won't sleep knowing the windows are open. It's too dangerous."

So she's cautious in some ways, but not when it comes to me. I wonder why she trusts me so much? And why I trust her? I told myself I'd live like a hermit in this town, hiding away in that house and never going out. Yet here I am, only my second night here, and I'm hanging out with my neighbor and have revealed more about myself than I wanted to.

"What if I stayed?" I ask, despite knowing it's a bad idea.

"Stayed where?"

"Here." I look around. "You have a sleeping bag? I could sleep on the floor."

"Why would you stay?"

"So you could keep the windows open. Air the place out."

"You'd really do that?"

"Sure. Why not? Your floor's probably more comfortable than Miller's bed. The thing's gotta be at least thirty years old. It sinks so low in the middle I almost couldn't get out of it this morning."

"Maybe you should buy a new mattress. I'm sure he wouldn't mind."

"Maybe I will." I walk over to her and open the window she was trying to close. "What do you think?"

She looks at the window, then up at me. "I don't know. I'm not sure if it's a good idea...you spending the night."

"You don't feel safe with me?"

"Um..." She bites her lip. "It's not that. Well, maybe it is a little. I mean, we did just meet and although you seem safe, sometimes looks can be deceiving."

"I totally get it," I say, glad that she's being cautious. I'm not a threat but some other guy could be so it's good she's not as trusting as I originally thought. I just met her but I already feel this need to protect her, and honestly, I don't like her living out here by herself with nobody around. I'm her closest neighbor and my house is two miles away.

"I'll close the windows for you before I go." I move the window side to side, then shove it down to get the lock to slide in place. The windows are so old the frame is warped and doesn't fit right when you try to close it.

"Actually, if you wouldn't mind," she says in a hesitant tone.

"Wouldn't mind what?"

"If you wouldn't mind staying, I *would* like to air the place out. Closing that window just now made it seem stuffy in here. I'm already smelling the couch again."

"You could just open the windows tomorrow. Keep them open during the day."

"I can't. I'll be at work. I don't want the windows open while I'm gone." She walks over to the hall closet and opens it up. "I don't think I have a sleeping bag but I have lots of blankets and quilts, if that works." She pulls out a quilt and brings it over to me.

"You sure about this?"

"As long as you promise to be on your best behavior." She smiles.

"So no dancing to loud music or raiding your fridge in the middle of the night?"

She laughs. "My fridge is full of food you paid for so that's not a problem. As for the music, you can play it as long as I get to come out here and dance with you."

"Deal." I shake her hand, and when our eyes meet I feel the need to kiss her again. From the look on her face, I think she's waiting for me to do it, but I won't. I'm not saying it won't happen again in the future but for now, I want her to know I'm here to keep her safe and nothing more.

I let go of her hand and she looks away. "Do you need to go get anything?" she asks.

"No. I can sleep in my clothes."

"Okay, well, if you need anything, I'm down the hall on the right."

"Got it. Thanks!"

She nods quickly, then hurries down to her room. I think she's nervous having me here, not because she's scared, but because we both want to give in to our attraction to each other and don't trust that we can make it a whole night without something happening.

It was probably a bad idea for me to stay here, not only because of what might happen between us, but also because I'm the last person who should be protecting her. I can barely protect myself.

As of now, I think I'm safe. But I know it won't last. They're looking for me. I know they are. And if they find me, they'll kill me.

CHAPTER TEN

Sage

"Kyle?" I say softly, not sure if he's awake in the chair or just sitting there. The room is dark except for the light of the TV so it's hard to tell.

"Hey," I hear him say. He stands up. "You okay?"

"Yeah." I pull the blanket around me and sit down on the chair that's opposite his. Now that the couch is gone, I should probably move the chairs to be beside each other, facing the TV, but last night, I didn't move them because being that close to Kyle could've led us to do things it's too soon to do. I'm not even sure he wants to do those things. I thought he did when we kissed, but ever since then, he's kept his distance from me, almost like he's trying to avoid me.

"What time is it?" he asks, sitting down again.

"A little after five."

"What are you doing up so early? Do you have to get to work?"

"Not until seven. I couldn't sleep and I got tired of lying in bed. I usually get up around five and watch TV until I have to get ready for work."

"Here." He hands me the remote. "There's not much on other than informercials and the ag report."

"Yeah, I don't have money for cable." I flip the channel to the ag report. "This may sound strange but I actually like the farm news. Sometimes they even give recipes." I turn the volume up because he had it on mute. "Did I wake you up?"

"No. I was awake."

"Did you get any sleep?"

"A couple hours."

"That's it? It was the floor, wasn't it? I shouldn't have asked you to stay. Now you didn't get any sleep."

"The floor was fine. And you didn't ask me to stay. I offered. As for sleeping, I'm not someone who sleeps a lot. I'm lucky if I get more than a couple hours a night."

"That's it? How do you write on such little sleep?"

"Caffeine." He chuckles. "Coffee is a writer's best friend."

"Would you like some now? I can make some."

"That'd be great."

I go to the kitchen and take out the can of coffee, then pull the coffeemaker out from under the counter.

"On second thought," he says, getting up, "maybe I should go. You need to get ready for work."

"I have plenty of time. And actually, I kind of like having someone to have coffee with in the morning." As I say it, I realize it sounds like I'm asking him to be here every morning so I quickly say, "Maybe I should get a dog. They don't drink coffee but they're good companions."

He comes over to the kitchen and sits down at the table. "I had a dog when I was a kid. His name was Lumpy because when we got him, he had all these knots in his fur which made him feel lumpy. We found him behind our apartment near the dumpster, looking for food. He didn't have a collar so we assumed he was a stray. My father threw a fit when he saw him. He's a neat freak and a germaphobe. He saw that dirty mutt and almost made us get rid of him but my mom somehow talked him into keeping it."

I continue making the coffee, acting like his story is no big deal when actually it's a huge deal. This is the first time he's told me something about himself without me having to pry it out of him. Maybe the fact that he's tired has his defenses down.

"Do your parents still have him?" I casually ask as I get some mugs out from the cupboard.

"No. He died when I was seven."

"Oh. That's too bad. Did they get another dog?"

"No. My father wouldn't allow it. He hated that dog." He clears his throat. "Anyway, what about breakfast? Can I make you something?" He gets up and goes to the fridge and opens it. "Hmm. You don't have eggs. I should've got breakfast stuff when I was at the store."

I reach around him to get the milk. "Coffee is fine. You don't have to make breakfast. I usually just skip it."

"I could run down to that bakery you mentioned and get something."

"Going into town would take too long. Plus, you'd have the whole town wondering who you are and where you came from. It's better if I have Nina send your story through the gossipers in town so they at least have an idea of who you are, and then you can make an appearance."

"Are you serious? I can't just go in and buy donuts?"

"No. I mean, you could, but trust me, the other way is better."

"Maybe it's best if I just never leave the house."

"That'd be worse. Everyone knows you're staying at Miller's house and they'll want to know why. I'm sure they've already started rumors about you after they saw you at the grocery store. I'll call Nina this morning and have her get the word out about you. You should be able to show your face in town in the next day or so."

"That's kind of ridiculous that people are so into other people's business."

"It is, but that's just how it works around here. But your celebrity status won't last. After a week or two, you'll be old news."

"Doesn't sound like *you're* old news."

"Because my dad stole from people here in town and they feel the need to get revenge. It was only a few families but the town feels loyal to them, which is why I'm an outcast. But Nina's made things a million times better. She keeps people from bothering me so now I can go into town without people looking like they want to kill me." I open a cupboard and take out the oatmeal cookies Nina's aunt gave me a few days ago.

"What's that?" Kyle asks as I set the cookie tin in front of him.

"Breakfast." I take the lid off. "They might be a little stale but they're still good. And they're oatmeal so they work for breakfast."

"Thanks." He takes one.

"I'll get the coffee." I fill the mugs and bring them to the table and sit down. "So what are you up to today?"

"I'll try to get some writing done, and if I can't, I'll probably do some yard work. The lawn's starting to get overgrown."

I take a cookie and break it into two, dipping one half into my coffee. "Don't take this the wrong way but you don't seem like someone who does yard work."

"What makes you think that?"

"Have you ever used a lawnmower?" I bite into my cookie, which is the perfect level of softness now that it's been dipped in coffee.

"Of course I have. I've mowed the lawn plenty of times."

I nod, and dunk my cookie in my coffee again. "Have you ever been in a fight?"

"That's kind of disgusting."

"What?"

"That." He points to my cup. "Dipping that in your coffee."

"It's not disgusting. It's good. People dip donuts in coffee. Why not cookies?"

"Dipping donuts in coffee is also disgusting. Pieces of it break off in the coffee and then you're left drinking soggy bread."

"That doesn't bother me." I point to his cookie. "They'll break your teeth if you don't soak them in something."

"They're not that stale. Not even close to breaking teeth, unless you have soft teeth, which is a much bigger problem than stale cookies."

I laugh. "There's no such thing as soft teeth."

"Which is why there's no need to dunk your cookie in hot coffee, no matter how stale it is."

"I don't care. I'm still doing it." I pick up another cookie and dip it in my coffee then take a bite, closing my eyes and murmuring, "Umm, it's so good."

It comes out sounding sexual and when I open my eyes, I see Kyle staring at me, his lips parted. I set the cookie down and pick up my coffee. It startles him from whatever it was he was thinking about and he quickly gets up from the table and walks over to the coffeemaker.

"Need some more?" he asks, picking up the carafe.

"Yeah. Thanks." I hold my cup out for him. "So you never answered my question."

"About the lawnmower? Yes, I've used one before."

"Not about the lawnmower. About the fight. Were you in a fight? Is that how you hurt your head?"

"Yeah." He sits down again. "I was attacked when I was filling my tank with gas. It was night and nobody was around and the guy wanted money."

"So what'd you do?"

"I punched him and knocked him out, then drove off. Never saw him again."

I don't like violence but I find it kind of hot that he was able to fight off an attacker.

"How'd you know how to do that?"

"Do what?"

"Fight like that."

He shrugs. "I grew up doing martial arts. I did it for fun but it can be used as a weapon if needed."

"I should tell Jesse that." I sip my coffee.

"The garage guy?"

"Yeah. It might keep him from doing something stupid. I think he sees you as a threat. I wouldn't be surprised if he tried to fight you."

"Why? Because he thinks I'm trying to take his girl?"

"Are you?" I cock my head in a flirtatious way.

"Since when are you his girl?"

"I'm not. But he thinks I am." I set my coffee down. "You're an expert at not answering questions, you know that?"

He looks down, then back up. "I can't get involved with someone right now."

I nod, trying to hide my disappointment. "Makes sense. You're not staying here. It wouldn't be right to—"

"No. It wouldn't. Like I told you last night, it's not fair to either of us to start something we can't finish." He pauses. "But if you want to use me to get Jesse to leave you alone..." He doesn't finish the thought.

"You'd pretend to go out with me?"

He shakes his head. "Never mind. It's a bad idea."

"Actually, it's brilliant." I move my coffee mug aside and rest my arms on the table. "If Jesse thought I was with you, he'd stop harassing me at work. It's not like we'd have to put on a big show. You could just stop by the garage now and then and we could be seen around town a few times."

"I don't think that's a good idea. Just forget it. I shouldn't have even suggested it."

"But you did, and it's a *great* idea. It would really help me out. How about if we just pretend to go out one time and see what happens?"

"Where would we go?"

I pause to think. "The fire department is having a fundraiser this weekend. The whole town will be there. You could go as my date. I was going to go with Nina but we can all go together. It'll be fun! Nina's a blast. You'll love her."

"I'm trying to keep a low profile here. Do the whole reclusive writer thing. I don't think going to a town function is a good idea."

"It's just one night and I promise it won't be that bad. If it is, we'll leave. And if you do this for me, I'll make you grilled cheese every night for a week."

He smiles. "Well, that might've just sealed the deal."

"So you'll do it?"

"Okay, I'll do it. But if it doesn't go well, we're not staying."

"Agreed." I hold my hand out and we shake on it.

"Do we need to come up with some kind of story before Saturday? About how we met or when we started dating?"

"We probably should. People will ask questions and we need to have the same answers." I tap my hand on the table as I think. "Why not just tell them the truth?"

"Meaning what?"

"We'll say I stopped to help when I saw you on the side of the road. Except in our fake story, we'll say you happily accepted my help instead of telling me to get lost."

"Sorry about that. I just really wanted to be alone. It'd been a long day."

"You never told me about that day. What exactly happened?"

"I'll tell you some other time. So what else do we tell these people? Is Saturday going to be our first date?"

"No, let's tell them today was. We'll say I invited you over for dinner and that we hung out the next night too."

"Meaning tonight."

"Yeah."

"Are we?"

"Are we what?"

"Hanging out tonight?" He gets the slightest hint of a smile.

"Of course we are," I say, playing along. "We had a good date last night. So good that you asked me out again for tonight, but this time I'm going to your place."

"You are, huh?" His smile grows. "Am I supposed to make dinner?"

"That's up to you. I planned last night's date. You plan tonight's."

"I can't cook. Is there any place that does take-out?"

"Tony T's Barbecue, but Tony's wife works the register and she's really nosy. If you go in there, she'll ask you tons of questions. I'll just go there myself and bring the food to your place. Sound good?"

"Yeah. Let me give you some money." He takes out his wallet and hands me a hundred dollar bill. "It's all I've got. Sorry."

"It's okay. I'll just bring back the change."

Who carries around hundred dollar bills? The one he gave me wasn't the only one he had. I saw several in his wallet.

He gets up from the table. "So what time will you be over?"

"Around six. I need to go home first and change. I'll text you when I'm heading over."

"I don't have a phone."

"Oh, that's right. Then I'll call Miller's number. His phone is still working, right?"

"Yeah." He chuckles. "It's bright yellow with a ten foot cord and these massive buttons with huge numbers."

"His eyesight isn't so great. My grandma used to have a phone like that too." I get up and take our mugs to the counter. "So I'll call you on the phone with the giant numbers around six. Does that work?"

"Yeah. I'll see you then." He turns to leave.

"Wait, before you go, could you help me close the windows? I have trouble getting them closed enough for the lock to turn."

"Sure." He walks into the living room and begins closing the front windows.

"It smells so much better in here," I say, as I try to close the side window. It closes, but not all the way. "Thanks for staying last night. It really helped having the windows open."

"I think they could use another night of being open. I can still smell that couch."

"You want to stay another night?" I joke.

"If you want me to, I will."

"I was just kidding."

"Really, Sage. I don't mind. Do you want me to stay tonight?"

"Um...you really don't have to. I'll just wait until the weekend and air the place out when I'm home."

"I heard we might get a storm this weekend. Tonight would be better."

I didn't hear anything about a storm. Did he just say that so I'd let him stay here again? But why would he want to stay here? Is he thinking we'll do something? Even after he told me he didn't want that?

"I'll think about it," I say, still fighting with the window. "I can't get this one closed."

He comes over to me. "Let me try."

I step aside and watch as he lifts it up, then shoves it down, his arm and shoulder muscles flexing with the movement. I feel a flutter in my stomach. The same one I felt when I met him, when I saw his face for the first time. I felt it again when I kissed him, along with an arousal so strong I couldn't deny it. Seeing his muscles flex has me feeling it again.

"It's locked now," he says, motioning to the window. "The other ones are good too. Need anything else before I go?"

"No. That was it. Thanks for your help."

He walks to the door. "Have a good day at work. Tell Jesse your boyfriend wants to know when his motorcycle will be done."

I laugh. "I think it'd be best to hold off on telling him about you until your motorcycle is fixed. But I'll check on when it'll be done."

"Thanks. See you tonight."

Once he's gone I hop in the shower and get ready for work. When I arrive at the garage, Jesse is working on Kyle's motorcycle.

Usually I go straight to the office, but today I stop and talk to Jesse. "Think you can fix it?"

"I can fix anything," he says, picking up some wrench-like tool. I know almost nothing about cars or what you use to fix them. Luckily, I don't have to know any of that to work here.

"What's wrong with it?"

He stops what he's doing and looks at me. "Since when are you so interested in repair jobs?"

"I'm not. I was just making conversation."

He sets his tool down and stands up. "You never make conversation, at least not with me."

"Seriously, Jesse?" I roll my eyes. "It was a simple question. Do you have to read so much into it?"

"When it's you? Yeah, I do, because I'm trying to figure out what's going on with us."

"Nothing's going on with us, and nothing ever will. I'm your employee. That's it." I walk off. "I have to get to work."

"Is this about that guy?" I hear him ask.

"What guy?" I ask, still walking.

"The asshole frat boy you were drooling over yesterday."

I stop and turn around. "Why'd you call him a frat boy?"

"The way he was dressed? That haircut? He looks like one of those stuck-up frat boys."

"Whatever." I turn back and head toward the office.

"You can tell him his bike will be done by noon," I hear Jesse yell from behind me.

"Okay," I yell back.

"And Sage," he says.

"Yeah?" I turn around.

Jesse glares at me. "Tell him you're off limits."

I huff. "You don't own me, Jesse. I'm not yours." I storm off and yell, "And I'm never going out with you."

"We'll see about that," he calls back.

If he's threatening me, or tries to fire me for not going out with him, I'll go to the police. I know they're all friends with Jesse but there has to be at least one cop who would agree that Jesse's harassment is wrong and illegal.

As soon as I'm in the office, I look up Old Man Miller's number and call it. It rings several times before Kyle finally picks up.

"Hello?" He sounds different. His voice sounds deeper and he said 'hello' really fast like he's in a hurry.

"Kyle? It's Sage."

"Hey." He sounds more relaxed now. That's weird.

"Hi. I was calling about your motorcycle. Jesse said it'd be done by noon."

"That's great. I didn't think it'd be ready that fast."

"Well, that's what he said. Can you pick it up at noon or do you want to get it later?"

"I'll swing by around noon."

"Okay, see you then."

At noon I spot Kyle through the glass partition in the office door. He goes up to Jesse and I watch as the two of them talk. Jesse, who usually slouches, stands up straight, sticking his chest out, and I feel like I'm watching some nature show where one of the male gorillas tries to assert his dominance over another. It's so ridiculous.

Kyle is standing there with a smirk on his face, obviously humored by Jesse's attempt to show off his manliness. Not at all intimidated by it, Kyle steps closer and talks with his hands, forcing Jesse to take a step back.

They continue to talk, and Jesse nods a couple times, then hands Kyle the keys to his bike and motions to the office. They both glance my way and I quickly look down and pretend to be typing.

A few moments later, Kyle walks in. "I'm here to pay my bill. Turned out to be five-eighty so I owe you eighty."

I look up and see him smiling, almost about to laugh.

"Something you want to share?" I ask.

"Nope. Just here to pay my bill." He gets his wallet out.

"C'mon. I saw you with Jesse just now. What did he say to you?"

"It was guy talk. It's private."

"Oh please," I say, taking his invoice from the printer. "Don't give me that. You two were talking about me, weren't you?"

"Why would we talk about you?"

"You know why." I hand him his invoice, but as he takes it, I hold onto it and narrow my eyes at him. "You better not have done something Neanderthal, like place bets on who would end up with me. That's totally something Jesse would do but—"

"But it's not something *I* would do." He yanks the paper from me. "And I'm insulted you would think otherwise." He looks over the invoice.

"Sorry," I mutter.

"I'll let it slide this time," he says, glancing up from his invoice, his lips creeping up.

"This time?" I huff. "Meaning what? I'm in trouble if I ever offend you again?"

"Yes," he answers, trying to be serious.

"What are you going to do to me?" I ask, my face heating up because that sounded totally naughty, which is not how I meant it to sound.

"I'm not sure yet," he says casually, as if he didn't take my comment in a sexual way, but the spark in his eyes tells a different story. There's that flutter again, but now it's not in my stomach. It's lower, in a place it shouldn't be when I'm here at work with a guy I'm not dating. A guy I still don't know that well, despite spending all of last night with him.

I wish he'd tell me more about himself, but he hasn't, and I get the feeling he won't. The only thing I know for sure is that he's just as attracted to me as I am to him. And maybe, if this becomes just a summer fling, then the fact that he wants me is all I need to know.

CHAPTER ELEVEN

Sage

Kyle sets the invoice down and picks up his wallet. As he opens it, I see it's full of hundred dollar bills, even more than he had this morning. What's the deal with this guy? Does he just walk around with a stash of hundreds?

He takes one out and hands it to me. "That should cover it."

"Do you always pay in cash?"

"I don't like credit cards," he says. "I don't like having debt."

"Most people don't, but can't really avoid it."

His smile disappears as he shoves his wallet in his pocket. "Is that it?"

"Um, no, I need to get your change." I hurry over to the drawer where we keep the cash.

"Forget it. I don't need change. It's yours. A tip for good service."

I sigh. "Are you only doing this because of what I told you last night?"

"What did you tell me?" His brows furrow. "Was it the part about you finding me cute? If so, then yes, that's the reason. I'm giving you $20 to thank you for the compliment. It's been a long time since someone's called me cute. I think it was probably the seventh grade."

I swat his arm. "Stop teasing me about that. I was being nice."

"Why are you hitting me?'

"You were being sarcastic. And you know I wasn't referring to that."

He grins, which is both annoying and hot. Why does he have to be so damn good-looking?

"What are you smiling at?" I ask, crossing my arms over my chest.

"You know what that was?"

"I have no idea what you're talking about."

"What we just did. That was our first fight. Our first couple's argument."

I can't help but smile at that. He called us a couple, and even though he's just playing along with our fake arrangement, I like the sound of us being a couple.

"We're not dating," I remind him. "And that wasn't a fight. I just asked a simple question and wanted an answer, and as usual, you didn't give me one. That's really annoying, by the way. Why can't you just answer questions the way normal people do?"

"Are you saying I'm not normal?"

"See? Once again, you didn't answer my question. Instead you responded with another question." I return to my desk. "It's so freaking annoying."

"And yet you still find me cute," he says with a smirk.

"Ugh," I groan. "So annoying."

"I'll let you get back to work." He turns to leave.

"It's after twelve. I'm on my lunch break."

"Okay, well, have a good lunch." He opens the office door.

"Wait," I say.

He turns around. "Yeah?"

Why did I stop him? I should let him go home and write or do whatever it is he does at this time of day. But I don't want him to go, which makes no sense and sounds pathetic if I think about it for too long. So I scratch the logic from my brain and go with my initial thought.

"Do you want to have lunch?"

"You're already starting your get-Jesse-to-leave-you-alone plan? I thought that wasn't starting until Saturday."

"It is. This isn't about Jesse. I just didn't want to eat lunch alone."

"What do you normally do?"

"Eat at my desk. But it's a nice day out and I feel like getting some sun."

"And you want my company." His mouth ticks up into that annoyingly sexy smile.

I sigh. "I'm not going to beg, so if you don't want to then just forget it."

"I don't have a lunch, but I can sit with you while you have yours."

Shoving his money into the cash drawer, I say, "Never mind. I'll just eat here." I close the drawer and open the one above it that has my lunch, which consists of PB&J with a bag of chips. I have it every day and am sick of it but it's cheap and easy to make.

"Let's go," Kyle says as he sees me opening my lunch sack.

"Forget it. I'll just see you tonight."

He comes over and snatches my lunch sack just as I was about to reach into it. "Hey! Give it back!"

"You wanted to eat outside so we're eating outside."

"I'm not sitting there eating while you watch."

He thinks for a moment. "Is there a vending machine?"

"Yeah, but it doesn't have much in it."

"I'll make it work. Where is it?"

"In the garage by the break room."

"Head outside. I'll meet you in the back parking lot."

"We can't eat out there. Jesse will come out and bother us. We'll have to walk down to the lake. It's just beyond the parking lot, through the trees. It's not far."

"I'll meet you there."

He hands me my lunch sack and leaves the office. I go to the mini fridge and get my can of soda.

"Who's that?" Helen asks as she walks in the office. Her lunch break is right before mine. She always walks at lunch. She's in really good shape for 68, which I think is how old she is. She told me once but she kind of mumbled it so I'm not sure if I heard her right.

"Kyle," I tell her.

"Kyle who? What's his last name?"

Older people are all about last names. I never even think to ask for a last name, and if I'd asked Kyle when I met him, he probably wouldn't have told me, given his refusal to answer questions. The only reason I know his last name is because he had to give it to me to get his motorcycle fixed.

"Shadwick," I say. "Kyle Shadwick."

She scrunches her brow. "Is he related to the Mannings?"

"No. He's new in town. He's not related to anyone here."

"Then why is he here?"

Kyle's going to get this question a million times unless I tell Nina to spread his story through town so people won't have to ask. I forgot to call her this morning. I'll have to do it after lunch.

"I'm not sure," I lie, not wanting to be delayed by a lengthy conversation. Once Helen starts talking, it's hard to get her to stop. "You'll have to ask him on Saturday. He'll be at the fundraiser. I'll see you later, Helen. I need to get to lunch or my break will be over."

"You're going out?" she asks, surprised because I almost always eat at my desk.

"I'm just going to sit outside. Get some sun."

She nods and goes to her desk.

When I get out back, Kyle is already walking along the small path that goes through the trees.

"Hey!" I yell. "Wait up!"

He turns and I see he's carrying what looks like a sampling of everything in the vending machine.

I catch up to him, laughing. "You hungry?"

"Not really, but I wasn't sure what to get and I thought maybe you might want some. How far is this pond? I'm not sure how far I can carry this stuff without dropping it."

"Here." I open my lunch sack. "Toss in whatever fits."

He drops some candy bars in there. "You can have whatever we don't eat."

"Another gift for calling you cute?" I ask, scrunching up the bag.

He chuckles. "Exactly. But I still haven't fully repaid you for that so expect to get more."

We continue along the path.

"You don't have to keep buying me stuff. I may be broke but I do have a job."

"Fine," he says in a stern tone. "I'll never buy you another candy bar as long as we both shall live."

I laugh and jab his arm. "You know what I meant."

"Why do you keep hitting me?"

"Why do you answer every question with a question?"

"Why do you eat lunch at your desk every day?"

"Why do you pay for everything with hundred dollar bills?"

He stops abruptly and I prepare for him to get mad at me for what I assume he considers to be prying. But he doesn't. Instead he turns to me, his eyes on mine.

"Why do you have to look so goddamn hot and adorable at the same time?"

I'm so surprised by the compliment I pause a moment then say, "Why do you have to be such an ass and then be really sweet so that I don't know which is the real you?"

He steps closer. "Why do you pretend you don't like me when you really do?"

"Why did you agree to pretend to go out with me?"

"Who said it was pretend?" He drops the bags of chips he was holding and cups my face, his eyes locked on mine.

My lunch sack falls to the ground and I look up at him, breathing hard, completely turned on by our rapid-fire banter and the sexy look he's giving me.

"Why'd you show up here?" I ask. "Why now? When neither one of us is looking for a relationship?"

"Who said it'd become a relationship?"

"If it's not, then what is it?" I shoot back.

"Why do we have to know?"

"So you're okay with this just ending when one of us leaves?"

"Are YOU?"

"Why don't we just go with it and see what happens?"

He pauses, his eyes lowering to my lips. "Why don't we stop talking?"

I swallow. "Why don't we?"

"Can I kiss you now?"

I close my eyes and whisper, "Enough with the damn questions."

He kisses me and I feel it all the way down my core, warmth spreading between my thighs. He grabs me around the waist and pulls me into him. I feel how hard he is, the length of him pressing against me, and want him even more than I did last night. But we're out in broad daylight and not that far from the garage. We're deep in the trees but I can't risk someone seeing us.

"We can't do this here," I say as his hand disappears under my skirt, a light-weight billowy skirt that keeps blowing up in the breeze.

"You want me to stop?" he asks, kissing my neck.

"Yes," I moan, loving the feel of his lips on my skin, trailing down the deep neckline of my shirt. I tilt my head back as he kisses between my breasts.

"Sage," he groans. "Fuck, you turn me on."

I grip his hair as his hand skims up my inner thigh. He tugs my panties aside and slides his fingers over my slick center, then plunges one inside me.

"Kyle—" I was going to tell him to stop but he's already started and there's no way I'm ending this now. What he's doing feels so amazing I can barely keep myself up. I lean back against the tree and let him keep going.

When the pleasure overtakes me, I have to bite my lip to keep from making too much noise. A quiet moan escapes me as I collapse back against the tree.

"Still want lunch?" Kyle asks. I open my eyes and see him smiling at me.

I smile back, my heart still struggling to recover from what he did to me. "I should eat before my break's over." I pick up my lunch. "Do you have to go?"

"I can stay." He gathers up the bags of chips and we follow the path to the pond. There's a small bench there where we sit down.

He rips open a bag of chips. "Want some?"

"I have my own, but thanks." I pull out my sandwich and take a bite.

"So..." he says, grinning as he munches on a chip, his eyes on the lake.

"So..." I say, mimicking him.

"Not your typical lunch."

I laugh. "No. Not at all." I turn to him. "Just so you know, I don't normally do this."

"Do what?"

"I don't normally move this fast with a guy. I think the only reason I am now is because I know our time is limited."

"And because we share an attraction that's so intense it's nearly impossible to be around each other without getting physical."

"Yeah." I sit back. "There's that too."

His eyes remain on the lake and he takes a drink of his soda. "So...one day at a time?"

"One day at a time."

"And when it's over?"

"It's over." I'm already dreading the end. It's just a few months away, maybe less if he decides he's tired of being in this town. How much time do you really need to research a small town? He could finish writing his manuscript anywhere. He wouldn't need to stay here.

He opens three bags of candy and sets them between us. "Dessert."

"Thanks, but I'm not quite finished with the main course."

"You eat that every day?" He points to my sandwich.

"Unfortunately, yes. It's the only lunch that fits in my budget."

"Why don't you let me take you out sometime? After our fake relationship is made public?"

"I guess we could do that." I wipe the crumbs off my hands. "As long as you're okay keeping the fake relationship going."

"We kind of have to, don't we? Otherwise, that idiot will ask you out again."

So now Jesse's an idiot, and Kyle said it in an angry tone, almost like he's jealous.

"Does it bother you?" I take some candy from the bag.

"That he flirts with you? Yeah. It does. He's out of line and being disrespectful. You told him you weren't interested and he won't take no for an answer. And he's breaking all kinds of HR laws, which you know, given that it's your major. So why haven't you reported him?"

"Because it wouldn't do any good. The whole town would be on Jesse's side and I'd be the enemy for reporting him."

"That's messed up."

"That's just how it is. But if he ever tries anything, like tries to grab me or kiss me, I'll take him down."

"I'll do it for you. Just say the word. It'd be good to put all that martial arts training to good use."

"You'd get arrested for sure. The cops here wouldn't even listen to your side of the story. They're all friends with Jesse and his dad."

"Okay, so, we'll have to find a different way to deal with him. I can't be getting arrested." He runs his hand through his hair, then along his stubble-lined jaw.

He seems nervous. Was it because I mentioned the cops? Or was it something else?

"Maybe just pretending to date me will be enough to keep Jesse away from you."

"I hope so. Or it might make him try even harder."

My phone rings. It's Nina, so I send her a text, telling her I'll call her later.

"You need to get that?" Kyle asks.

"It's Nina. I'll call her back in a minute."

"I should get going." He puts the cap on his bottle of soda. "I'm guessing your lunch break is over?"

"Not yet, but I do need to call Nina. She needs to start telling people your story so they'll leave you alone." I stuff my trash in my lunch sack. "Anything else you want the town to know besides that you're a writer from California here to finish your book?"

"No." He stands up. "They don't need to know any more than that."

"Okay. Well, I'm going to stay here and call her quick. I'll see you later."

"Bye." He leans down and gives me a kiss on the head. The type of kiss a boyfriend would give his girlfriend. A kiss that means you care about the girl.

Am I reading too much into it or does Kyle already have feelings for me? I have feelings for him but I tend to fall for guys way too fast. With Kyle, I'm trying not to do that, knowing this isn't going to last, but I can't seem to stop it from happening. We got off to a rocky start but the more I get to know him, I'm finding he's a really sweet guy.

"Hey, it's me," I say when Nina picks up. "Sorry I missed your call. I was having lunch."

"Then why didn't you answer?"

"Because Kyle was here."

"He had lunch with you?"

"He was here to get his motorcycle so he stayed for lunch."

"Why would he stay for lunch? What's going on with you two? Are you friends now?"

Friends. Is that what you call it when a guy kisses you, spends the night at your house, and pleasures you on your lunch hour? I'm blushing just thinking about that.

"Sage? You still there?"

"Yeah, I'm here."

"So what's the deal with you and this guy?"

Do I tell her about the arrangement I have with Kyle? I have to. She's my closest friend and she'd know if I were lying.

"We're friends. And we're kind of dating."

"You're what?" she yells into the phone. "You're dating the psychopath? Since when?"

"He's not a psychopath and we're not really dating. We're just going on a few dates around town so people, specifically Jesse, will assume we're dating."

"This is all to make Jesse leave you alone?"

"I'm tired of him hitting on me at work. It needs to end, and this may be the only way to do it."

"So you're not dating him."

"Not really."

"*Not really?* What does that mean?"

"It means we kinda kissed, which I guess could mean we're dating, but we're really not."

"Okay, back up. You kissed him?"

"Yes."

"When?"

"Last night, when he was over for dinner."

"Damn! I knew I should've went over there."

"To keep me from kissing him? Why do you care?"

"I care because you're my friend and you're in a vulnerable state right now. I don't want Mr. Psycho Biker Guy taking advantage of you."

"I'm not vulnerable. And he's not taking advantage of me. We kissed. That's it."

"If you keep hanging out with him, he's gonna want to do more than that."

"Maybe that's what I want too."

"You want to have sex with a complete stranger you found on the side of the road? Have you lost your mind?"

"He's not a stranger. I've been getting to know him, and so far, I really like him. He helped me get that stinky couch out of my house and he offered to haul it off to the dump."

"In exchange for sex."

"That's not why he's doing it."

"Trust me, that's why he's doing it. Guys don't do stuff just to be nice."

"That's not true. Josh used to do nice things for you."

"Because he wanted sex."

"You were dating. He would've got that anyways."

"Whatever. The point I'm making is that you don't know enough about this guy to be getting close to him. And you definitely shouldn't have sex with him, at least not until you know more about him."

"So exactly how well did you know the guy you met at the bar we went to a few weeks ago?"

A few Saturdays ago, Nina convinced me to drive to some town that was forty minutes away and go to this bar that had live music. The band was pretty good so we stayed a few hours. This guy kept buying her drinks and she ended up going home with him.

"That's different. I was drunk, and I swear I'd met him before. I think he used to be friends with my cousin, Ray."

"Doesn't matter. You still had sex with a guy you barely knew."

"Then do as I say, not as I do, and don't do anything with this guy until you know for sure you can trust him."

"And how would I know that? Am I supposed to hook him up to a lie detector?"

"Just stay away from him. He's not going to stick around and neither are you so why waste your time with him?"

"Because I like him. He's a good kisser. And he's hot." I smile as I say it.

"Okay, fine, so there's that, but you could find plenty of other guys that are hot that aren't all mysterious and weird."

"Kyle's not weird. And he's not mysterious. He's been telling me more about himself, and I'm sure he'll tell me even more if we spend more time together."

"I doubt that," she mutters.

I don't know why she hates him so much. She hasn't even met him.

"So what happened last night?" she asks. "You had dinner, made out, and then what?"

"We hauled the couch out, then opened all the windows to get rid of the smell. Turns out the couch is what was making the house stink. Not that it smells great now, but it's better than it was."

"And then he went home?"

"Um, no. He ended up spending the night."

"You already slept with him?" she yells.

"No! He stayed in the living room. I wanted the house to air out but I didn't want to sleep there alone with the windows open all night."

"So you invited a serial killer to stay with you?"

"Would you stop calling him that? He's not a serial killer. He's a writer, and not a psychopathic killer writer. Just a writer. But since you refuse to believe that, I'm bringing him to the firehouse event on Saturday."

"You're supposed to go with me! And now you're ditching me for some guy?"

"I'm not ditching you. We're all hanging out together. The three of us."

"Great. So I'll be going on your date with you. I'm sure he'll love that."

"He knows it's not a real date. And this will give you a chance to question him to death, although I'll tell you right now that he's not great about answering questions. He doesn't like talking about himself."

"Because he's hiding something."

"That's not why. But if it is, I'm sure you'll find out what that something is. If anyone can get the truth out of someone, it's you."

She sighs. "Okay. He can go with us, but I'm going to grill him all night."

I laugh. "I'm sure you will."

"Maybe I'll sic Josh on him. He's good at reading people. He'll know if this guy is being real or not."

"You can't ask Josh. He'll be on a date," I remind her to see if she'll show even a hint of jealousy. She tried to hide it the other night when Lacey asked Josh out, but I could see her jealously brewing.

"With Lacey?" she scoffs. "That's not a date."

"Then why did he call it that?"

"Because that's what Lacey wants it to be. Josh was just being nice."

"Lacey wasn't around when he called it a date."

I hear her take a deep breath. "Then maybe it is. I really don't care. It doesn't matter to me. I've moved on."

She hasn't moved on. I saw her with Josh. She still likes him, and there was definite jealously in her tone just now. She doesn't want him going out with Lacey. She still wants him for herself. Maybe on Saturday night she'll be so busy watching Josh that she'll leave Kyle alone.

I doubt that'll happen. In fact, I'm worried she's going to badger Kyle so much that he'll want to leave. But before he does, I'm kind of hoping she'll get more out of him than I've been able to so far. I still want to find out more about him and Nina may be my best chance of doing that.

CHAPTER TWELVE

Kyle

What the hell was I thinking? I can't be getting involved with Sage. So why did I agree to have lunch with her? And what the fuck was I doing kissing her? Again!

Every time I'm around her, I want to touch her. I can't seem to stop myself. But then the touching leads to kissing, and today led to even more than that. If I keep this up, we'll be having sex tonight, and as much as I want that, I shouldn't do it.

Sage is a great girl but not for me. If the circumstances were different and I wasn't running for my life, then yeah, I'd be doing everything possible to make Sage mine. She's the type of girl I've always dreamed of meeting but didn't think existed.

The girls I've dated in the past have all been shallow and demanding and wouldn't give a shit if they saw some guy walking down the side of the road, nearly dying of heat stroke. But Sage did. And then she stopped at my house and gave me water and bandaged up the gash in my head. How many people would do that? Almost none, especially if they thought I was dangerous. Dirty and sweaty with a broken-down motorcycle and all my possessions in a duffle bag, I probably looked like I'd just been let out of prison.

And yet still, Sage stopped for me, because she's that type of person. The type that stops to help random strangers. I didn't think those type of people existed. They don't in my world. The world of rich, haughty, elite snobs who are only interested in people who can make them more money. I could never figure out how my father fit in that world. He grew up poor, begging for money, digging food out of dumpsters so he wouldn't starve. He used to tell my brother and me those stories all the time. About how much he had to struggle and how lucky we were to grow up with everything we could ever want.

When I asked my father how he made it out of poverty, he never really explained it other than to say that he met the right people. I asked who those people were but he wouldn't tell me. Now I know those people were crooks, liars, murderers. People who made their money through illegal activities and lured poor desperate people like my dad to do their dirty work. Now he's one of them. A filthy rich asshole pretending to be someone he's not.

It sickens me to know people like that exist. I feel even more disgusted knowing my father is one of them. But then I meet someone like Sage and am reminded there are still good people out there. She's proof of that a million times over.

Sage lost everything she had and yet she's still kind and selfless, wanting to help others. Her own father robbed her blind, which you think would make her bitter and angry, wanting to get back at the world she'd trusted that turned against her.

That's how I felt when I learned the truth. I still feel that way. When your own father betrays you, it's hard to feel anything but anger and distrust. But Sage has managed to stay positive. I think that's why I'm so drawn to her. I admire her. I admire her spirit, her determination to keep going when it'd be so much easier to give up. I want to be like her, still smiling despite my circumstances, able to feel something other than anger and hate.

Those were the only emotions I felt after I left and I was beginning to think that's all I'd ever feel again. But then I saw Sage's beautiful face with that beautiful smile, and as much as I tried to be angry at her, I felt a sense of peace come over me. A calmness I haven't felt in years.

It's alluring, addictive, and one of the many reasons I can't seem to stay away from Sage. It's why I feel so close to her, even though we just met. She doesn't know my story but I feel like she understands me. I feel like we understand each *other*, both having gone through the pain of betrayal by someone we were conned into trusting.

I pull into the driveway of Miller's house. Knowing where I came from, it's hard to believe this is where I'm living. The house is one level with a roof that needs to be replaced and brown siding that probably hasn't been painted in twenty years. The place is a run-down shithole. The inside isn't much better but at least the old man splurged on a big-ass recliner that's so comfortable that I've been sleeping in it instead of the bed.

The chair is dark brown and has cupholders built into it. Fabric pouches hanging off each side to hold your remote and whatever else you want to put in there. You could basically live in the chair, only getting up to use the bathroom. His other splurge was the 60-inch flat screen that's mounted directly across from the chair. When I asked to rent out his house, he told me he just bought the TV and if I damaged it, I'd owe him twice what it was worth. The man loves his TV.

Unlocking the door, I go inside then freeze when I hear a noise coming from the kitchen.

My heart jumps to my throat, my pulse skyrocketing. How the fuck did he find me? Out in the middle of fucking nowhere?

My eyes frantically search for a weapon. I have a knife in my bag but it's in the bedroom. Why is it in my fucking bedroom? It should be with me at all times, but I didn't carry it today because I knew I'd be seeing Sage and I didn't want her to find it on me.

I hear glass shatter and then, "Gawd-dammit."

It's an old man's voice. Why would he send an old man?

As I turn around to bolt back outside I drop my keys, the sound of them hitting the floor enough to be heard by whoever's in the kitchen. Shit!

"Hey!" I hear the old man behind me.

I turn, expecting to see a gun, but instead he's pointing a bottle of beer at me. He's gotta be in his seventies, with a full head of white hair. He seems fit for someone his age; lean, with a slight outline of muscle along his arms.

"Who are you and what you are doing here?" I ask, my body tensing, ready to fight.

"I'm Hank. Miller's friend." He takes a few steps toward me. "What's wrong with you, kid? You're white as a ghost."

I take a moment to breathe, then say, "You broke into my house. Scared the shit out of me."

He lets out a laugh. "Miller didn't tell you?"

"Tell me what?"

"I have a key. I come over every Friday and mow his lawn." He holds up the bottle. "Help myself to his beers."

"I don't need you to mow the lawn. I'll do it myself."

"It isn't up to you. It's Miller's house and I'm doing what he asked. I've been mowing his lawn for ten years."

"Then take the summer off. I won't tell him."

"You want me to lie to my friend?" He narrows his eyes at me. "Is that what people do wherever you're from? They lie to their friends?"

"I'm not trying to cause problems between you and Miller. I just want to be left alone. I don't like coming home and finding some stranger in my kitchen."

"I'm not a stranger. I'm Hank Folts." He extends his hand to me. "And you are?"

Shaking his hand, I say, "Kyle."

"No last name?"

I sigh. "Shadwick. Kyle Shadwick."

He grins, causing the wrinkles on his tan face to become even more pronounced. "Nice to meet you, Kyle Shadwick."

"Yeah," I mutter, glancing around the room, wishing he'd leave.

"You're still white as a ghost." He chuckles. "No need to be scared around here. The only burglars that'll be sneaking around are cat burglars, as in actual cats. I caught one trying to come in when I came through the back door today. I shooed him out before he got in."

Great. So now I have cats trying to get in my house. I'm allergic to cats.

"So you come here every Friday?" I ask.

He nods, then takes a drink of his beer. "Every Friday at one. I work down at the hardware store but get off at noon on Fridays. I have lunch, then come over here, have a beer with Miller, then mow his lawn. The old man hurt his leg years ago on some farm equipment and has trouble pushing the mower so I volunteered for the job, in exchange for beer." He gives me a wink. "That's a hint to keep the fridge stocked."

So now I need to buy this guy beer? I don't even want him here but it sounds like I'm not going to be able to get rid of him. He's loyal to Miller, and trying to get him to go away will cause more trouble than it's worth.

"How about I leave the beer out back in a cooler before you come over so you don't have to go in the house when I'm not here?"

"What do I look like?" he asks with anger in his voice. "Some farm animal? I'm not allowed to go in the damn house? What if I have to use the toilet?"

I let out a long sigh. "Fine. But it needs to be the same time each week, and no coming here outside of that. You nearly gave me a heart attack showing up here without telling me."

He shakes his head. "You big city people need to learn how to relax and stop thinking you're important enough for crooks to come after you. Unless you're famous or have a lot of money, nobody's interested in you. And out here? I guarantee nobody's going to be breaking your windows to get in. They've got better things to do."

He doesn't get that it's not the townspeople I'm worried about. It's the people my father knows. The people looking for me. Trying to kill me.

"How long do you think you'll be?" I ask.

He shrugs. "I usually spend about an hour on the beer and a couple hours on the lawn, but since your conversation skills are sorely lacking, looks like I'll be finishing the beer and getting to work."

"Sounds good," I say, going around him to the table where the answering machine sits. Miller still uses an answering machine, the kind with the tiny tapes. The red light isn't blinking, which means there aren't any messages. I was wondering, or maybe hoping, that Sage would call. I know I just saw her but I thought she might call and ask if she could come over earlier tonight, in which case the answer would be yes.

I shouldn't do that. I shouldn't be wishing she'd call, but damn, I can't stop thinking about her, and thinking about her makes me want to see her.

"I suppose I could sit for a minute or two," Hank says, taking a seat in the recliner.

What the hell? I can't rid of this guy.

I stand beside him. "I'm kinda busy so..."

He looks up at me. "You don't *look* busy."

"Well, I am. I have a lot to do."

"What exactly do you do?" He takes a swig of his beer.

"I write." I cross my arms over my chest. "I'm a writer. And I'm on a deadline. So I really need you to leave so I can work."

"What do you write?" he asks, ignoring my request.

"Fiction. Novels."

"About what?"

My God, he's never going to leave. I'll have to pry his ass out of the chair and throw him out the door.

"Just stories," I tell him. "Stories about people."

"What kind of people?"

I sigh in frustration. "Just people, okay? I don't want to get into it. It's not even done yet."

"Seems like if you want to sell some books you should talk about it. Get people interested."

"Well, it's not published yet so I'm not ready to start selling it to people. Now I really need to—"

"I read crime dramas. Been reading them since I was a kid. We didn't have all those channels on the TV back then so people read more, you know?" I don't answer so he keeps going. "I got so into those stories I wanted to be a cop. Solve crimes. But then I went to the police academy and found it wasn't for me. It's different when it's in a book. Cops always catch the bad guys and everyone's happy in the end. It's not that way in real life. People go missing and are never found. Murders go unsolved. It's depressing."

"But you still read the books?"

"When I have the time. Reading keeps the mind sharp and I like trying to figure out the mystery." He winks at me. "I have an inquisitive mind."

"Yeah, I figured that out."

He laughs. "You're a strange kid but you're starting to grow on me." He motions to the chair next to him. It's also a recliner but really old and worn out, the fabric faded and the seat cushion sunken down. "Grab a beer and sit a minute."

"I can't. Like I said, I have work to do."

"Work can wait. Besides, don't you have to be inspired before you write?"

"Not really. I usually just sit down and write."

"If that were the case, you'd be done with your book by now. Word around town is that you're behind schedule and here to finish it."

So I guess Sage was right. Gossip travels fast in this town. She told Nina my story and now everyone knows. But Sage was talking to Nina when I left. How did she get the word out so fast?

"If you already knew that about me," I say, "why'd you pretend you didn't?"

"I wanted to hear it from you. You can't always trust the town gossip."

"Well, it's true that I'm behind on my book, which is why I need to get writing. My agent will kill me if I don't turn in some chapters."

He pulls the lever on the chair and reclines back, getting comfortable. At this rate, he's seriously never going to leave.

"My wife always says I should write a memoir. Tell my life story? I think she's crazy. No one would want to read that. She says the grandkids would but they're not interested in reading. Today all kids care about is whatever's on that goddamn internet. It's a damn shame."

I'm wondering why his wife would want his story told. I want him to leave but my curiosity has me asking the question, "What would you write about? What's your story?"

He looks at me, seeming pleased that I asked. "It's not so much my story as the people I dealt with on a daily basis. Lawyers, criminals, witnesses."

"Wait, so you haven't always worked at the hardware store?"

He laughs. "Heavens, no. That's my retirement job. The wife and I moved here when we retired because we wanted to go back to small town living. We both grew up here. Knew each other since we were kids."

"Where did you used to live?"

"St. Louis. I was a judge. Criminal court. Saw things and heard stories you wouldn't believe."

"I don't get it. You said you didn't want to be a cop because it was too depressing. Isn't being a judge just as depressing?"

"I wasn't in charge of solving crimes. I was in charge of locking people up or letting them go free. I wasn't out looking for criminals. I saw them after they'd been caught. There's a difference. It's hard to explain unless you know a lot about the criminal justice system, but the bottom line is that yes, it was depressing at times, but it also gave me hope."

"How so?"

"I saw that people can change. Criminals can be reformed. Not always, but sometimes. And people who grew up in horrible conditions can get out and make something of themselves. For every bad story, there's a good one, and that's what kept me going every day."

"When did you retire?"

"The day I turned sixty. I could've waited but I'd had enough. I wanted to relax and enjoy my golden years before I got too old to appreciate them."

He's a retired judge. I never would've guessed that. I thought everyone in this town was a farmer or somehow involved with farming. There's wheat fields everywhere you look, in every direction. I can't imagine retiring here, but I guess if you grew up here and liked it you might want to move back.

The phone rings but when I go to pick it up, I realize it's not Miller's phone. It's Hank's. His cell phone sounds like Miller's landline phone except it's really loud.

Hank fishes it out of his pocket and answers. "Yes, sweetheart, what do you need?" He listens and nods. "Fine. We'll bring them over tonight." He nods again. "I'll stop and pick some up." He smiles. "Love you, too. Be home soon." He hangs up. "That was the wife."

He really loves her. I could tell by the way his face lit up when he answered the phone and by the way he talked to her, with so much love in his voice. When my mom was alive, I never heard my father talk to her that way. Most of the time, he wasn't even home, and when he was, he mostly ignored my mom.

"She needs me to haul some tables over to the firehouse," Hank says. "They're having a fundraiser and Lois is in charge of setting everything up. You should come. You should at least stop by for some food."

"I'll be there. I'm going with Sage and her friend, Nina."

"Two girls?" He smiles. "And you've only been here, what...not even a week?"

I smile back. "We're just going as friends."

He cocks his brow. "That's not what I heard."

"Okay, yeah, Sage and I are going as a couple but it's not a big deal. We just met."

"I think you two would be good together."

"Why is that?"

He shrugs. "I just do. I have a feeling about these things."

"What things?"

"People. How they work together. Whether they're a good fit. Believe me, I've seen just about every type of person come through my court and after a while you start to see which types go together and which don't. Some people shouldn't even be in the same room together. Others *should* be together but are too blind or stubborn to see it. Like these two lawyers that were always in my court. A defense attorney and a prosecutor. They acted like they hated each other in the courtroom but it was clear they were meant to be together."

"How could you tell?"

"There was a spark between them. Mutual admiration. Respect. When she'd be talking, he couldn't take his eyes off her. When it was his turn to speak, he'd be so flustered from watching her that he'd have to take a moment to compose himself. One day I called them both back to chambers and told them they needed to cool it in the courtroom. They didn't understand so I explained that their attraction to each other was too much for the court. They were heating the place up so much it was becoming a distraction. I practically ordered them to go out for a drink to deal with this issue, which they did. And six months later? They were married."

"And did it last?"

"They've been married twenty years. Have a kid in college and two in high school. They send me a Christmas card every year. So I know these things, and even though I haven't seen you two together, I get the feeling you and Sage would make a good couple."

"Maybe so, but neither one of us plans to stay here so it'd never work out."

"It'll work out if you want it to." He shoves his feet down on the footrest, popping the chair back up to a sitting position. "Well, I suppose I better get out there." He stands up. "Good luck with your writing."

"Thanks." I follow him to the kitchen. "Oh, and if you need to use the bathroom, just knock or ring the bell or something so I know you're coming in."

"Will do." He sets his empty beer bottle down, then grabs another from the fridge. As he pops the cap off, he winks at me. "Last one."

"Got it. I'll make sure to get some more."

He exits out the back door and heads to the shed.

The guy scared the shit out of me showing up here like that, but he turned out to be a nice guy. The problem is, he's a judge, and judges can read people. They look for signs you're lying. Signs that say your story isn't true.

So as much as I like Hank, I need to watch out for him. He can't find out the truth about me.

CHAPTER THIRTEEN

Sage

"What'd you think?" I ask, getting up from the table.

Kyle and I just finished off a rack of Tony T's famous ribs, some pulled pork, potato salad, and Tony's homemade cornbread. I'm stuffed.

"It was great." Kyle brings his plate to the sink where I'm rinsing mine off. "Let me do that. You're my guest tonight. You shouldn't be cleaning."

"When you were *my* guest, I made you carry my couch outside, open all my windows, and spend the night on the floor."

"True." He gives me a smile. "You kind of suck as a host."

"Hey! You offered."

"Just kidding. Oh, that reminds me, I need your help loading the couch in the truck. I was going to drop it off at the dump tomorrow."

Returning to the table, I get our glasses and bring them to the sink.

"You want to do it right now?"

"Sure, if you're up for it."

"Why wouldn't I be?"

"You seem kind of tired."

"I am," I say, drying my hands on the towel. "I didn't sleep well last night."

"Because *I* was there?"

"I don't think that was it. I was just tossing and turning a lot." I go around him but he takes my hand, pulling me back. "What are you doing?"

He looks me in the eye. "Are you afraid of me?"

"*Afraid* of you?" I let out a nervous laugh. "Why would I be afraid of you?"

"I don't know. Sometimes I get the feeling you are."

"If I was afraid of you, I wouldn't have let you stay at my place all night."

"You're acting nervous."

It's because of his intense stare, and the tight hold he has on my hand. He hasn't let go and now his other hand is wrapping around my arm.

"Is there something you're not telling me?"

"No." I pull on my arm until he lets go. "I don't know what you're talking about."

"If you want to know about me, then ask me. Don't go behind my back."

"I didn't go behind your back. And for the record, asking you questions gets me nowhere because you never give me answers."

"Let's go." He turns and walks to the door.

I follow him outside and watch as he locks up. He'll only be gone a few minutes so I don't know why he's bothering to lock it. I also don't know why he's acting so strange. I thought after dinner we'd end up kissing, or maybe do more than that, but he hasn't even touched me all night.

When we get to my house, he backs up next to the garage. I park my car, and when I get out, I see Kyle is already loading the couch in the truck.

"Want some help?" I ask as he lifts up the couch.

"If you could, then yeah."

I lift up the other end and we slide it into the bed of the truck.

"Thanks for getting rid of it," I say as he closes the tailgate.

He nods. "See you later."

He gets in his truck and drives off, leaving me in the dark driveway. I forgot to leave the house lights on and now I can't see. As I search my purse for my house key, headlights come up behind me. I turn around and see Wilson's truck pulling up. Kyle jumps out, leaving the truck on.

"Sorry," he says, coming up to me.

"For what?" I ask, squinting from the bright headlights of the truck.

"I should've made sure you got inside."

"Oh, um, that's okay. I'll be fine."

"You got your key?"

"Yeah." I hold it up.

He takes it from me and walks to my door and opens it. He hands me the key. "Go ahead."

I walk past him into the house. "You didn't have to come back."

"I had to make sure you were safe. It's dark out here."

"Well, thanks. That was nice of you."

He pauses, remaining outside my door. "I'm not dangerous, Sage. I'd never do anything to hurt you."

I just nod, feeling odd we're even having this conversation. Was I acting afraid of him earlier? I didn't think I was, but maybe I did.

"Goodnight." He leans down and kisses my cheek.

"Goodnight."

I close the door and lock it behind me, then hear his truck pulling away. As I'm walking to the kitchen to set my purse down, my phone rings. It's Nina.

"Hey," I say, answering it.

"Is he there?"

"No. Why?"

"You didn't answer my texts earlier so I assumed he was either over there or he killed you."

"You thought he killed me but didn't bother to check that I was okay?"

"I didn't think he killed you, but I was starting to get worried when I didn't hear from you. So what were you doing?"

"I brought dinner to his house, we ate, and then I came home."

"Did you get anything out of him?"

"Not really. We just talked about random stuff. Nothing too personal."

"And you don't find that strange?"

"Guys never say much. That's just how they are."

"Not when the subject is them. Guys love talking about themselves. They're egomaniacs."

"Not all of them. Stop reading so much into this. He's just a private person."

"Did you guys do it?"

"No. We didn't even kiss. It was a totally platonic evening."

"That's boring."

"It's what you wanted! You keep telling me to just be friends with him."

"I don't think you two should even be friends, but it's no use telling you that. You don't listen to me."

"There's no reason we can't be friends. We're both outsiders in this town so it makes sense we'd bond over that. It's nice to finally have someone who knows how I feel. So did you tell people about him?"

"Yep. I went straight to my number one gossipers. Ralph's wife, Patty, and Alice from the sewing shop. Oh, and Ted from the hardware store. He gossips more than the women. Telling those three, the whole town should know about Kyle by now."

"You told him he's a writer from California. That's it, right?"

"I added a few more details."

"Nina! I told you not to make stuff up."

"I didn't. I just said he had a motorcycle and that he was renting out Miller's place for the summer. And I might've mentioned you had him over for dinner."

"Nina, that was not part of the plan. Why'd you tell them I had him over?"

"What's the big deal? You're going to show up with him as your date tomorrow night."

"Yeah, you're right. Never mind. It's fine. So did they ask you questions about him?"

"A few, but I didn't have any answers."

"What did they want to know?"

"Where he grew up. What his parents do. That type of thing."

"People in this town are so nosy. Why can't they mind their own business?"

"Because nothing ever happens here. When someone new comes to town, it's like free entertainment. And no offense, but you haven't been that entertaining. You're kind of boring."

"Thanks," I say with a laugh. "I'll try to stir up some trouble to be more interesting."

"I'm sure Kyle will. That guy sounds like trouble."

"He's not. He's just as boring as me. Nina, I have to get to sleep or I'll never get up in time for work."

"Before you go, what time are you coming over tomorrow?"

"Since I'm going with Kyle, I was thinking we'd just meet you there. Maybe around seven?"

"You're making me go alone? We were supposed to ride together."

"We could come pick you up."

"Forget it. I can't believe you're making me be a third wheel on your date with the roadside serial killer."

"Please do not call him that tomorrow night. Or ever again. And please try to be nice."

"I have to be myself, Sage. You know I say what I think."

"You have to at least give him a chance. And don't question him all night."

"I can't promise you that. If you're actually going to date this guy for real, I need to know more about him."

I'd like to date him for real but I don't think he'd agree to it, especially given how he acted tonight.

"So tomorrow around seven," I say. "Text me if you change your mind and want us to pick you up."

We say goodbye and I go to bed, my mind still on Kyle. It's been on him all day. I keep thinking about him and I don't know why. I've dated plenty of guys in the past and never thought about them this much. Maybe it's because Kyle is still such a mystery. I'm actually hoping Nina is her usual prying self tomorrow and finds out as much as she can about him.

***

The next night, Kyle picks me up just before seven. He called me earlier in the day, asking what to wear. I told him a t-shirt and jeans was fine but he showed up in jeans and a black button-up shirt.

"You look nice," Kyle says, glancing at me from across the seat of Miller's truck. We're on our way to the firehouse, which is on the other side of town.

"Thanks." I'm wearing a dress tonight but it's nothing fancy. Just a casual cotton sundress that's white with small red flowers all over it. It has straps at the top, leaving my arms and shoulders exposed so I brought a jean jacket in case it gets cold later.

"You look nice too," I say.

"I know you told me to wear a t-shirt but it didn't feel right for going out."

"Around here, t-shirts are acceptable pretty much anywhere, even church. People don't dress up, especially guys."

"Well, where I'm from, t-shirts are for working out so wearing one to a function doesn't seem appropriate."

"People in L.A. don't wear t-shirts outside of a gym?"

"If they do, they're designer and cost a couple hundred dollars."

"Is that what yours cost?"

"No, but *this* shirt did."

Taking a closer look at his shirt, it *does* look expensive. It's some kind of cotton blend but doesn't have a single wrinkle and has unique buttons that are black, outlined with a thin silver. The shirt fits him perfectly. There's no bagginess in the shoulders. The sleeves aren't too long. The chest part is fitted. It looks really good on him with his tan complexion and dark hair and eyes. He looks hot.

"How do you afford expensive clothes on a writer's salary? I thought writers didn't make much, unless they're really famous and have sold a lot of books."

I wait in silence for an answer. I'm sure he didn't like the question. It's personal and he hates personal questions. And probing about his financial status probably wasn't appropriate.

He confirms this by saying, "People don't like being asked about money."

"Sorry. It just came out. I'm so used to talking about my own money situation that I just assume others are as well, but I shouldn't assume."

"So what exactly is this thing we're going to? You said it's a fundraiser, but what goes on there? Is it just a dinner?"

"It's a dinner and dance and they'll have some items to auction off. People donate things like pies or quilts, and the businesses in town donate stuff."

"I don't dance."

"That's fine. We don't have to dance. But Nina will probably force me on the dance floor for a few songs."

"Why isn't she bringing a guy?"

"Because she's dated all the eligible guys in town and she refuses to date outside a twenty mile radius."

"Then she'll always be single."

"I keep telling her that and she says she doesn't mind but I know she does. It'll be interesting to see how she acts around Josh tonight. Her ex."

"The cop?"

"Yeah. He'll be there with this girl who went to high school with Nina."

"Does she still have feelings for him?"

"Nina? Yeah. Totally, but she refuses to admit it. I'm predicting she'll get really drunk to cover up the hurt she's feeling seeing Josh with someone else, and then we'll end up driving her home."

"I'm not sure I want to stay that long. I was hoping we might leave after dinner."

"Oh. Then I'll just stay there with her and take her home in her car."

"It's not that I don't want to be there with you. I just don't want people bothering me all night."

"I understand." And I do, because I've been in his shoes. When I moved here, going into town made me sick to my stomach. But unlike Kyle, who will be bombarded with questions all night, people avoided me, assuming I was a horrible person because of my dad. Now it's a month later and things are much better. A lady even smiled and said hi to me at the store the other day.

"This is it," I tell him as we approach the field across from the firehouse. "You can just park out here and we'll walk. Everything's set up behind the firehouse."

"It's outside?" He pulls up next to a truck and parks.

"Yeah. Is that a problem?"

"No, but you might get cold later."

"I brought a jacket." I pick it up from beside my feet where I had it sitting. "I'm going to leave it in the truck for now."

It's nice that Kyle worried I might be cold. Just like it was nice he made sure I got safely inside my house last night. He really is a nice guy.

Kyle opens my door and helps me out of the truck. As we walk toward the firehouse, he takes my hand.

"We're starting already?" I ask, holding our joined hands up and smiling.

"Is that a problem?"

"No. I just know you're not really loving the idea of being my fake date tonight so I thought you'd want to put off the act as long as possible."

"It's not an act. As far as I'm concerned, this is a date. A *real* date."

"But I thought you didn't want that."

He stops and turns to me. "I can't give you a longterm relationship, so if that's what you're looking for, then we can't do this. I thought we already discussed this."

"We did. And I'm fine just keeping this casual. Dating for the summer or however long you're here. I just wasn't sure you still wanted that. You kind of blew me off last night at dinner."

"I didn't blow you off, or I wasn't trying to. I just had my mind on some things and wasn't completely there."

"What was your mind on? Your book?"

He pauses. "Yeah. My book. I've been thinking more about the story and I think I'm going to take it in a new direction. I didn't like where it was going."

"So you started writing again?"

"Not yet but I will tomorrow."

"That's great!"

"Yeah." He gives my hand a squeeze. "We should get going. Your friend's probably waiting for us."

We walk past the firehouse to the back field, which is lit up with colorful lights strung along poles that outline the picnic tables and dance floor. Tall field lights are set up farther back and will turn on when it gets darker.

"Sage!" I hear Nina's voice and see her hurrying over to us, almost tripping on her high heels. A dusty field is not the place to be wearing high heels but I'm guessing they're meant to attract the attention of Josh. The same is true of her dress, which is a very short, tight red dress that belongs at a dance club not a town fundraiser.

"Nina." I give her a hug. "You really dressed up tonight."

"This?" She shrugs. "It's nothing special. It belongs to my cousin but she never wears it so she let me borrow it."

"Are you going to a club later?" I kid with a smile.

She smirks, eyeing me up and down. "Are you going to a hoedown?"

"Actually, yes." I look around. "That's what this is, right?"

"Doesn't mean you have to dress like it." She yanks the hem of her dress down. She'll be doing that all night. It's so tight it keeps riding up when she moves.

"Hi." Kyle holds his hand out to her. "I'm Kyle."

"Nina." She takes his hand and uses it to pull herself closer to him, motioning him to lean down.

"What is it?" he asks, now face-to-face with her.

She lowers her voice. "I told everyone here to leave you alone. If they step out of line, let me know. I've got dirt on everyone in town. If they bother you tonight, they risk their secrets getting out."

"Thanks," Kyle says, standing up straight again.

"Yeah, thanks, Nina," I say. "Not sure I agree with your methods but whatever works."

She keeps her eyes on Kyle. "Don't assume this means I like you. I'm only helping you because Sage asked me to. You hurt her and you'll be on my shit list. And ask anyone here, that's not a good list to be on."

"Got it," he says, putting his hands up in surrender.

She laughs. "Scared you, didn't I?"

"Kind of." He takes my hand and Nina notices.

She leans into us and says in a hushed tone, "You two look like a real couple."

We are a real couple, at least according to what Kyle said earlier. He keeps confusing me. Sometimes he acts like he doesn't want us going out but then he acts like he does.

As far as Nina's concerned, I need to play it cool and pretend Kyle and I are just friends. She knows we kissed but I made it sound like it wasn't a big deal, which it wasn't. We're still getting to know each other, so for now, we're friends who share an attraction to each other. Where it goes from here I'm not sure.

CHAPTER FOURTEEN

Sage

"Jesse's going to be pissed," Nina says. "Seeing you two together like this? I wouldn't be surprised if that boy tries to fight you," she says to Kyle.

"Bring it on," he says. "I can take him.

"No, don't." I look up at Kyle. "Getting into a fight with him will make people hate you, even if Jesse is the one who starts it."

"So if he takes a swing at me I'm just supposed to stand there and take it?"

"Just try to avoid it. If he starts talking to you, just walk away."

"And if he tries something with you? Tries to touch you? You really think I'm just going to stand here and do nothing?"

Nina's watching us, her eyes going between Kyle and me. She can tell from the concern in his voice how protective he is of me, a clear sign he has feelings for me. Now she's going to think Kyle and I are more than friends and I'm going to get a lecture about how I'm setting myself up to get hurt.

"We should go sit down," I say, walking toward one of the tables.

Nina and Kyle follow. Kyle sits next to me with Nina across from us.

"Do you want to get food now or later?" I ask.

"Later," Nina says, her eyes fixating on something behind me.

I turn and see Josh by the food tables, handing a plate to Lacey. Josh is wearing jeans and a black t-shirt that fits tight to his chest. He must be lifting weights because he didn't look that muscular in the pictures Nina has from when they were dating. She still has those photos on her phone. When I ask her why she hasn't deleted them, she says she hasn't gotten around to it, as if it's a time-consuming task to press the delete button.

Lacey has on a low-cut frilly pink blouse and denim mini skirt. The top and skirt don't really go together but she doesn't seem like someone who has great fashion sense. I would know because I don't either, although tonight I think I did an okay job, but I copied this look off a fashion website.

"That shirt doesn't go with the skirt," Nina says, tapping her nails on the plastic picnic table.

"What are we talking about?" Kyle asks.

"Josh's date," I tell him. "They're behind us at the food tables."

"Why would he drive all this way to go out with her?" Nina asks. "She's not even his type."

"Maybe he came here for you." I smile. "To make you jealous."

"If so, it's not working. I'm not jealous."

"You sure about that?" Kyle asks in a kidding tone.

She leans toward him across the table. "Are YOU sure that your relationship with Sage is fake and not real?"

He looks at me and smiles. "No comment."

Nina sits back, folding her arms over her chest. "I'm not jealous. I don't care who he dates. Josh and I are ancient history."

Kyle glances at the line of guys waiting for drinks. "Should I get us something from the bar?"

"I'll take a beer," I say.

"Whiskey straight up for me," Nina says, her eyes going to Josh again.

"Be right back."

When Kyle's gone, Nina leans toward me across the table. "I can't believe him."

"Kyle?"

"No! Josh! You don't see *me* flaunting a date in front of *him*. He's so inconsiderate."

"If you had a date you would've had no problem bringing him tonight, and you would've paraded him in front of Josh to make Josh jealous."

"I would not," she insists.

"Really?" I ask, giving her a deadpan stare.

"I don't play games like that."

"Then what's with the dress? That is not what you wear to a country jamboree or whatever you guys call this. That dress is so tight and short I don't know how you can walk in it."

"I felt like wearing something nice tonight. It had nothing to do with Josh."

"Then if you're not bothered by him being here, go up and talk to him. Go say hello."

"I'm not going over there. He's busy. And I'm busy getting to know Kyle, who by the way is freakin' hot." She lowers her voice. "Has he always been that hot?"

"Well, yeah. You saw him in the truck that day."

"From across the street. I didn't get a good look at him. But seeing him now...damn, he's something to look at. I get why you want to do the nasty with him." She pauses. "Did you already do it?"

"No. We're not in an relationship. We're keeping it casual."

"Meaning casual sex. No strings."

"That's not what I meant."

"If you ask me, you two are already past casual."

"What do you mean?"

"The way he was holding your hand, acting all protective. The way he was looking at you. He's got a thing for you. And you feel the same way about him. This isn't gonna end well."

"It's not like that. We're getting closer, yes, but it's not going to go anywhere. We both know it'll end so there's no use making it into something it's not."

"You say that now, but what are you going to do if you fall for him? Like fall in love?"

"That won't happen. I won't let it."

"Like you can control it?" She laughs. "Yeah, okay. You're already halfway there and don't even know it, so if you think you can stop it, you're wrong."

"I'm not—"

"Whiskey," Kyle says, setting the plastic cup in front of Nina, "and a beer." He hands me a bottle, keeping the other one for himself.

"So Kyle," Nina says, "what's your story?"

"I thought Sage already told you."

"What's your *real* story? Why are you here? Why this town over some other small town? If you wanted to research small towns, you could've done that in California. Or Arizona. Nevada. Someplace closer to home."

"My book is set in Kansas. I needed a small town in Kansas."

"Huh." She stares at him a moment, then downs her whiskey all at once, slamming the cup down when she's done.

"You might want to slow down there," I tell her. "The night just started."

"What about your family?" she asks Kyle. "Brothers? Sisters? Parents still around?"

"I have a..." He coughs. "I have a sister. Older. She lives in France. Works for a company there."

"Really?" I turn to him. "What company?"

"Just a small clothing company. She majored in fashion."

"That's cool. Do you ever go visit?"

"Not very often. I don't have time." He fidgets with his beer bottle, tearing at the label.

"What about your parents?" Nina asks. "Are they in California?"

"Sacramento. My dad sells insurance." His tone is curt. He's annoyed by her questions and starting to get angry. I don't know why it bothers him so much to talk about himself, but since it does, I'm wishing Nina would back off a little. I wanted her to get information from him, but not if he's going to get this upset.

"And your mom?" Nina asks.

I try to intervene. "Nina, why don't—"

"Passed away," he says, looking her in the eye. "A few years ago."

"Oh," Nina says, biting her lip.

"I'm sorry," I tell him. "We didn't know."

"Done with the questioning now?" he asks Nina before taking a long swig of his beer.

She gets up. "I'm gonna get another drink."

While she's gone I turn to Kyle. "I'm really sorry about that. Nina tends to go a little overboard sometimes. She's just trying to get to know you."

"I thought you told her I hate talking about myself."

"I did, but...I mean, her questions are pretty basic. Most anyone would ask about your family. Obviously if she knew about your mom, she wouldn't have asked but—"

"That's why she shouldn't be asking. You never know what kind of answer you'll get when you ask about someone's personal life. And you don't know if asking the question will affect someone in ways you didn't expect. People will tell you what they want you to know. And if they don't, it's because they don't want you knowing."

So is he saying he doesn't want me knowing anything about him other than where he's from and what he does for a living? Because that's basically all he's told me about himself. If that's all I'm allowed to know about him, we won't have much of a relationship. Or even much of a friendship.

"Why don't we get some food?" Kyle stands up. "We can eat and then go."

"Go?" I get up from the bench. "We just got here."

"And I'm already feeling uncomfortable. Everyone's staring at me and I'm not in the mood to answer their questions."

"Then don't answer them. But no one's going to ask. You heard Nina. She told them to leave you alone."

"Then what do you want to do?" he asks, sounding annoyed.

"For one, I think you need another drink to loosen up. You're too tense."

"I don't need another drink."

"Well, *I* do." I hold up my empty beer. "A stronger one this time."

"I didn't know you drank that much."

"I don't usually, but these town events tend to make me drink."

"Because you hate being here as much as I do, which is why we should just leave. Look around. Nobody wants us here."

Glancing around, I see a few people glaring at us and whispering to each other, but that's nothing new. I'm used to that.

"If we go, we're just giving them what they want. They don't own this town. We have just as much right to be here as they do."

"Then let's just go somewhere private for a minute." He takes my hand. "I need a break from these people."

As we're walking away, I hear my name.

"Sage!" I turn and see Josh waving at me.

"It's Josh," I tell Kyle. "He wants to talk. C'mon. Let's go over there."

"No." Kyle pulls hard on my hand. "We're leaving."

"We're not leaving." I yank on his hand, just like he did to mine, then say, "Stop acting like this. This was supposed to be a fun night but you're ruining it by being all cranky and moody."

He sighs, his eyes on Josh. "One hour. And then we leave."

"Sage," Josh says as he walks up to us. He has a big smile on his face but no date on his arm. Maybe Lacey had to use the restroom.

"Hey, Josh. This is Kyle." I point to him. "He's new in town."

"That's what I hear." Josh eyes Kyle in a suspicious way. It could just be something cops do, or it could be because Nina told Josh her concerns about Kyle. "So you came here to finish your book, huh?"

"That's the plan." Kyle looks directly at Josh, as if trying to prove he's not lying. He must sense Josh is suspicious of him.

"How long are you here for?"

"I don't know yet."

"Got tired of California? Just thought you'd check out rural Kansas?"

Kyle's jaw tightens and he moves it side to side just slightly, then says, "My book is set in a town like this. It's research."

"How'd you find Miller's place? It wasn't even up for rent."

"I drove through here when I was looking for a place to stay. Saw Miller sitting out on his porch and stopped and asked if he'd like to rent me his house."

"You must've paid him a lot to get him to agree to that. As far as I know, the man's never left the state. Never had much desire to."

Kyle doesn't answer.

"You must be doing well financially," Josh says.

"Yeah, that's why I rented out a shitty run-down house," Kyle says in an angry tone.

"Kyle." I hold his arm. "Why don't we get some food?"

"What do your parents think of this?" Josh asks. "You running off to the middle of nowhere?"

"I don't give a shit what my parents think. I'm 25. I can do what I want. And it's parent, singular. My mom is dead."

"I'm sorry to hear that."

"Yeah." Kyle smirks. "You seem real sorry."

"Kyle." I tug on his arm. "Let's go."

"I don't know if I'm allowed to. I don't think your cop friend is done interrogating me."

"I wasn't interrogating you," Josh says casually, lifting his beer to his lips. "Just trying to get to know you." He swigs his beer.

Kyle stares at him. "I'm not looking for friends."

"Then I guess that means you're looking for enemies. Keep that attitude up and they'll be easy to find."

"Josh," I say, trying to diffuse the tension that's erupted. "You should go find Lacey. She's probably looking for you."

"I doubt it. I think she's with Kevin now."

"*Kevin?* The baseball coach?"

"Yeah." He motions behind him. "They're over there dancing."

I look back and see Lacey slow-dancing with Kevin, her arms hooked around his neck.

"Why is she dancing with Kevin? What happened?"

"She thinks I'm still hung up on Nina so she moved on with someone else."

"Why does she think you still like Nina? Did you say something?"

"No. She said she could tell because I kept looking at Nina and not listening to whatever it was she said. I didn't think I was doing that but I guess it's possible. It's kinda hard *not* to look at her in that dress she's wearing."

"So is Lacey right? You want Nina back?"

He chuckles. "Even if I did, she wouldn't agree to it. When Nina makes her mind up about something, she doesn't go back."

"She might if you tried a little harder."

"Did she say that?"

"No. But you know Nina. She doesn't like to make things easy. If you put in the effort, I think she'd come around. And if not, just sheer persistence would do it. You could wear her down to the point she'd go out with you again."

"Huh." He rubs his chin. "You might have a point there."

"Touch me again and your balls will be up your ass!" we hear a girl yell. It's Nina. I can tell without even looking.

"Sounds like your girl could use some help," I say to Josh.

He laughs. "I think she's got it under control."

I turn and see a guy on his knees, doubled over in pain. Nina is storming away from him, a drink in her hand.

"On second thought, you might want to wait a few minutes for her to cool down before going over there."

"I can handle it," he says, walking off. "I've seen worse than that from her."

"She's crazy," I say to Kyle, laughing.

"No offense, but I can't say I'm liking your friends too much. And I'm pretty sure they don't like *me*."

"They're just being cautious and watching out for me. If you spent more time with them, they'd like you." I slip my hand in his. "Let's get some food. I'm starving."

We go up to the food table and Kyle buys our meals. The suggested donation is ten dollars a person, but Kyle drops a fifty dollar bill in the jar.

"Thank you!" Mary Oberson says. She's an older woman who's supervising the food table. She's also the kindergarten teacher at the local elementary school.

"The food looks great, Mary," I tell her.

"Oh, I didn't make it. I'm just helping to serve." She points to Kyle, who's walking away. "Who's the young man?"

"Kyle. He's new in town. He's a writer, here to finish his novel."

"How exciting!" Her eyes widen. "A writer! Has he been published yet?"

"No, not yet. Hey, Kyle!" I call out, but he's already heading to a table. "I'll see you later, Mary."

I catch up to Kyle. "You could've been friendlier to her. Mary is one of the nicest ladies in town. And unlike most people here, she doesn't pay attention to gossip. That's why she didn't know you."

"Good for her," he says, taking a seat at the table.

"You're still in a bad mood? Is this how you're going to be the rest of the night?"

"If I keep getting interrogated, then yes." He scoops up his shredded pork with his plastic spoon and shoves it in his mouth.

"Then just leave," I say, getting angry. "Nina will give me a ride home."

"Nina's drunk. She's not giving you a ride home."

"Then Josh will. He's not an *ass* like *some* people."

"I'm the ass?" He drops his spoon and turns to me. "I'm standing there, minding my own business, and Mr. Big Bad Cop comes storming up to me, asking questions and demanding answers like I'm a damn criminal."

"Okay, yes, I agree that he needed to back off on the questions but he was just trying to get to know you."

"And what if I don't want him to? What if I have no interest in being that guy's friend? What if I don't want to tell him my life story? Does not answering his questions make me a criminal?" He huffs. "Is he going to arrest me now?"

"No, of course not." I take a breath. "I'll tell you what. If you agree to stay here an hour and not be in a bad mood, I promise I'll keep Josh away from you."

"I don't need you to keep him away from me. I can handle him myself. But I shouldn't have to. I shouldn't have to even be here."

"But you are because I asked you." I soften my voice. "Because I like spending time with you. Not so much when you're an ass but..."

His body relaxes and he gives me a slight smile. "Why do you like me? I seriously don't understand why."

"I don't either." I sigh, pretending to be annoyed with myself. "But for some reason I do. So I really don't want you to leave."

"Then I'll stay." He leans down and gives me a kiss. "Because I like you too. And I love spending time with you."

CHAPTER FIFTEEN

Sage

"Guess I was right," a voice says from behind me.

I turn and see Jesse standing there, a bottle of beer in his hand. From the drawl in his voice, it's clear he's had too much to drink.

"Hey, Jesse," I say in a carefree tone, as if the kiss he just witnessed isn't a big deal. It's good he saw me with Kyle but I don't want him overreacting because of the kiss.

He motions to Kyle. "That's why you won't go out with me?"

"I wouldn't go out with you even if I wasn't with Kyle. I told you that before Kyle even came to town."

"You think he's better than me?" Jesse says, glancing at Kyle. "I have a business. I got my own place. What's this guy got?" He swigs his beer. "Nothing. He's got nothing, Sage."

Kyle stands up. "Why don't you go hang with your buddies? Sage and I are trying to have dinner."

Jesse pokes him in the chest. "Who the fuck do you think you are? Coming into town and taking my girl."

"I'm not your girl." I get up and put myself between Jesse and Kyle. Jesse was just supposed to see me with Kyle, not get in a fight with him, but I should've known this would happen. When Jesse gets drunk, he gets stupid and does stupid things.

"Let's not start something here," Kyle says to Jesse. "I don't want you getting hurt."

"You seriously think you could take me?" Jesse asks, sticking his chest out. "I could fucking knock you out so fast you wouldn't even have a chance."

"Think so?" He chuckles.

"Kyle." I lean toward him and lower my voice. "Don't provoke him. He's drunk."

Jesse sets his beer down on the table. "I'd be more than happy to beat the living shit out of you." He leans his head to one side, then the other, and shakes his shoulders out. Kyle just stands there, a smug grin on his face.

"Hey!" Josh yells from behind Jesse.

"Stay out of it," Jesse yells back. "You're not on duty, shithead."

Josh comes up beside Jesse. "Calling a cop a shithead isn't the smartest idea."

"You're not a cop here. You can't arrest me."

"No, but there are plenty of people here that could."

"All friends of mine. Friends who'd love to see me kick this guy's ass." Jesse sways side to side, like he's trying to figure out the best angle to hit Kyle. But he can't because I'm still standing between them.

"C'mon," Josh says, gripping Jesse's shoulder.

Josh yanks away from him. "Don't fucking touch me."

"Lance," Josh yells, turning back and waving at Lance to come over. Lance is a local cop. He's probably around thirty and friends with Jesse. Not best friends, but they play basketball together.

"Go ahead and call him over," Jesse says. "He'd love to see this." Jesse raises his fist. "Get out of the fucking way, Sage."

Lance appears. "What's the problem?"

Jesse answers. "Officer Dipshit here is trying to tell me what to do. Do me a favor and throw his ass out of here."

"Jesse, you need to stop," Lance says. "You want another arrest on your record?"

Another? He's been arrested before? I didn't know that. I'm surprised Nina didn't tell me.

"You'd fucking arrest me for hitting this asshole?"

"He could charge you with assault. Is that what you want?"

"I don't give a fuck. It'd be worth it if it got his ass out of town."

"I'm not going anywhere," Kyle says, cool and collected, not at all intimidated by Jesse. "At least not until I'm ready."

"Let's go." Lance pulls on Jesse's arm.

Jesse turns and swings at Lance, hitting him right in the middle of his face. Lance falls to the ground.

"What the fuck?" Lance says.

"Okay, that's it." Josh comes up behind Jesse and wraps his arm around his chest, yanking him back. "You're done."

"Fuck off, asshole!" Jesse fights against Josh, kicking him while wrestling to get Josh's arm off him. He manages to free himself, then whirls around and punches Josh.

"Jesse, stop it!" I go up to him and he whirls toward me. It's like slow motion. I see Jesse's arm rise up, ready to take a swing at anything and everything, which right now happens to be me. I'm right in the line of fire and just as I tense up to take the blow, Jesse drops to the ground. Like flat to the ground, landing so hard he's knocked out.

"What just happened?"

I look and see Kyle beside me.

Josh is next to him staring down at Jesse. "Shit, where'd you learn that?"

"I took martial arts," Kyle says.

"I might have to sign up for that."

"What'd you do?" I ask Kyle.

"Kicked him at the knees."

"And caused that?" I point to a still unconscious Jesse.

He grins. "There might be a little more to it than that, but basically, yeah, that's it."

"Wow."

I hear Nina's voice. "What happened? What's going on?"

Lance stands up, his nose bloody and swollen. He talks to Josh, "I'll get the other guys to carry him back to the car."

Josh nods.

"Holy shit," Nina says to Lance. "Did Jesse do that?"

"Yeah. I didn't see it coming. The fucker's fast." He walks off, wiping his nose on his sleeve.

"You guys okay?" she asks Kyle and me.

"We're fine," I answer.

"What about me?" Josh asks her. He has some blood on his lip but that's it. "Aren't you going to ask if *I'm* okay?"

She rolls her eyes. "You're fine. And besides, it's not my job to ask if you're okay. That's your date's job. Where is she, anyway? Shouldn't she be here cleaning that blood off your mouth?"

"Lacey found someone new." He points to the dance floor.

"She dumped you already?" Nina laughs. "That's hilarious. What'd you do wrong? Did you make those stupid duck noises? I told you girls don't like that."

"It's for hunting," he says to Kyle and me. "And other than the ducks, I've only shared that talent with Nina, who you can tell was impressed by it. She's still talking about it."

"I wasn't impressed. It was stupid." She looks at Lacey again. "So what happened? Why'd she dump you?"

Josh shrugs. "Don't know. But her loss." He wipes his mouth, which seems to be bleeding more.

Nina looks at him and sighs. She grabs his arm. "C'mon. I'll clean you up."

"I thought that was my date's job."

"It was, but she dumped you for another guy and I'm about to vomit looking at all the blood on your face." She drags him away.

"It's not that much," he says as they walk toward the fire station. "I can probably clean it up myself."

"Just shut up and let me handle this."

I laugh. "Those two are meant for each other."

Kyle isn't laughing. He pulls me off to the side, away from Jesse's lifeless body. "We should get out of here."

"Why? You don't have to worry about Jesse."

"It's not about Jesse. It's about being here. I want to leave. We accomplished your goal of convincing Jesse we're going out, so there's no need to stay here."

"It's something to do. We can eat, drink, listen to music. There's nothing to do at home."

"We can watch TV. Watch a movie. Anything's better than hanging around with people who don't want us here." He turns me toward him. "I'd rather just be with you. Just the two of us."

Looking at the scene around us, I realize I want that too. I thought coming here would be fun, but the whole thing with Jesse kind of ruined it. Now people are staring at us like it's our fault Jesse reacted that way. I guess in a way it was, but Jesse didn't have to react violently. His jealousy got out of hand because he was drunk, and that's not my fault.

"Okay, let's go."

We walk back to the truck and drive home in silence. When we get back to Kyle's place, I stop him before he gets out.

"Are you mad at me?"

"For what?"

"Making Jesse almost hit you?"

"You didn't make him do anything. He was drunk and being stupid."

"But I made you go there so Jesse would stop harassing me. And then he ended up almost punching you."

"I expected that would happen."

"You did?"

"If a guy like Jesse wants you and then sees you with someone else, there's a good chance he'll start a fight with the guy."

"And that didn't concern you?"

"As you saw tonight, I can take care of myself. He didn't stand a chance. Even if Josh hadn't held him back and Jesse was able to get a swing at me, he still would've ended up unconscious on the ground."

"Have you ever done that before? Used your martial arts training like that?"

"A few times." He opens the door and gets out.

"So you've been in fights before?" I ask as we walk to the house together.

He opens the door and we go inside.

"Have you or not?" I ask, wanting him to answer the question.

"Yeah." He walks past me to the kitchen. "You want something to drink?"

I meet up with him at the fridge. "Why do you always do that?"

"Not give you a thousand word answer to every question you ask?" he asks in an angry tone as he moves stuff around in the fridge.

"I didn't say it had to be a thousand words, but more than one would be nice."

He slams the fridge door shut. "How many times do I have to tell you I don't like talking about myself before you'll finally accept it?"

"And when are you going to realize that I can't be around someone who keeps secrets? After what I went through with my dad, I can't do that again."

He sighs, rubbing his hand over his jaw as he walks past me. "Then this isn't going to work."

I follow him to the couch and sit beside him. "I don't understand. Why is everything such a secret with you? Can you at least tell me that?"

"Why?" He looks at me. "Why is it so important that you get to know me?"

"Because I..." I look away. "Because I like you."

"Yeah, I kinda guessed that when you kissed me." His tone is lighter, and when I look back at him, I see him smiling.

"I didn't kiss you. You kissed *me*."

"You didn't push me away."

"Because I like you, which is why I want to know more about you. So why won't you tell me anything? If you're worried I'd tell other people in town, I swear to you, I wouldn't. Whatever you tell me will stay between just us."

He lets out a breath and looks down at my hand, which is now wrapped around his.

"Sage, I—" He stops suddenly.

"You what?" I ask softly, feeling like he's on the verge of finally telling me something.

He shakes his head. "I can't."

"You can't *what*? What is it you're afraid to tell me?"

He looks up, his eyes searching my face like his mind is trying to decide what to say next.

"What is it, Kyle? Just tell me. I promise I won't tell anyone."

He gets up and walks to the side of the room. "I'm sorry, Sage, but I don't want to talk about it."

"About what? Is there something in particular or do you just mean in general?"

"I don't want to talk about my past. It wasn't good, and it's something I'd rather not relive by telling someone else. If you want to know my favorite color or favorite food or what side of the bed I sleep on, then go ahead and ask. But as for my past and my family? I don't want to talk about it and I'm asking you to respect that."

"Come here." I motion him to sit beside me. When he does, I say, "I understand what it's like to want to hide stuff from people. Believe me, if I could've hidden the fact that I'm the daughter of a con man, I would have. Unfortunately, photos of me with my dad were plastered all over the news. But if I'd been able to hide it, I wouldn't have told anyone, except maybe someone I felt close enough to tell. Someone I trusted." I pause. "Maybe over time you can trust me enough to talk about it. Because not talking about it can sometimes be worse than keeping it a secret."

He's looking at me, his eyes on mine. His lips part like he's about to say something, but then he quickly looks down.

"I can't talk about it," he says.

I put my hand on his. "Okay."

What he said about his past not being good makes me wonder if he has issues with his family. His mom is gone so maybe it's his dad. Maybe his dad was abusive and Kyle left California to get away from him.

"Blue," I say.

Kyle's brows draw together. "Am I supposed to know what that means?"

"I'm guessing that's your favorite color."

He leans back against the couch, smiling. "Why blue?"

"It's the color of the ocean and you chose to live near the ocean which means you must like it. And you're moody, which reminds me of a storm brewing, when the sky goes from bright blue to dark blue. Blue fits your personality."

"Well, I hate to say it but you're wrong. On all accounts." He leans toward me, putting his face close to mine. "First of all, I don't like the ocean. Just looking at the waves makes me seasick. And forget about getting me on a boat unless you want to see me hurl for hours."

"Huh. Okay, what else?"

"I'm not moody. I'm just going through a time of transition right now where I'm not sure about some things. I'm asking myself a million questions to figure out what I'm going to do next and I don't have the answers. Then I move here and have people asking about my past, which I'm trying not to think about. I'd say all that gives me an excuse for not always being in the best mood."

"So coming here wasn't just about your book. It's about getting away. You're running from your—"

"No!" He stands up. "That's not what I said!"

"Why are you getting so angry?"

"I'm not." He takes a calming breath. "Sorry. I didn't mean to yell." He rubs his hand over his jaw. "I'm not running away. I came here because I need time to think."

"And write," I add.

"Yes." He sits down. "I need time to write."

"And blue isn't your favorite color."

"No." He gives me a slight smile.

"Orange?"

"Nope."

"Yellow?"

"*Yellow?* Is that *anyone's* favorite color?"

"I don't know. Probably. Why? What's wrong with yellow?"

"It's the color of pee."

"And sunflowers. People like sunflowers. Yellow is cheery."

"But not my favorite color."

"I give up. What is it?"

"Black."

"Black?" I scrunch up my nose.

"What's wrong with black?"

"It's depressing. It's the color of death. And darkness."

"You asked me my favorite color and now you're making fun of it?" he asks like he's offended. "You see why I don't answer questions?"

"Sorry. You're right. I should accept your answer without judgment, even though just seconds ago, you passed judgment on yellow, which could be *my* favorite color."

"Is it?"

"No. I like red."

"Red," he repeats. "The color of passion."

"And roses. Hearts."

"So you're a romantic?"

"I used to be, but then I saw my dad break my mom's heart and ever since then, I've kind of lost hope in love and romance. It's nice to read about or see in movies, but in real life? I'm not sure it exists."

"That's a cynical view."

"Do you believe it exists?"

"I think it does, but I personally haven't seen it. I don't think my parents were in love."

"Ever?"

"Maybe before I was born but not when I was older. They definitely weren't in love by the time my brother was born."

"You have a brother?"

He pauses, his eyes moving around like he doesn't know how to answer. Why is that a hard question? He either has a brother or doesn't. Or maybe he had a brother but he died.

"What's wrong?" I ask.

"Nothing." He shakes his head.

"You don't want to talk about your brother?"

"No. We're uh...not really speaking right now."

"Oh. That's too bad. Is he younger or older?"

Kyle doesn't answer.

"You don't want to talk about him."

He still says nothing, so I do.

"I'm an only child," I say. "My dad took off when I was little. That was the first time he broke my mom's heart. And then he did it again."

"I can see why you're losing faith in men."

I shrug. "I don't think all men are bad. But I am more cautious now than I used to be. I worry that guys are lying to me. I worry I can't trust what they say. That's why I keep asking you questions. I want to prove to myself you're nothing like him. But that's not fair to you and it's wrong of me to make assumptions about you that aren't true. I know that, and I keep reminding myself not to do it but sometimes I still do."

"It's not a bad thing to question what people say. People lie. It's a fact of life."

"I know, but I can't have a relationship built on suspicion. It has to be built on trust and I'm not sure I'm there yet, which is why I agreed to keep things casual with you. I want to get to know you but if you're not willing to share much then I guess I'm okay with that, knowing this isn't going to last." I smile.

"We'll just be two mysterious strangers, keeping each other company for the summer."

"We're not strangers," he says seriously. "I already have feelings for you, Sage."

"You do?" I ask, my heart skittering with excitement because before now I wasn't really sure if he had feelings for me. I definitely have feelings for him. I can't quite define them yet, but I love spending time with him and when he's not around I can't stop thinking about him. "What kind of feelings?"

He rubs my hand. "The kind that makes me wish the situation were different. That this wasn't just for the summer."

"What if it wasn't?" I ask, my eyes meeting up with his.

"That's all it can be." He looks down. "I'm sorry, Sage, but the summer is all I can give you. And it may not even be that long."

I don't ask what he means by that because I don't want the answer. I don't want this to end. It just started, and although Kyle is confusing and frustrating and sends my emotions all over the damn place, I still want him around. I don't want him to leave.

CHAPTER SIXTEEN

Kyle

I wake up suddenly and forget where I am for a moment, my body tense and rigid. Looking around, I remember I'm not home. Not in my room. Not in that house. Only then do I let myself relax, taking a deep breath.

Feeling something against me, I look down and see Sage nestled under my arm, her head on my chest. She's sound asleep, looking both beautiful and sweet.

The TV is making a low humming noise and I see it flickering with static. I search for the remote to turn it off but can't find it. Then I see it on the couch cushion, sticking out from under Sage's leg. I reach down and try to gently slide it out from under her without waking her up.

She moves a little, her eyes still closed, and mumbles, "Kyle."

Hearing her say my name in her sleep makes me smile. Maybe she's dreaming about me. If so, I hope it's all good. I don't want her thinking bad things about me. I'm not a bad person. My father is, but I'm not. I may be lying to her but it's for her own good. For her safety.

When we got home earlier I almost let the truth slip out. I wanted to tell her everything; what I've been through, where I'm really from, and why I had to go into hiding. I'm sick of keeping all this a secret. If I could just tell one person I'd feel better and could maybe get another opinion on what to do.

But I can't tell Sage. I can't get her involved in this. Even just knowing the truth could put her in danger if my father ever found out. Making money is all that matters to him and if anyone interferes with that, or even poses a threat of interfering, he'll go after them. He'll make sure they keep quiet.

I already told Sage too much. I didn't mean to. It just slipped out. When I'm around her I start to relax, and when I relax I tell her things I shouldn't.

When I mentioned my brother I wasn't even thinking. When it slipped out and she asked about him, I didn't know what to say. When I lied about having a sister in France, the made-up story came easily, maybe because I was telling it to Nina and not Sage. Lying to Sage is harder because I really do want to be truthful with her. I just can't.

Thinking about it now, it's really not a big deal if Sage knows I have a brother. Knowing that doesn't give anything away so I shouldn't have reacted the way I did. Luckily, I found a way to explain my reaction by pretending my brother and I are no longer speaking. It's true but it's not because we're fighting. It's because talking to him could put us both in danger. I haven't spoken to Cain since the night I was almost killed.

"Kyle?" Sage lifts her head off my chest.

"I'm right here."

"What time is it?" she asks, sounding groggy.

"I'm not sure. Probably around two or three."

She yawns. "I should go."

"Why don't you stay? I don't want you driving home this late."

"I live two miles away."

"Still. Going home to a dark house late at night doesn't sound safe."

"You're saying I'm safer here with you?" She lays back on my chest.

"Much." I kiss her head without even giving it a thought. It's something I'd only do with a girlfriend, with someone I really care about. I'm not supposed to feel that way about Sage. I'm not supposed to be getting closer to her.

"Could we move?" She rubs her eyes. "My neck is starting to hurt sleeping that way."

The bed would be more comfortable but we'd probably end up having sex. Given our attraction to each other, I have a feeling that'll happen eventually but I don't want it to be tonight. It's too soon and I don't want her thinking that's all I want from her. Truthfully, I don't know what I want from her, or what she wants from me. Right now I'm just going with what feels right in the moment, and right now, holding her in my arms feels right. I don't want it to end.

She stands up. "Lay down."

I do as she asks, laying on my side to give her room in front of me.

"Do you have a blanket?" she asks.

"Just the one on my bed. I'll go get it."

"I'll do it." She's gone before I can stop her and I panic. My duffle bag is in there and I don't want her seeing what's in it.

Bolting up from the couch, I run to my room. "Find it?"

The blanket is off the bed and wrapped over her arm. "You didn't have to come all the way in here."

"I thought you might need help."

"You're strange," she says with a smile as she walks past me.

We lie down on the couch, Sage in front of me, my arm holding her close, the blanket over us. It's perfect, and something I wish we could do every night.

I've never slept with a girl like this, meaning actually fallen asleep together. I've had girlfriends but nothing serious. Nothing that made me feel the way I feel with Sage. There's something about her that makes me want to be with her. To hold her. To protect her. Take care of her.

A loud noise comes from the kitchen. I immediately sit up, causing Sage to fall back where my body had just been supporting her.

"What are you doing?" she asks.

"I heard a noise."

"Yeah? So? It was probably an animal."

"It sounded like it came from the kitchen." Looking back there I don't see anything but I can't see the back door from here. If someone came in that way, I wouldn't know.

"It was probably a raccoon trying to get into the garbage. You can't leave your garbage can out. They're always trying to tip it over."

"The garbage is in the garage," I say, slowly getting up.

"I'm sure it's nothing. Just go to sleep."

I look around the living room for a weapon but it's too dark to see anything. Even if I could, there's nothing here I could use. I need a gun, and I need to get it illegally since going the legal route puts me at risk of being found.

"Stay here," I tell her, keeping my voice down.

"What are you doing?"

"I just need to check something."

I walk quietly to the kitchen, my heart pounding, hoping Sage is right and it's just an animal that made the noise. I flip the light switch on and search for any signs of an intruder. Nothing seems out of place. I know because I memorize how things look and where they're placed every time I'm about to leave the house. Then when I get home, I make sure nothing's changed.

Going over to the door, I check that it's locked. It is, but I unlock it to check the screen door. It's loose, flapping in the wind. That must've been the noise I heard.

I slip the metal hook on the screen door into the metal hole attached to the doorframe, securing it in place, then I close the back door. As I turn the lock, I freeze, realizing the metal hook should've already been secured. I'm almost positive I checked it before I left tonight. So if it was secured when I left, how did it get undone? It couldn't just happen. Someone had to have done it.

"Are you coming?" I hear Sage yell.

"Just a minute," I yell back.

Going over to the kitchen window above the sink, I slowly move the curtain aside just enough for me to see the back yard but it's too dark to see if someone's out there.

"What's going on?"

Sage's voice startles me and I rear back, almost hitting her. I turn and wrap my arms around her, for my own comfort more than hers. In her mind, nothing's wrong. In mine, I'm imagining men with guns surrounding the house, waiting to break in and shoot me. But how would they have found me? And if they were here, they wouldn't be waiting outside. They'd break through the door and finish the job.

"Kyle," Sage says softly. "What's wrong?"

"Nothing." I hold her tighter. "Everything's fine."

"You're shaking," she says, her hand moving softly over my back. It's soothing. Comforting. A feeling I'm not used to.

"I just got a chill. I opened the door to lock the screen and the air was cold."

"C'mon." She backs away and takes my hand. "We'll get the blanket over us."

We return to the living room and lie back on the couch. Once Sage is tucked in my arms, her body against mine, I immediately start to relax. This is why I can't get enough of her. Just her very presence calms me like nothing else can. And holding her calms me even more.

She falls asleep before I do and I listen to her softly breathing. The sound lulls me to sleep and I don't wake again until hours later when the sun's coming up.

"I need to go," Sage whispers. "I have to get to work."

She turns and kisses me on the cheek.

I open my eyes and see that beautiful face of hers, the highlights in her hair glistening in the soft morning light.

"Why are you working on Sunday? The place should be closed."

"It normally is, but the Sunday after the firehouse fundraiser, the garage always does free oil changes all day with the donations going to the firehouse. I think Kenny will even be there today. Jesse said something about his dad showing up for the event. We'll have free food in the waiting area. I'm in charge of that. I'm also in charge of the kids' area. I'll have games set up and a movie playing."

"Sounds like a busy day."

"It will be, but I don't mind. It's for a good cause."

I hold out my arms. "Come here."

She smiles and sinks down in my arms.

"Thank you," I say, hugging her to my chest.

"For what?"

"Staying."

She pulls back. "You don't have to thank me for that."

"I liked it," I say as my eyes wander over her face.

"I did too," she murmurs.

I focus on her mouth, her slightly parted lips. She tilts her head and strands of her hair fall over those soft, sweet lips. I reach my hand up and slowly move her hair aside. When I look up I see her watching me, and hear her breath getting heavier.

"I should go," she says, but it's not convincing. I can feel what she wants. I can see it in her eyes. She doesn't want to go. She wants to stay, and do what we didn't do last night.

I want that too, but now isn't the time. In the light of day my mind is back on full alert, wondering how the hell that screen door came undone and who was responsible.

I need to call Hank. Maybe he stopped by to get something and forgot to latch the door.

"Can I call you later?" I ask.

"Yeah, of course," she says as she hurries to move off me.

I pull her back into my arms. "I really liked having you here."

She smiles. "Then maybe we should do it again."

"I think we should."

She sits up. "Like maybe tonight? There's supposed to be a thunderstorm and I hate being alone during a storm. It scares me."

"Then I'll come over. I'll bring dinner. Or is that too early?"

"No. Dinner would be perfect."

I kiss her. "I'll see you tonight."

She gets up and finds her purse and I meet her at the door.

"Have a good day," she says. "Hope you get some writing done."

"I hope so too. And hey, if Jesse gives you any trouble at work today, call me. I'll come take care of it."

"I doubt he'll bother me. He'll be embarrassed about last night. He'll want to pretend it never happened." She reaches up and kisses my cheek. "Bye."

As soon as she's gone I call Hank. "Were you here yesterday?"

"Who *is* this?"

"Kyle. I was wondering if you stopped by yesterday."

"No. I was helping my wife with the fundraiser. Why do you ask?"

"The screen door wasn't latched and I always latch it so I thought maybe you were here and forgot to latch it before you left."

"Wasn't me. Was Sage there? Maybe she's the one who forgot."

"It wasn't her. She didn't come over until last night."

I shouldn't have said that. Now he's going to think Sage and I did something last night. But we're supposed to be a couple so I guess people wouldn't be that surprised she was over here.

"You two were looking pretty cozy at the party last night," he says. "Is it getting serious?"

"No. We just met."

"Sometimes you know right away. I knew I loved my wife from the moment I saw her."

"Love at first sight? That really happens?"

"It did for me. And we've been married now for over fifty years."

"That's a long time. Congratulations."

"Could be you someday. I think you and Sage would be good together. A lot better than her and that mechanic."

"You don't like Jesse?"

"He's a troublemaker. He's immature and lets his temper get out of control. The boy's been arrested at least twice, maybe more."

"For what?"

"Mostly misdemeanors. Public intox. Disturbing the peace. Resisting arrest. I don't think he's been in trouble for fighting before but the way he was acting last night, I'm surprised he didn't do more damage than he did."

"I would've stopped him. I can protect myself."

"I have to say, I was impressed with that move you did. Took Jesse down before he even knew what happened. How long have you been doing martial arts?"

"Ever since I was a kid. It was a way to burn off steam."

It was also one of the few activities I did with my dad. He took me to his gym and got me started with classes.

"Well, you've certainly mastered it," Hank says. "I've never seen someone drop that fast to the ground."

"Hank, I need to get going. I just wanted to check about the screen door."

"Like I said, it wasn't me. Maybe you just didn't latch it completely and the wind blew it off."

"Yeah, maybe."

"I'll see you on Friday."

"Yeah, see ya."

I go to the back door and check the screen. It's still latched, despite the strong winds whipping around outside. It couldn't have been the wind. It was definitely unlatched by someone, and maybe that someone was me. My mind has been distracted by thoughts of Sage for days now. It's possible, in my distracted state, that I left yesterday and didn't check the latch.

Living like this is driving me crazy. I'm always paranoid. I never feel safe. It would be nearly impossible for them to find me here but that doesn't mean it can't happen. Impossible things happen every day.

I need protection. I can't keep living here without a weapon. A knife isn't good enough. I need a gun. If someone shows up here to kill me I'm not going to give him a chance.

But where the hell am I going to get a gun? Illegally? The irony that the son of man who sells contraband weapons can't figure out how to get a gun would be humorous if it were someone else. But I don't find it the least bit funny because the only reason I need the gun is to protect myself against my father.

Who the fuck does that? How evil do you have to be to want to kill your own son? Even after I told him I'd keep quiet, he still wanted me dead. He doesn't trust me to keep quiet. And maybe I shouldn't. Maybe I should go to the police and turn him in, except I have no proof. It'd be his word against mine and they'd have no reason to believe me.

To the outside world, my father looks like a model citizen. He has a successful import business, donates a ton of money to charity, and is involved in numerous civic organizations. My claims against him would go nowhere, which is why he shouldn't be threatened by me. Even if I wanted to report him to the police it wouldn't do any good. And yet he still feels the need to get rid of me.

If I go to Kansas City there's a good chance I'd find a place that would sell me a gun, but going to a large city puts me at risk. I'm sure my father has put alerts out, asking people if they've seen me. And those people could very well be the people I'd be trying to buy a gun from. Those are his people. Criminals who are able to make a good living doing illegal activities while circumventing the police. I don't know that much about my father's business but I'm sure he's well connected in that world. He'd have to be in order to do what he does without getting caught.

The phone rings and I nearly jump from the sound. I'm not used to the loud ring of a landline phone. My father had one in his home office but I was never allowed to go in there so I didn't hear it ring.

I'm hesitant to answer it. There's no caller ID. It could be anyone. What if it's them? But how would they get this number? Even if they had the number, they wouldn't call. They'd just show up.

I answer the phone. "Hello?"

"Hi." I immediately recognize her soft sweet voice. It instantly calms me.

"Hey. Are you on break?"

"No, but it doesn't matter. I'm allowed to make phone calls during work. Anyway, I was wondering if you want to come by for lunch again?"

I'd much rather have lunch with Sage than be off searching for a place to illegally buy a gun, but I need protection. This can't wait.

"Sorry, but I can't today."

"Too busy writing?" Her voice is cheery. It makes me smile. Given my life right now, I shouldn't be smiling, and I didn't until the day I met Sage. Now just the sound of her voice makes me smile.

"Yeah. I just started a new chapter." How I came up with this writer story I have no idea. It's not something I'd planned ahead of time. Before I got to town, I should've figured out a story to tell people but I was too focused on staying alive. I assumed I'd have at least a few days to myself, hidden away in Miller's house, before I had to interact with anyone. But then Sage showed up and insisted on getting to know me.

"You still need to eat lunch."

"I'll just eat something here. If I go out, I'll lose momentum. Once I start writing, I need to keep going."

"What about tonight? Are you still coming over?"

"I'm not sure. I'll have to see how the writing's going."

"But you'll let me know if you're coming over, right?"

How am I going to let her know? I don't have a phone. If I end up having to drive hours to find a gun I won't make it back until late.

"Tell you what," I say. "Don't plan on me coming over tonight. If I'm able to, I'll call and let you know. If you don't hear from me it means I'm making progress on the book and can't get away."

"Oh. So I probably won't see you then." Now she sounds sad. I hate making her sad but I don't want to say I'll be there and then not show up.

"Probably not. But maybe tomorrow."

"Okay." She still sounds sad. "Then I guess I'll see you tomorrow."

If I'm not dead by tomorrow. Going on this journey to find a gun could end up getting me killed.

CHAPTER SEVENTEEN

Sage

I'm disappointed I won't be having dinner with Kyle. When I left him this morning I already couldn't wait to see him again. That's a sure sign I'm falling for him. I don't normally miss a guy right after seeing him. But with Kyle it's different and I still haven't figured out why. I don't know him well enough to like him this much. He still hasn't told me much about himself and when I try to get him to talk, he shuts down.

But he did share how he felt about me. And I was shocked. I still am. He likes me far more than he was letting on but I don't know why he decided to tell me that, knowing our relationship won't last. But at least he said he wished it could, which makes me sad but also happy. I'm sad knowing this will end sooner than either of us wants. But I'm happy that we both like each other enough to wish this could continue longer than a few months.

All morning I've been trying to think of ways we could continue this relationship past the summer. We could call and text and maybe visit each other every few weeks. But traveling costs money and I barely have money for food so trips to California are definitely not in the budget.

I don't know why I'm even thinking this way. I just met Kyle and here I am trying to find a way to see him after he leaves. I need to slow down and make this relationship what it was supposed to be. Just a casual summer romance to keep my mind off the situation I've found myself in.

As I'm driving home, my phone rings. Hoping it's Kyle, I quickly answer it. But it's not Kyle. It's my mom.

"Hey, Mom, where have you been?" I ask because I haven't talked to her for a few days. She texted and said she was super busy getting ready for the gallery event, which was last night. I've been dying to hear how it went.

"Sorry I haven't called. There was just so much to do."

"It's fine. I was just kidding. So tell me what happened."

"Honey, you're not going to believe it!" she says, her voice brimming with excitement.

"You sold a painting?"

"Not just one, but two! I sold both of them!"

"Are you serious? Mom, that's great!"

"I was so shocked I didn't think it was real. I thought maybe the person meant to buy someone else's painting and got mixed up."

"Did the same person buy both?"

"No. One sold last night to a woman from Connecticut. And then today, a business man who was at the showing called and asked if the other one was still available. It was, so he bought it!"

"Mom, that's amazing!"

"It really is. Claire said new artists rarely sell two pieces in one night, especially if there hasn't been much buzz about them in the art community. And I've had no buzz other than Claire talking about me to some of her friends."

"So what happens now?" I slow down as I pass Kyle's house. I don't see his motorcycle out front. Maybe it's in the garage.

"I've already started another painting. If I'm lucky, I'll sell one or two before I have to move back."

Have to, meaning she doesn't want to. She loves it there. I can tell. Every time we talk she always sounds so happy. So full of life.

"At this rate you might sell ten by the end of summer." I pull into my driveway and park.

She laughs. "I doubt it. I think last night was a fluke. But a good one. We made five thousand dollars."

"Mom, that's awesome. And it wasn't *we* it was you. You did all that yourself. Because you're talented and the people there saw that. That's why your paintings sold. It wasn't a fluke."

"You're sweet for saying that but I'm not counting on selling any more. If it happens, great, but if not, at least now we have money to put toward an apartment and maybe a small down payment on a car."

"I'll have money by then too so at least we won't be completely broke."

"Your money goes for college. I'm not letting you spend it any other way. I don't want you waiting years to go back."

"Mom, it won't be years. I'm still planning to go back in the spring."

"Did you tell your advisor that?"

"Yes. We talked last week. He said I'll be fine. And this will actually work out better. If I finish up in the spring I'll graduate in May, when they have a bigger ceremony. The December one is lame."

"You're always seeing the positive. I love that about you, honey."

"Where do you think I learned it?"

I hear her sniffle. "Don't make me cry. I miss you so much. I wish I could fly back there and see you."

"We can't afford it. And you can't leave your studio. You've got paintings to do."

"I really do love it here," she says, getting excited again. "This city has so much energy and such a diverse mix of people. Last night I met this woman who sings in the opera and writes children's books on the side. She was fascinating to talk to. We're meeting for coffee next week."

"Sounds like you're making friends."

"I am. I've joined an artists' group that meets every Saturday morning where people share their work or just talk about what inspires them. I went to the first one yesterday and loved it."

Walking into the house I smell a hint of that stinky sofa. Its stench still lingers in the air. I need to open the windows again. It's going to take awhile to get rid of that smell.

"So how about you?" my mom asks. "How was the firehouse event?"

"It was okay. I didn't stay long."

"Did you go with Nina?"

"I met her there. I went with my new neighbor."

"Oh, that's right. The young man that's renting the house."

"Yeah, that's him."

"How much do you know about this boy?"

"Um, let's see. He's a writer from L.A. doing research for his book, which is about a small town in Kansas."

"Seems rather extreme to move somewhere to do research. He could've just interviewed some people. Done research online."

"He's also here to finish his book. He's behind on his manuscript and thinks he'll get more done here than back home."

"What's his name? Maybe Hattie would know him."

"Hattie?"

"My new friend. The opera singer."

"Why would she know him?"

"She's an author. Authors might know other authors, or maybe she's at least heard of him."

"He's not published yet so I doubt she's heard of him. But his name is Kyle. Kyle Shadwick."

"I'll just mention him to her. You never know. So was this a date you two were on last night?"

"Not really. I mean, I guess it was but...it's complicated."

"What do you mean?"

I always tell my mom everything but I'm not sure if I should tell her this.

"Sage, what is it? What are you not telling me?"

I sigh. "I've been having some issues at work. My boss, Jesse, keeps asking me out, even after I tell him to leave me alone. I know I should report him but it wouldn't do any good. In small towns like this, the locals take the side of the people who are from here and since I'm not, they'd take Jesse's side. I know it's not right but it's just how it is."

"Honey, why didn't you tell me this?"

"Because there's nothing I can do about it. It is what it is. Anyway, going back to last night, I brought Kyle to the fundraiser so Jesse could see us together and hopefully give up trying to date me."

I'm not going to tell her about the fight they had. She doesn't need to know.

"And did it work?"

"So far it has. I had to work today for that oil change fundraiser and Jesse didn't even talk to me. I guess he didn't really have time with all the oil changes but still, I don't think he'll bother me anymore."

"So you and Kyle aren't dating. You're just friends."

"We're friends but it might turn into more. I'm not sure yet."

"You said he's from California?"

"Yeah, so if we start something it won't last."

"Then maybe you shouldn't. I don't want you getting hurt."

"Getting hurt is part of life, Mom. You and I know that more than anyone."

"I know, but I'd hate to see you get hurt by this boy. You've already been through so much."

"So have you."

"But I feel so much better now. Coming here was the right decision. I wasn't sure at first but now I know this is just what I needed. Now I need to make sure you're doing okay too."

"I am. I have Nina and now I have Kyle. I don't feel so alone here anymore."

"That's good, honey. Just be careful with this boy. Maybe just be friends with him."

"Mom, I'll be fine. You don't have to worry."

"I always worry about you. I'm your mom."

"My mom, the famous artist." I smile as I think about that. She sold two paintings in one night! I'm so proud of her. "You better get back to work."

"Except it's not work. It's fun. I absolutely love what I'm doing."

"That's great, Mom. I'm really happy for you."

"What are you doing tonight?"

"Staying in. Having dinner."

"What about Nina? Is she coming over?"

"No, she has family dinner at her aunt's house on Sundays. I'll probably just watch some TV then go to bed. I'm tired."

"Well, get some rest. We'll talk soon."

"Okay, bye."

I go in my room and peel off my stinky garage clothes, then jump in the shower. When I get out I go to my dresser to find some clothes. I'm going for comfort tonight. I put on some gray drawstring shorts made of sweatshirt material and a loose white t-shirt.

Just as I'm finished dressing I hear a knock on the door. It's still light outside so I shouldn't be scared but living alone in the middle of nowhere I'm always worried when someone comes to the door.

Going over to my window, I peek out the side of the drapes but can't see anyone. And I don't see a car.

The knocking continues. "Sage?"

Is that Kyle's voice? It kind of sounds like him.

"Who is it?" I call out from behind the door.

"It's Kyle. Everything okay?"

"Yeah, just a minute."

What is he doing here? He said he wasn't coming over. I'm not dressed for company. I'm not even wearing a bra.

As I race to my room to put one on, I hear him talking. "Can I come in? My hands are full."

His hands are full? With what?

Hurrying back to the door, I open it and see him holding a large pizza box and a six pack of beer.

"What are you doing here?" I ask, taking the beer from him.

"What do you mean? I told you I was coming over."

I step aside and let him in. He's wearing jeans today, but not the ones he wore the other night. These look new, like he just bought them. They're dark and fit tight on his ass. He has a nice ass.

"I'll put this in the kitchen." He walks over there and I follow him with the beer. It's warm so I put it in the fridge.

"I thought you said you'd call if you were coming over."

"I did." He turns me toward him and puts his arms around my waist. It feels like something a boyfriend would do. If we're keeping this casual is that allowed? I don't know what the rules are for a casual, short-term relationship. I've always gone into relationships thinking they'll last.

"I didn't get a call from you."

"I left a message like a half hour ago."

"Oh. It must've been when I was on the phone with my mom. I didn't even notice you'd called. After we hung up I went right in the shower." I look down at my clothes. "As you can see, I'm not really dressed for company."

"You look great. We're just eating pizza and watching movies, right?"

"Well, yeah, but I'm not wearing, um...undergarments."

He laughs. "Undergarments? You mean like a bra?"

"And um, other things."

"Going commando, huh? You do that often?"

"No." I push him back. "And stop talking about this. It's embarrassing."

"I say you stick with what you're wearing. You put it on so you'd be comfortable so why put something on that makes you uncomfortable?"

"Because it's even more uncomfortable to be on a date when you're not wearing a bra and panties."

He smiles. "I think that's hot."

"It is if you're..." I go around him. "Never mind. Let's eat."

"We need to let the beer chill."

"Then the pizza will get cold."

"Then we'll heat it in the oven."

"What do you want to do while we wait?"

"Play charades?" he says with a smile.

"Yeah, that's funny. How about we go sit in the living room?"

"Only if you sit on my lap."

He's being very flirtatious tonight and he's in a good mood. He's not so serious. He must've had a good day of writing.

"Why would I sit on your lap?" I ask.

"Because you don't have a couch anymore and the chairs are placed six feet apart."

"Then we'll move them closer."

He walks over there. "Okay, but I liked my idea better."

So did I, so why did I say that? He's acting all flirty and sexy, which is just what I want, and then I shut him down.

Once the chairs are moved and we're seated, I turn to him. "Did you accomplish your goal?"

His brows furrow. "What goal?"

"Your writing goal for today. I assume you did or you wouldn't be over here."

"Yeah. I did."

"And you're happy with what you wrote?"

"I don't know yet. I'll find out when I read it tomorrow. I need time away from it before I read it again."

"So tell me more about your writing process."

"I don't really have a process. This is my first book."

"But you've been writing a long time, right? Like in college? You never told me where you went to college."

"I didn't."

"You didn't go to college?"

"No. But I've taken writing classes and gone to some writing workshops."

"Weren't your parents—I mean, your dad—wasn't he upset you didn't go to college?"

"Not really. He knew it wasn't right for me."

"Huh. I just assumed you went to college, not that it's bad you didn't."

"Why'd you assume I went?"

"I don't know. You just seem like someone who went to college. I imagined you going to some East Coast school, the kind that has stone buildings with ivy growing up the sides."

"Where every day I wear a navy blazer and khakis to class?" he kids. "And at night I put on my polo shirt and drink until I pass out?"

I laugh. "Yes. Exactly. That's how I pictured you spending your college years."

"Sorry to disappoint you but that didn't happen."

"But your sister went, right?"

"My what?"

"Your sister. She went to college, right?"

He sits up straighter. "Design school. She didn't go to a traditional college."

"Which school?"

He nudges my foot. "Why are we always talking about me? Let's talk about you. How's your mom? You said she called?"

"Yeah, before you got here. She was so excited. She sold two paintings last night!"

"This was at a gallery in New York?"

"Yes. Her friend, Claire, owns it. She told my mom it was rare for a new artist to sell her work that fast."

"It IS rare, although if one influential person buys a painting, then usually whatever else is available will also sell. Word spreads and soon everyone wants the artist's work. Well, not everyone, but people in the art community who want whatever's in demand. Did she say who bought her paintings?"

"No, but if she had, I'd have no clue who the people are. Why do you ask?"

"No reason."

"You wouldn't have asked unless you thought you might know the people who bought the paintings."

"How would I know them? I don't live in New York."

"You might know people in the art community. You said you like art."

"I do, but I'm not familiar with the art scene in New York. I asked because I thought maybe someone famous bought your mom's painting. Famous people often buy works of up-and-coming artists hoping the piece will go up in value. It's less about the art and more about the investment value."

"If it was someone well known, she would've told me."

"So is she going to stay there? In New York?"

"You mean beyond the summer?"

"Yeah."

"She didn't say she was."

"She should. If she gets a name for herself in the art world she could make a lot of money. And it sounds like she likes what she's doing."

"She loves it. And she loves New York."

But I hope she doesn't stay there. It's too far away. It's her decision to make and I'll support her if she decides to move there for good but I don't know what I'll do without her. For most of my life it was just my mom and me so we've always been close. She's not just my mom. She's my friend. So I hope she doesn't move. I'd miss her way too much.

CHAPTER EIGHTEEN

Kyle

After dinner Sage and I attempt to watch TV but she doesn't have cable so there's nothing to watch. That means we'll end up talking, which is my least favorite thing to do. If we were just talking about her, or about random things like movies or sports, I'd have no problem. But unfortunately, when we talk, the conversation keeps steering back to me. She keeps asking questions I can't answer so then I have to lie to her, which I hate doing.

Sometimes she catches me off guard and I almost give her an honest answer. Like when she asked if I accomplished my goal today, I almost told her about getting the gun because that was my *real* goal for today. Obviously, I would've stopped myself before I told her but my initial instinct was to tell her the truth. That's what happens when you get comfortable with people. You let your guard down. You say too much.

"How late are you staying?" she asks, flipping through the channels.

"I thought I was staying over tonight."

"That was only if we got a storm. But I don't think we're getting it now. It's just supposed to rain." She sets the remote down.

"Are you afraid to be alone when it's raining?"

She looks at me. "No."

I raise my brows. "You sure?"

She smiles. "Oh. Yeah. Actually I am. Very afraid."

"Then I guess I have no choice but to stay. Or we could go to my place."

"Maybe tomorrow." She faces the TV again.

"You're coming over tomorrow?"

"I heard it's supposed to be a lot cooler tomorrow. You said you get cold easily."

"Uh, no, I never said that."

She turns to me. "You're from California. It's a given."

I reach over and take her hand. "So you're coming over to keep me warm?"

"I have to. I don't want you getting cold."

"That means you'd be sleeping in the same bed as me."

"Yep." Her eyes are still on the TV.

"What about tonight?"

"What about it?"

"Where am I supposed to sleep? You got rid of the couch and I can't sleep in this chair."

"Sounds like there's only one option."

"Which is what?" I want her to say it. I don't want to assume.

"You'll sleep on the floor."

I look at her, trying to see if she's kidding. She seems serious.

"Why are you giving me that look?" she says. "I have blankets and pillows. It's not like you'll be directly on the floor."

"If *I'm* sleeping there, *you're* sleeping there."

"No way! I'm not sleeping on the floor."

"Then how can I protect you? You said you have a fear of being alone when it's raining. If I'm here and you're in your room, you're alone."

"Yeah, I guess that's true."

I squeeze her hand. "So what's it going to be? The floor or your bed?"

"The bed. I can't sleep on the floor."

"Maybe we should go in there now."

"It's just after eight. It's too early."

"Not really. You have to be up early for work tomorrow and I want to get an early start writing."

She shakes her head. "I'm not tired yet."

So I guess we're just sleeping. I thought maybe she wanted more than that. She's been flirting with me all night. In the kitchen, she kept purposely brushing her body against mine, and when I'd sneak a kiss, she'd keep it going, making me think it would lead somewhere. But then she'd stop.

"You look cold," she says, getting up from her chair.

"I'm not—" I stop myself and smile as I realize what she's doing. "You're right. I'm freezing."

"Let me help." She straddles my lap and all I can think about is how she's not wearing panties. Just a pair of very short shorts. There's only a small piece of fabric covering the place I've been dying to touch all night.

She moves closer, right up against my crotch. I put my hand on the back of her head and gently pull her mouth to mine and kiss her. With my other hand I grip her ass and pull her even closer. She softly moans as we kiss and begins moving her hips, rubbing herself against me.

I break from her lips and slowly kiss my way to her ear, whispering, "You're beautiful, Sage."

She tips her head back and I kiss down her neck, her shoulder, along the area that's exposed from her loose-fitting shirt. Knowing she's not wearing a bra, I slip my hand under her shirt, up the side of her ribcage, over her soft smooth skin. She breathes out a moan as I cup her breast and rub my thumb over her nipple. She likes that, her moans getting louder.

When I take my hand away, she lets out a sigh of disappointment, but then softly moans again when my hand goes to her upper thigh, my fingers slipping under her shorts. I immediately feel how wet she is, which shoots my arousal into overdrive. This no-panty thing has got me hard as steel. I'm ready to do it here in this chair but that wouldn't make for a very romantic first time together, and this chair smells like an old person.

"Yes," she whispers as I slide a finger in her, and then another. "Don't stop."

I love that I'm pleasing her and I love that she tells me. I thought she'd be shy when it comes to this, but she's not and it's just another thing I love about her. Not that I actually love her. I just met her.

She trembles a little right before she comes, then cries out as her body's overcome with pleasure. I keep my eyes on her the whole time. It's beautiful. *She's* beautiful.

"You still thinking it's too early to go to bed?" I say in her ear as she catches her breath.

She laughs a little. "Actually, bed sounds great. I'm suddenly really tired."

"Oh," I say, disappointed. "Okay."

It's fine she doesn't want to do it. I understand. But I might have to excuse myself and finish what she started.

She gets off me and holds out her hand. "C'mon."

When we get to the bedroom, I strip down to my boxer briefs because that's what I wear to bed. She watches, her eyes going to my chest, then my abs, then down to what's bulging from my boxers.

"Everything okay?" I ask, smiling at her.

"Yeah." Her eyes move up to my face. "Why?"

"You're not getting into bed."

"Right," she says, seeming flustered. She gets into bed, and just as I'm about to, I see her fling her shorts to the floor. Then she sits up and slips her shirt off, tossing it aside. So I guess she sleeps naked.

I get in beside her and pull her warm, naked body against mine. The feel of her has me so hard it's practically shoving its way out of my boxers. She feels it against her belly and I hear her swallow, then take a breath. Is she nervous? Or just turned on?

"So..." I say, lightly kissing her neck. "I should probably let you sleep. Since you're tired."

"Or you could maybe..." She runs her hand over the front of my boxers, "take these off."

"I could," I say, my mouth finding hers, kissing her until I hear that soft little moan again. I slide my hand down between her legs. "But if I do," I say over her lips, "things are gonna happen."

"The nightstand," she whispers, clearly wanting this. I assumed she did but wanted to make sure.

I turn just enough to reach over and open the drawer. There's a strip of three condoms in there. I tear one off, then reach under the covers and yank off my boxers, finally freeing what will soon be inside her. Just the thought of that turns me on even more. She's so damn beautiful and I want her. I want her so bad.

She must read my mind because she wastes no time, taking the condom from me and sliding it on. As I position myself over her, she reaches down and guides me inside her.

Closing her eyes, she makes those soft moans I love so much. As I thrust into her, she grabs hold of me and her hips rise, moving in sync with mine.

"Kyle," she says between breaths.

I thrust deeper, harder, unable to hold back.

"Yes! Right there," Sage says. We've only been going at this a few minutes and she's already making the sounds she did right before she came on my lap. It's good she's fast because I'm about to come. "Yes!" she says as I thrust faster. "Yes! Yes!"

She does that slight trembling again, then cries out like she did before. When she's done, I let myself go, coming hard and fast.

Shit, that was good. Better than I've had in a long time.

"Now I'm *really* tired," she says with a contented sigh.

I move off her, laying on my back. She turns and hugs me from the side, her head on my chest. It's nice. I haven't laid like this with a girl for a long time. Usually, the girl gets up and leaves, saying she needs to get home. Or sometimes I was the one who left. Looking back, my past relationships really weren't that intimate. They were intimate in a sexual way but not in a way like I'm experiencing now. Sharing a quiet moment, wrapped in each other's arms.

Within minutes, Sage is asleep while I lie there listening to the rain. It's getting heavier, pelting against the house. The wind rattles the window next to me and I jump at the sound, waking up Sage.

"What's wrong?" she mumbles.

"Nothing. Go back to sleep."

I've got to stop being so jumpy or people are going to think something's wrong. They're already suspicious of me. I don't need to be making it worse.

Nobody's going to find me here. I keep telling myself that, hoping I'll eventually believe it. I feel better having the gun, except now it's not with me. It's back at my house, hidden so no one will find it.

Getting a gun turned out to be easier than I thought it would. I was sure I'd end up coming home without one. But I not only got a gun, but also an untraceable phone that I can use to call my brother. I can't tell him what's going on, not over the phone. I probably won't even talk to him. But I can at least hear his voice and make sure he's okay.

Honestly, I don't think my father would ever hurt Cain. He's always liked Cain better than me. He rarely gets mad at him. When Cain screws up, I'm the one who gets yelled at because my father assumes it's my job to watch him. And I did. I basically raised him after Mom died.

But now I'm not there and I'm worried my dad's anger over my disappearance might get out of control. I don't want that anger being taken out on Cain. That's another reason I needed the gun. When I figure out a plan for going back there to get

Cain, I'll need the gun to take down whoever tries to stop me. I've never shot someone before but I'm willing to do it to get my brother out of there.

I bought the gun from a guy at a bar in a town about two hours from here. It's not even a town. It was more like a deserted stretch of road with some old abandoned buildings that went on for about a block. I went down a side street to turn around and that's when I saw two guys in a parking lot behind one of the buildings. They were exchanging something. I assumed it was a drug deal.

Normally if I saw that I'd get the hell out of there, but these were the type of guys I needed. Drug dealers have guns and they aren't buying them at the local sporting goods store.

I pulled into the parking lot as the one guy was leaving in his pickup. The other guy looked at me as he stuffed a wad of cash in his pocket.

"We're closed," he yelled at me.

I looked behind him and saw a neon beer sign flickering. I hadn't realized there was a bar inside. It was only eleven-thirty so it made sense the bar wasn't open. What didn't make sense is that it was there, in the middle of nowhere. People wouldn't drive out there to get a beer. It had to be a front for drug dealing, and maybe more than that.

"You sure?" I yelled back. "Because I could really use a cold one right now." I got off my motorcycle and walked up to him. He was older, maybe fifty, with tan wrinkled skin and a scar along his neck. He had a gut that jutted out from his black t-shirt and he was sweating a lot. He kept wiping his face with his hand.

He looked pissed as I approached him. "I told you we're closed. You deaf?"

"You own this place?" I asked, pointing to it.

"None of your damn business. What are you, a cop?" He squinted at me because the sun was shooting right at him.

"I'm not a cop. I just need a drink. Can I come inside?"

He waved me away. "Get the fuck out of here and don't come back."

I remained in front of him. "I'll give you a fifty for a bottle of beer."

He stared back at me as he considered my offer.

"And I'll give you a lot more for what I really came for."

His lips turned up just slightly on one side and he said, "Come on in."

The cash for the gun was wedged against the inside of my ankle, held in place by my sock. Over that was my boot, and then jeans, so the money was well hidden.

I took a hundred dollar bill from my wallet and slapped it down on the bar. "Make it two."

"Who sent you?" he asked, grabbing the beers from the cooler. He set them in front of me, then picked up the hundred and stuffed it in his pocket.

"No one. I came on my own."

"You can't find this shit at your college?" He stood across from me behind the bar, his arms crossed.

"I don't go to college." I took a long drink of my beer. It was good. I was hot and thirsty and nervous as hell. The beer calmed me down a little, but I was still very aware I might not leave there alive.

"You just ride around on your motorcycle all day, stopping at random bars?"

He was fishing for information. Trying to figure out if he could trust me enough to let me buy from him.

"I felt like taking a drive," I said, not willing to tell him more. "So what do you got?"

He paused a moment, his eyes on mine, then said, "I got it all. Ecstasy, coke, heroin, pain pills. What exactly you looking for?"

I finished my beer. "I'm not looking for drugs."

He put his hands on the bar and leaned toward me. "Then why the hell you here?"

"I need a gun," I said flatly. "Something small. Easy to conceal."

He nodded, not at all surprised by my request. "How much you got?"

In my head I was smiling like an idiot. I'd done it. I found someone who could get me what I needed.

"Depends on when I could get it," I said.

"You could get it today, for the right price."

"Which is what?"

"Two thousand."

That's it? I was prepared to pay five. Not wanting him to know that I pretended to bargain with him.

"Is it here?" I asked.

"Maybe."

"I need to know. If I'm paying that much I'm not taking extra steps. I want to know I can get it right here, right now."

"Show me the cash."

"I need to know I can walk out with it today."

He wouldn't budge. "Show me the damn cash or we don't have a deal."

I reached down into my boot and pulled out what felt like half of the money. Keeping my hands hidden under the bar, I counted out the bills and set two thousand on the table.

"It's all there."

He picked up the stack and counted it out. "That's twenty five hundred."

"A tip for good service." I paused. "And a bonus for your silence. I was never here. You never met me. Never saw me before."

"That's how I do business. I don't rat out my customers." He held up the cash. "But thanks for the extra."

"No problem. Now can I see it?"

He crouched down, disappearing behind the bar. I heard something click and assumed it was a lock. He must have a safe hidden there.

When he stood up he held the gun in his hand. It was a type I'd used before. I'd grown up going to the gun range with my dad, thinking it was just a fun activity, not realizing he was practicing to protect himself from whoever might come after him. I had no idea he was dealing with criminals, selling weapons on the black market. I thought he was just a boring businessman who imported junky souvenirs for tourist shops. And he *does* do that. That's his main job, but his side job is where he makes his money. The job I didn't know about until just recently.

"We good?" the guy asked.

"How do I know it works?"

"Go out back in the alley. There's some cans set up. Go try it out. See what you think." He eyes me. "I don't sell defective product. If I did, I'd be out of business."

I got up to leave, but then remembered the other thing I needed. "A phone. I need a phone that can't be traced."

He smirked. "Left a girl behind, huh?" He opened a drawer under the bar and pulled out a small flip phone like I hadn't seen in years. He set it on the counter. "You love her?"

My mind immediately thought of Sage, which was fucked up for many reasons. One, because I shouldn't have been thinking of her during this transaction. And two because she's the first person that popped in my head when he asked if I loved her.

"Yeah," I said, going along with his assumption that I needed the phone to call a girl. "I love her more than anything."

He shook his head. "Another dumb fucker."

"Meaning what?"

"Love has taken down more men than I can count. Half are in prison and the other half are dead."

"I know how to be careful."

"We'll see about that. Send me a postcard in a couple years so I know you're still alive." He chuckled. "I tell everyone that. Have yet to get one."

"How much?" I said, holding up the phone.

"Five hundred."

I gave him six, then got the hell out of there. He locked the door behind me and I went straight to the alley and fired off a couple shots. The gun worked fine but I'd need more ammo. I could get that later.

I left with exactly what I'd been searching for. Like I told Sage, I'd accomplished my goal. She just didn't know what goal I was talking about. If she did, she wouldn't be in my arms right now, looking beautiful. Sweet. Like an angel.

An angel I could fall in love with. If I wasn't living in hell.

CHAPTER NINETEEN

Sage

It's been a month since I met Kyle but it seems longer than that, probably because we spend so much time together. What was supposed to be a casual relationship doesn't seem so casual anymore. We have dinner together every night, breakfast together every morning, and take turns spending the night at each other's house. We're basically living together, which is not how I would describe a casual relationship.

The only thing casual about it is the fact that Kyle still won't open up to me. He still says nothing when I ask about his family and he almost never talks about his past. If there's no future for us I guess I don't need to know all that stuff, but I'd still like to. I want to know everything about him. I find him fascinating. And smart, funny, sexy. He's just what I've been looking for, but in a couple months it'll all end. He'll go back to California and I'll move in with my mom and this summer will just be a memory.

"Going to lunch?" I ask Helen as she grabs her purse from under her desk.

"Yes. I just need to refresh my lipstick." She takes out her tube of red lipstick and smears it over her lips.

"Got a hot lunch date?" I tease.

"Actually, I do. Marv's friend is in town and I agreed to have lunch with him."

Marv is one of her cousins. She has a million cousins and talks about them all the time.

"So it's not really a date," I say.

"He asked me out, I said yes, and he's picking me up. It's a date." She puts her lipstick away.

"But he doesn't live here so it's not like this date could lead to anything."

"Why couldn't it?" She stands up and smooths her skirt. She dresses up every day. I think it's because she's old. Old people like dressing up. I always wear jeans to work or a casual skirt with a t-shirt.

"Where does he live?"

"Branson."

"That's like three hours away."

"That's nothing. If he likes me enough, he'll make the drive." She goes to the window that looks out at the front parking lot. "He's not due to show up for another few minutes." She comes over to my desk. "So how about you and the writer?"

"Kyle? What about him?"

"I assume you two will continue your romance when he leaves? Or when *you* leave?"

"No," I quickly say, pretending to type on my computer. I don't want to talk about this. I like to live in my happy little bubble where Kyle and I get to stay together after this summer.

"No?" She laughs. "But he's your love."

I stop typing and look at her. "What do you mean?"

"He loves you. You can't let miles come between that."

I don't think Kyle loves me but I don't bother correcting her.

"He lives in California. I can't afford to go see him. And he can't afford to fly back to see *me*."

Actually, I don't know if he could afford it or not. He's never talked about money but he seems to have plenty. His wallet is always full of what seems like an endless supply of hundred dollar bills, and one day he drove into Kansas City and bought all new clothes from very expensive designer brands.

So he definitely has money but I don't know how much or where it came from. It's one of the things that bothers me about him, mainly because of my dad. My dad showed up in expensive clothes and an expensive car and it turned out they were paid for with stolen money. But I can't make assumptions about Kyle based on what my dad did. It's not fair to him.

"Let me tell you a little story," Helen says, pulling up a chair. "Years ago, I met a young man the summer after I graduated high school. We hadn't dated long but I knew he was the one. He loved me. Cherished me." A longing look comes over her eyes. "And I loved *him*, but I didn't want to admit it."

"Why? Because it was too soon?"

"Because he was leaving. He was drafted and sent overseas. Before he left, I tried to end things between us. I told him it would never work and that it wasn't fair to either of us to continue what clearly wasn't meant to be. I said if it was, he wouldn't have been taken from me."

"And what did he say?"

"He said 'bullshit!' and slammed his fist on my mother's dining room table."

My eyes widen, surprised that Helen cursed. I've never once heard her swear and the few times *I've* done it, she's scolded me, telling me there are better words to express myself.

"What'd he do next?"

She shrugs. "He proposed."

"After you tried to break up with him?"

"Loren was a stubborn fool." She smiles. "But he was *my* stubborn fool."

Loren was her husband. He died over ten years ago.

"But that's not what you wanted, so what made you say yes?"

"I didn't really want to end things with him. I loved him. I wanted to spend my life with him. But I didn't see how it was possible with him going overseas. Loren said my logic made no sense and he was right. Because it wasn't about logic. It was about not getting hurt. I was trying to protect my heart. If I stayed with him, I'd miss him every second of every day that he was away."

"The same thing would happen if you broke up with him."

"Yes, but I thought it would get better over time. Back then, I didn't realize that if you really love someone, it doesn't just go away if you don't see them anymore."

"It's not the same with Kyle and me. He isn't being sent off to war. He's leaving because he wants to. Because he has to. He has a life in California. And I have a life here. I still have to finish school."

"If he knew you wanted him around for longer than a summer, he would find a way to make it happen."

"I don't think so. We agreed this would end in August or whenever one of us leaves."

"But that's not what you want, is it?"

I shake my head.

"So tell him. Don't be some shy wallflower waiting on the side of the room hoping the boy you love will ask you to dance."

"It's not the same as—"

"Tell him how you feel. The man shouldn't have to guess what you're thinking. I was lucky enough to have a man who forced me to tell him how I felt but not all men are like that. Some have to be told, plain and simple, then pounded over the head a few times until they get it."

I laugh. "I get that, but Kyle and I have already agreed that this will end after the summer."

"That was before. This is now." She stands up. "Talk to him. There's no harm in being honest with him, is there?"

"I guess not." Other than the harm of embarrassing myself if he doesn't feel the same way.

She walks to the window. "My date is here." She goes to the door. "I'll try not to be late getting back."

"Take your time. I'll cover for you until you get back."

"You're such a doll." She winks at me. "That boy would be a fool to let you go."

When she's gone, I'm about to call Kyle but Nina calls. "What's up?"

"What do you think about going out tonight?"

"Where?"

"I don't know. You can pick."

"Why?" I ask, because she never lets me pick. "What are you up to?"

"Josh is coming to town and I don't want to be alone with him."

"You want me to come with you on your date with Josh?"

"Not just you. You and your boyfriend."

"Wait. Hold on. Why is Josh coming to town?"

"He wanted to talk so I kinda told him we could."

"So you're talking again?"

A few days after the firehouse fundraiser Nina and Josh went out for dinner and briefly got back together, but then got in a fight. She wouldn't tell me what the fight was about and ever since then, the two of them have been on-again, off-again, but mostly off. She hasn't talked to him for over a week.

"We're trying to be friends," she says. "So far, it's not working."

"Because you keep arguing?"

"Yes."

"Which leads to you two having sex."

"Correct."

Nina and Josh both get turned on by arguing. It's their thing. And whenever they're together, they argue, so a friends-only arrangement doesn't work for them.

"You two will argue even if Kyle and I are there."

"Not if you stop us."

"That's impossible. Once you two start, it never ends. And I don't know why it bothers you so much. It always ends with sex. *Great* sex, according to you."

"Yes, but we can't have a relationship, even just a friendship, if all we do is argue. It's gotta stop."

"It's not like you guys are mean to each other. It's more like flirty teasing than arguing. And I can tell you both like it. If you didn't, you wouldn't keep it up."

"Will you do this or not? Tonight at seven. You pick the place."

"I'll call Kyle and ask him."

"Let me know."

"I will. Bye." I call him up. "Can we go out tonight?"

"Is this my hot sexy neighbor?"

I smile. "I think so, unless you say that about all your neighbors."

"I was just thinking about you."

"You were?"

"Yeah. I was wishing you were here right now." He says it in a sexy voice that turns me on.

"If only my lunch hour were longer."

"We could make it work."

"Not today. Helen has a date and I told her I'd cover for her if she's late."

"Helen has a date?"

"I know. I was surprised too. It's some friend of her cousin's. Anyway, going back to tonight. Nina wants to have dinner with us. Josh is coming to town and she doesn't want to be alone with him."

"Because they'll end up having sex?"

"Yes." I've told Kyle all about Nina and Josh. I asked Nina before I told him and she didn't care. In fact she encouraged me to tell him so she could get a guy's opinion on what to do. He said she should just date him and stop finding reasons not to, which I've also said, but she doesn't listen. She's very stubborn.

At least she changed her mind about Kyle. I thought she'd never stop calling him a serial killer but she finally did after she saw how good he is to me. He not only buys me groceries but he also makes me dinner. He's not a great cook but he's better than me and keeps improving. He even had Nina over one night, which is when she finally took me aside and admitted he was a nice guy. And she likes his motorcycle. She thinks it's hot.

"I'll have to pass on dinner."

"Why?"

"I need to write. I'm in the middle of a chapter."

I'm dying to read his story but he won't let me read a single page. I've never even seen the manuscript or the laptop he uses to write it. Whenever I tell him I'm coming over, he hides everything away. And the few times I've stopped by to surprise him, I've seen nothing. Not even his laptop sitting out.

"We don't have to stay long," I tell him. "She said I could pick the place so I'll pick someplace that's fast."

"Which means pizza or barbecue, which we've already had this week."

"We can have it again. Would you please just go with me? It'll be awkward if it's just me and them."

"I can't. I need to get this done."

"It's only noon. Dinner isn't until seven. You'll finish the chapter by then."

He sighs. "Sage, stop pushing this. I don't want to go. I don't like that guy. I don't want to have dinner with him."

"You don't like Josh? You only met him one time."

"And I didn't like him."

"Why not?"

"Because he wouldn't stop asking me shit. I'm not going to sit there tonight and have him firing questions at me all through dinner."

"That won't happen. If it does, I'll say something to him, or we'll get up and leave."

"Or we could avoid that altogether and just not go."

"Would you please just do this for me? I never ask you to do anything, and this isn't that big a deal. It's just dinner."

He's silent.

"Kyle? Please?"

"Fine," he says in a curt tone. "But if he starts asking questions, we're leaving. Talk to you later." He ends the call.

What the hell? Why is he mad about this? It's just dinner.

"Got a new rule," I hear Jesse say as he walks in the office.

"What is it?"

"No more personal phone calls."

I roll my eyes. "And why is that?"

"You should be working, not talking on the phone."

"It's my lunch break so I can do whatever I want."

"Then when your break is over, there's no more calling your boyfriend until you're done for the day."

"And how exactly are you going to enforce this? Are you going to sit here and watch me all day?"

"If I have to, then yeah. Or I'll tell Helen to keep an eye on you."

Helen wouldn't tell on me. She doesn't like Jesse. She only works here because she likes Kenny, Jesse's dad. She's counting the days until he returns.

"Does this rule only apply to me? Because the guys in the garage are on the phone all the time during work hours."

"They're not your problem," he says in an angry tone. He's been like this since the firehouse event. I thought he'd get over it but he hasn't. He's just gotten worse.

"Why do you have to be like this? Just because you can't stand seeing me with anyone but you? I'm not interested in you, Jesse. I'm not trying to be mean. We're just not compatible. I don't see you that way. It was never going to happen."

"And you think you're compatible with *him*?" He folds his arms over his chest. "You don't even know him. No one does. The guy's so goddamn secretive. For all we know, Kyle isn't even his real name."

"Yeah, whatever." I put my eyes on my computer and pretend to work.

"I'm serious. Sage. Have you ever looked him up online?"

"Yes, but too many people have his name so I gave up trying to find which one was him."

"I didn't. I went through all of them, and not a single one matched up with a writer from California."

"That doesn't mean anything. Kyle is a private person. He's not someone who puts all his information out on the internet. He doesn't even have any social media accounts."

"You don't think that's strange? Everyone our age has that shit. The only people who don't are the ones who are trying to hide something."

"Like what?" I look back at Jesse. "What exactly would Kyle be hiding?"

"Who the fuck knows? But if I were you, I'd find out. This guy could be dangerous. He could be playing you. And when he's done with you, who knows what'll happen? You really want to put yourself at risk for this guy?"

"I'm not putting myself at risk. We're dating, not getting married. This isn't serious."

"Sure seems serious when you're spending every night at his house."

"How do you know that? Are you spying on me?"

"Seriously? Like you don't know by now that everyone around here knows everyone else's business?"

I look back at my computer. "I'm done talking about this. It's my break and I'm not going to spend it arguing with you."

"If this guy really likes you like you claim he does, he shouldn't be hiding shit from you. Other people? Yeah, fine. But his girlfriend? That's fucked up. It means he doesn't trust you enough to tell you. Is that really the type of guy you want to be with?"

I don't answer. I turn my back to him and look at my phone. When I turn back, he's gone.

As much as I hate to admit it, Jesse's right. Kyle shouldn't be hiding things from me. We've been dating for a month. We spend every night together. By now, he should be able to answer my questions but he won't. If I ask, he gets moody and quiet, so I just stopped asking. But it's not right. It's not right for him to be this secretive with me.

CHAPTER TWENTY

Kyle

Sage talked me into going to this dinner but I shouldn't have let her. Having dinner with a cop is one of the worst things I could do. What if my father filed a missing persons report? It'd be in the system. Any cop, anywhere, could see it. If Josh saw it and recognized me, he'd alert my father and I'd have to go on the run again, or they'd find me before I could and I'd be dead.

"They're late," I say, shoving my keys in my pocket.

We're sitting in a booth at the local pizza place. There are only five restaurants in town and this one has the fastest service.

"They're only two minutes late. It's not a big deal." Sage scoots away from me, just a few inches, but enough to let me know she's pissed.

I'm pissed too. I told her I didn't want to be here but she wouldn't take no for an answer. I'm also pissed at Nina. The girl is so damn pushy. She's always making Sage do things and Sage always just goes along with it.

It's not our job to babysit Nina and Josh. They have a fucked-up relationship that can't be fixed by anyone but themselves. If their constant arguing leads to screwing, then I say just go with it. If that's their biggest problem, then good for them. It's not like Sage and me, where I'm living a fake life every damn day, lying to the girl I love.

That's right. I love her. Which makes this whole situation even worse. I haven't told her I love her but I think she knows. Girls know this stuff. Us guys take longer to figure it out. Like with Sage? I have no freaking clue if she loves me. Given how she's acting right now, I'd say it's a definite no, but beneath her anger it's possible she loves me. And that too is a problem, because it means I'll break her heart when I leave. But mine will be broken too.

The door swings open and Nina walks in with Josh right behind her.

"Sorry we're late." Nina slides into the booth across from Sage. "Hey, Kyle."

"Hey, Nina."

Nina still doesn't like me. She pretends she does for Sage's sake but she really doesn't. She told me that when she came to dinner at my house. I was trying to win her over but it didn't work. She says she doesn't trust me. She has good instincts, I'll give her that. She knows I'm not being truthful, but since she can't prove it, she puts up with me.

Josh sits across from me. "Good to see you again."

"You too." It's such a lie. I'm already nervous having him here. He's doing that staring thing he did the night of the fundraiser, as if he can stare the truth out of me.

The girls start talking about Nina's dress, leaving us guys with nothing to say.

"So what's new?" Josh asks as the girls continue to talk.

"Not much. How about you? Catch any criminals today?" I meant it as a joke but it came out sounding condescending, which is probably what my subconscious was going for. It's not that I have anything against cops but I do when they can't get out of cop-mode when they're not on duty.

"Caught a drunk driver, a shoplifter, and went to the scene of a domestic abuse call."

"How'd that turn out?"

"He killed her." He watches me to see my reaction.

What the hell's that about? Does he think I'm going to kill Sage? Or does he think I'm just a killer in general? Seeing him look at me like that pisses me off even more.

"That's too bad," I say, clenching my hand under the table to control my anger.

"They got in a fight and the guy just went ballistic. Didn't have a history of violence. He just snapped."

"Did he say anything when you arrested him?" Sage asks. I hadn't realized she was listening.

"No, but we did some checking and it sounds like he'd been living a secret life. He had a woman he'd been seeing in a different state and had a kid with her. And we think he had another woman he was seeing in town. We think his wife was about to find out about all this so he killed her before she could. Of course, that's just a theory for now. We need to do some more investigating before we know for sure."

"That's horrible," Sage says.

"I wouldn't have let the bastard kill me," Nina says, adjusting the top of her dress. It's a cotton sundress with no straps and it keeps sliding down when she moves. She's someone who moves her hands and body a lot when she talks. "I would've shot him before he even had a chance."

"You're afraid of guns," Josh says.

"I'm not afraid of a damn gun." She points to his belt. "I'm sitting right next to one."

"Remember when I took you to the shooting range?" he asks.

She points her finger at him. "Don't you dare! That was one time and I was very emotional that week!"

"She cried," he says to Sage and me.

"Asshole!" She hits him, then faces forward, crossing her arms over her chest.

"Hey." He puts his arm around her. "A lot of people don't like guns. I get it. They're scary. They kill people."

"Just shut-up," she says, turning away from him, but she doesn't push his arm off her.

He pulls her closer and leans down by her ear. "Sorry, babe. I wasn't trying to embarrass you." He kisses her cheek.

"I hate guns," Sage says. "Just knowing you have one on you right now makes me nervous."

"If you know how to use one," Josh says, "and follow all the safety precautions, there's no reason to be afraid of guns."

"I still don't like them. I couldn't date someone who had a gun." She waves her hand at Josh. "Nothing against you! I didn't mean it like that. I just—"

"I know what you meant. And I totally understand."

Nina faces forward again. "It doesn't bother me that Josh carries one because he knows how to use it. And he doesn't just whip it out to show it off."

"Sometimes I do," he says to her with a smile. "Wait, are we still talking about the gun?"

"Shut up." She swats at him, rolling her eyes. "Anyway, I get what you mean, Sage. If I wasn't dating a cop, I wouldn't let a gun anywhere near me."

The table is silent. We all look at Nina.

"What?" she asks. "What did I say?"

"We're dating?" Josh grins at her.

She pauses, her eyes moving around the table. "No. I just, um...I got confused for a minute, because we used to date. I meant to say it past tense."

"Too late." Josh still has his arm around her and pulls her into his side. He kisses her head. "You already said it. We're dating. We have witnesses. It's official."

"Oh my God," she mutters, rolling her eyes for the third time tonight. I've never seen her roll her eyes this much. I think it's her coping mechanism to deal with the feelings she has for Josh but doesn't want to admit. It's clear she likes him. She might even love him, but again, with girls it's hard to tell. I know for a fact Josh loves *her*. It's written all over his face.

Sage laughs. "You two are hilarious. You guys should have your own reality show."

"Yeah, people would really want to watch a cop and a small town grocery store clerk," Nina says sarcastically.

"Are you kidding?" Sage perks up in her seat, which is adorable. I love it when she gets all excited about something. "People would totally watch! And it wouldn't have to be just you and Josh at home. They could follow Josh around at work, dealing with criminals, then they could cut to you at the grocery store, dealing with all the crazy people that come in."

"Speaking of that, you wouldn't believe what Ruth and her daughter did the other day. All six grandkids were with her and they were all screaming and crying and she—"

"How's the writing going?" Josh asks.

I point to Nina. "Don't you want to hear her story?"

"She already told it to me on the way here. Then she'll tell the one about Harold. He's in his seventies and always hits on Nina. The old man even slapped her ass today. If he wasn't so old and senile I'd drive out to his farm and punch him."

I was hoping I'd be able to just listen to the girls talk all night and avoid having to say anything. But of course, Josh wants to get to know me.

"So the writing," he says, "how's it going?"

"It's going well." I look around for the waitress, wishing she'd hurry up and take our order.

"You don't say much, do you?" he asks in a kidding tone, but I know he's not joking. He finds my lack of words to be suspicious. I'll have to make some shit up just to keep him off my back.

"I'm not a big talker. Writers tend to be introverts. And I'm really tired tonight. It's been a long week of writing."

"With all that writing you should be almost done by now. Does that mean you'll be going home soon?"

He's fishing for information about when I'll be leaving. I bet Nina put him up to that. She knows Sage will be upset when I leave and she thinks it'll be easier if I leave sooner rather than later. That might be true. The more time Sage and I spend together, the closer we get. It'd probably be easier on both of us if I left town sooner rather than later. But I can't do it. I can't leave, and not because of the situation with my dad. It wouldn't be hard to find another small town to hide in. The hard part would be saying goodbye to Sage. I'm not ready to do it. I don't know if I'll ever be.

"I'm not going anywhere anytime soon. I still have a long ways to go on the book and this is just a first draft. When it's done I need to go back and do some rewrites before I turn it into my editor."

"He hasn't even let me read it," Sage says, smiling at me as she sneaks her arm around mine. "I'm dying to read his stuff but he won't even let me read a page. And he won't tell me what it's about."

"That's not true," I say. "I told you what it was about."

"A guy who grew up in a small town who wants to run off to L.A. to be a famous musician. That's all I know."

"Because I haven't figured it all out yet. I'm still developing the story."

"You could at least let her read a page," Nina says.

"It's not ready yet. I don't like people reading my stuff until it's at a point where I'm ready to share it."

I've gotta get off this topic. All the attention is on me and I'm struggling to come up with information about a book I'm not even writing.

"So you must have a lot of stories," I say to Josh, trying to turn the attention back on him. "Being a cop, you must have enough stories to fill at least two or three books, maybe more."

"I do, but most are stories people wouldn't want to read about. Murders. Rape. Kidnapping. People don't want to read about that shit. It's depressing."

"People love crime books," I say, "especially real life crime."

"I don't get that," he says. "Why would you want to read about that? Unless it has a happy ending, like a kid who was kidnapped but then reunited with his parents. But even then, I don't get the appeal. As a parent, you'd read that and worry your kid's going to get kidnapped. Why is that fun to read? I don't get it."

"I don't either," Sage says. "I don't read much, but if I did I'd want to read something happy or funny, not something that makes me sad." She looks at Josh. "Like that guy you said murdered his wife? I don't want to read about that. I don't care how interesting the story is, with all the mistresses and whatever else he was hiding. I still wouldn't want to read it."

"It's hard sometimes," Josh says. "Some of the shit you see in this job is stuff you wish were fiction. Stuff that doesn't happen in real life. But unfortunately it does and that's the part of the job I hate."

"You ever regret being a cop?" Sage asks.

"No. It's tough but it's also rewarding, especially when we're able to help people. Like last year I found this kid who'd been missing. He wandered out of his babysitter's house and was gone almost a day. His parents, understandably, assumed the worst. I was on duty when they reported him missing. I did a search of the area and found him at a neighbor's house. The people weren't home but they'd left their door unlocked. I found him on their kitchen floor eating peanut butter out of the jar. He was only four and had no clue he'd done anything wrong."

"I'd be worried sick if I were his mom," Sage says.

"Yeah, she thanked me about a million times for finding him. That's the good part of the job. Being able to help out like that."

"How many missing kids are ever found?" Sage asks. "Do you know?"

"I don't have the exact number but I could find out. It seems like more and more kids go missing every year. Like just today, an alert came out about some kid who went missing in New York. A teenage boy. Been missing for a week now. His dad's so worried he's offered a reward of a million dollars for anyone who finds his kid."

My heart pounds faster, my hand clenching under the table.

"He has that much money?" Sage asks.

"He's some rich guy in Manhattan. A businessman. I don't know what business he's in but he obviously makes a lot of money."

Fuck, what if it's him? What if Cain ran away and my dad's trying to find him? I can't imagine Cain doing that. He has no reason to, unless my father did something that forced Cain to leave. But what would he do? My father's never hit me so I know he'd never hit Cain. But if Cain saw or heard something he shouldn't have, like I did...

I have to call him. I have to know he's okay. A couple weeks ago I called him on that phone I got and he answered and sounded fine. He was even laughing when he picked up, thinking it was his friend. When I didn't say anything, he realized it was a wrong number and hung up. I haven't called him since. I'm too paranoid someone might find out it's me or have some way of tracing the call to this location. I know that's unlikely given that it's a throwaway phone but I still worry.

"What's even sadder," Josh says, "is that the guy's a widower. He lost his wife years ago and now he can't find his teenage son."

Fuck, it's gotta be him. I clench my hand so tightly it's cramping up.

"What's he look like?" Sage asks. "If you have a photo I could send it to my mom and her friend. They live in New York. They could keep an eye out for him."

"If he's a runaway," Josh says, getting his phone out, "he's probably left the city. Same goes for if he's been kidnapped. They'll want to get him out of the local area where people are looking for him." He swipes through his phone and my heart beats so fast I can barely breathe.

"This is him." Josh holds his phone out to us.

I take it from him and see a kid with blond hair and braces. I let out the breath I was holding. It's not Cain. I hand the phone to Sage, my heart slowly returning to normal.

"Maybe he got messed up with a gang," I say. "Or got into drugs."

"It's possible," Josh says. "Or he could've run off with a girl. He'd been talking to a girl online the past few months."

Sage hands him the phone back. "I hope they find him."

The waitress finally shows up at our table.

"Sorry for the wait," she says. "We had to fill an order for the baseball team." She laughs. "I can't believe how much kids eat. They ordered enough pizza to feed the whole town. So what can I get you?"

"I think we need a minute," Sage says. "We've been talking and haven't looked at the menu."

"No problem. I'll come back." She walks off.

I lean over to Sage and lower my voice. "I can't stay. I'm not feeling well."

It isn't a lie. The stress I felt thinking my brother was missing has given me a horrible headache and made my stomach feel sick.

"What's wrong?" she asks.

"My head is killing me. I need to go lie down."

"Maybe you just need to eat. Low blood sugar can cause a headache."

"This is different. It's not from being hungry. I don't even feel hungry."

"What's going on?" Nina asks.

"I'm not feeling well," I say. "I'm gonna go. Could you give Sage a ride back?"

"I'm not staying," she says. "I'm going with you."

"You don't need to. I'll be fine. I just need to take some painkillers and lie down."

"I'm still going with you." She pushes on my side. "C'mon. Let's go. Get out of the booth." She turns to Nina. "Sorry. We'll have dinner some other time. Maybe next week?"

"Sure." Nina eyes me suspiciously.

"Feel better, man," Josh says as I get up. He actually wasn't that bad tonight. It's not that I think he's a bad person. He's just too damn inquisitive.

When we get home I go to my room. I want to call Cain and make sure he's okay but I can't because Sage follows me.

"Can I get you anything?" she asks.

"No. I just need to rest," I tell her.

"Then I'll rest with you."

She lies beside me and kisses my cheek. "If you need something, just let me know."

She's such a great person. Sweet, kind, caring. A great girlfriend. And way too good for me.

My life is a fucking mess. The past month I've been trying to pretend it's not, living this pretend life with my sweet beautiful girlfriend. But the reality is, my life is fucked up and I shouldn't be bringing Sage along for the ride. It's not fair to her, and it's time I do something about it.

CHAPTER TWENTY-ONE

Sage

I've been putting off this discussion long enough. Kyle and I have dated for over a month now and I need to know if our original agreement still stands. Are we going to end things after the summer or do we think we could make this work long-distance?

We need to figure this out, or at least talk about what we both want. As for me, I don't want our relationship to end. It'll be hard when Kyle moves away but I'm willing to do whatever it takes to make it work. I wanted to tell him that the other night but instead we went out with Nina and Josh and then Kyle didn't feel well and we ended up going home.

Kyle was sick the next day too so I stayed home and took care of him. Nina scolded me for it, saying I'm babying him and shouldn't have missed work to take care of a grown man. But I wanted to take care of him. Even though he slept most of the day, I wanted to be there in case he needed me. Besides, I still got paid. Jesse owed me a day off for that Sunday I worked after the firehouse event.

Now it's Friday and I'm back at work. When I left this morning, Kyle seemed a lot better. He even made me breakfast. It was just a bowl of cereal and some toast, but he still did it. He got out of bed and made it while I was in the shower so it'd be ready when I got out. I love that he does sweet things like that for me. It's one of the many reasons I love him.

Yes, it's true. I love him. I haven't told him that yet but I'm going to tonight when we talk. He doesn't know we're having this talk and I didn't tell him because I didn't want to make a big deal out of it. Because it *shouldn't* be a big deal. Trying to figure out a way to be together after this summer is something I know we both want so tonight is just about acknowledging that and discussing ways to make it happen.

At noon, I call Kyle to see what he wants to do for dinner. Miller's phone rings and rings and I eventually hang up. Kyle shut off the answering machine because it never worked right, so now the phone just rings forever. I wish Kyle had a cell phone. I've tried to convince him to buy one but he won't. He says if he had one his agent would call him every day and yell at him to hurry up with the manuscript. He said his agent still bothers him via email but he just deletes the messages.

I call the number again but he doesn't answer. He might be outside. Sometimes around noon he takes a walk to get some fresh air and clear his head before he starts writing again.

I'll call him later. I take my sandwich from my lunch sack, setting it in front of the computer. I need to do some apartment searching while I eat. My mom and I need to find a place and put a deposit down. September isn't that far away.

Just as I start to look, my mom calls.

"Hey, I was just thinking about you," I tell her.

"Hi, honey. How's your day going?"

"Good. But I'm tired. I don't think I slept well."

"Maybe you're getting whatever Kyle had. Is he feeling any better?"

"Yeah, much better. I don't think I'm sick. I'm just dragging like I need some caffeine." I take a drink of my soda. "So what's new with you? You don't usually call me at work."

"Is that okay? I don't want you getting in trouble."

"It's fine. I'm on my lunch break. So are you working on a new painting?"

"Yes. And the one I just finished has already sold. I didn't even have a chance to hang it in the gallery."

"Mom, that's great! Congratulations! That's your fifth one, right?"

"Yes, and this last one sold for five thousand!"

"Are you serious? That's awesome!"

The price of her paintings keeps going up. The first one sold for $2000, then the next one sold for $3000 and it's gone up from there.

"Claire said I'm starting to get a name for myself. If this keeps up, she said I could easily make a living as an artist."

"In New York," I say, trying not to sound sad but failing.

"Honey, I don't know what's going to happen so let's not worry about it just yet. And if it turns out I end up staying here, maybe you could join me after you graduate. New York is such a fun city. I know you'd love it. Unless you're planning to move to California to be with Kyle."

She knows how much I love Kyle. Every time we talk I gush about how great he is, something I never did with my other boyfriends.

"I don't know what I'm going to do yet. I need to graduate first and then figure it out."

"Haven't you two talked about it?"

"Not really. But we will. We have time."

"Isn't he leaving soon?"

"I'm not sure when he's leaving. It depends on when his book is done."

"I could call Lorraine and ask if you could stay in the house until Kyle leaves. I'm sure she wouldn't mind."

"Don't call her just yet. I'll talk to Kyle and see what his plans are."

"Okay. Just let me know. The other reason I'm calling is that I want you to come out here for a visit. Now that I have some money I'm buying you a plane ticket. I miss you and I really want you to see New York. What do you say?"

"That'd be great! When should I come?"

"The tickets are less if I get them a few weeks out so maybe the end of the month? Could you check with your boss and see if you can get time off?"

"Yeah, I'll check with him and call you back."

"Okay, honey. Talk to you later."

"Bye, Mom."

I go to find Jesse but one of the mechanics tells me he went home sick. I text my mom and tell her I'll let her know tomorrow. It isn't a matter of *if* I'm going but when. I won't let Jesse deny me the time off. I need to see my mom. Maybe I could even convince Kyle to go with me. I'd love for my mom to meet him.

Trying his number again, he finally answers.

"Hey, you okay?" I ask.

"Yeah, just tired."

"I called earlier and you didn't pick up. I was worried."

"I was in the shower."

"Maybe you could get a new answering machine so I could at least leave a message. Or how about getting a cell phone so I could reach you? "

"I have a cell phone. I don't need another one."

"Your phone is in California."

"Which is where it's going to stay." He sounds annoyed so I drop it and move on.

"So I was calling to ask about dinner, but before I do I wanted to tell you that my mom called and said she's flying me out to New York. Isn't that great?"

"Yeah. When are you going?"

"In a few weeks. And you don't have to decide now, but I was thinking maybe you'd like to come along. I really want you to meet her."

He's silent.

"Kyle? You still there?"

"Yeah. Um, sorry, I can't go to New York with you. I need to stay here and work."

"You could just go for the weekend. You don't have to stay the whole time. I'm not even sure how long I'll be there. I have to see how much time off Jesse will give me. Just think about it. Anyway, for dinner I was just going to bring something home. I could get soup at the diner."

"I don't want soup. I'm feeling better now. How about one of your famous grilled cheese sandwiches? Or is that too much work?"

"It's not work. It's super easy. Okay, we'll do that. I'll see you tonight."

I decide not to tell him I want to talk later. Doing so would make him think something's wrong, when in reality it's the opposite. Things are going great between us and tonight's talk will help us figure out how to keep our relationship going. I think he'll be happy about that. Actually, I know he will because I know how much he loves me. He hasn't actually said those words but I know he does.

When I get home Kyle has the bread and cheese out and is taking a skillet out of the cupboard.

"What are you doing?" I ask, going up to give him a kiss.

"I thought I'd try and make the sandwiches. I know you're tired from work. I've just been lying around all day."

"Because you're sick." I take the skillet from him. "Let me do this. You need to rest."

"I'm feeling better now." He tries to take the skillet but I won't let him have it. "What are you doing?"

"Just let me shower quick and then I'll make the sandwiches." I set the skillet down. "I'll be ten minutes, max." I walk off.

"You don't trust me to make them, do you?" he calls out. I hear him laughing. "You think I won't make them as good as you?"

I don't answer, but yes, I don't think he will. Kyle's an okay cook, probably better than me, but not when it comes to grilled cheese. I've perfected the art of the grilled cheese sandwich.

When I get back to the kitchen, he opens the fridge. "Do you at least trust me to do the drinks?"

"Yes." I close the fridge and give him a hug. "I'm sorry. I didn't mean to make you feel bad."

"I know. I'm just giving you a hard time. I only offered because I know you're tired from work, but I was hoping you'd volunteer to take over. You know how much I love your grilled cheese."

"And I love making it for you." I kiss him. "Because I love you."

I freeze. Did I just say that out loud? Did I just tell him I love him? I'd planned to tell him that later, not now, but then it just came out.

He pulls back and looks at me. "You love me?"

All I can do is nod. I can't tell if he's happy I said it or not. Now I'm getting nervous.

But then he smiles. "I love you too. But you already knew that, didn't you?"

I smile back. "Maybe."

He pulls me in for a hug. "You're hard not to love. Believe me, I tried, but I couldn't help myself."

"Why did you try?" I pull back enough to look at him.

"You know why."

"Because of our agreement?"

"Well, yeah. After this summer..." He doesn't finish the thought.

"Actually, I wanted to talk to you about that." I take his hand and keep hold of it as I walk around him. "C'mon."

"Where are we going?"

"To sit down. I want to talk to you about something." Once we're seated, I face him and say, "I don't want this to end after the summer."

He looks down and exhales a long breath. "Sage."

"What?"

"We knew what would happen. We had an arrangement."

"I know, but that was back in May. A lot has changed since then. We didn't love each other then. We do now."

"That wasn't supposed to happen," he says, his head still down.

"But it did." I scoot closer to him and slide my hand in his. "Now we just need to figure out how to see each other after the summer."

He's quiet. Why isn't he saying anything?

"What?" I ask, but get no response. "Kyle, what is it? What's wrong?"

He finally looks up. "It's not going to work."

"It won't if we don't have a plan." My voice sounds breathy and uneven, almost panicked, because he's not reacting the way I was hoping. "That's why I wanted us to talk. To figure out a plan for how to make this work. I was thinking we could try to see each other every other week. Like maybe you'll fly here once a month and I'll fly there once a month. I know it'll be expensive but I'll work two jobs if that's what it takes to see you."

He shakes his head. "That's not going happen."

"Why? I don't understand."

"We said it would just be casual. That we'd only do this for the summer. After that, we go our separate ways. That was the plan." His voice sounds normal but his expression is pained. His words don't match what he's feeling. What he really wants.

"But the plan changed." I look at him but he won't look back, his gaze on the floor. "Kyle, you just said you love me. If you love me, you wouldn't want to never see me again."

He closes his eyes and sighs.

"What does that mean? What are you thinking?"

He keeps his eyes closed. "I'm thinking we shouldn't have let it get this far. Once we felt it going beyond casual we should've stopped seeing each other." He opens his eyes. "Now we've just made it harder on ourselves."

I can't believe he's saying all this. It doesn't make sense. We love each other. We practically live together. And yet he wants us to break up when he moves back home? Why? Why would he do that?

"Is there someone else?" I ask, feeling sick just asking the question. "Is there someone you left behind? Someone you're going back to?"

"No! I wouldn't be dating you if I had someone back home."

"That's the only way this makes sense. That's the only reason you wouldn't want us to keep seeing each other." I get up and walk around the room. "Is that why you don't have a cell phone? Because you don't want her calling you while you're here?"

"No!" He stands up, watching me as I pace. "There's no one else. I don't have some secret girlfriend."

"Did you have an agreement with her too? Did you decide to be *casual* with her like you are with me?"

"Sage." He approaches me but I back away. "I swear, I don't have anyone else."

"Then why can't we keep seeing each other?" My heart is hurting so much it aches, tears streaming down my cheeks.

"Sage," Kyle says, stepping up to me and forcing me into his arms. "I'm sorry. I never wanted this to happen. This is exactly why I didn't want to start something with you. From the moment we met I knew I'd fall in love with you. That's why I kept trying to keep you away. But you kept showing up and inviting me over and..."

"So this is MY fault?" I try to push him away but he holds onto me.

"That's not what I said. What I meant is that I knew once we were together it'd be nearly impossible to say goodbye."

"But we don't HAVE to say goodbye." I finally push away from him and take a step back. "That's what I keep trying to tell you. There are ways to make this work but you're acting like that's not what you want."

He says nothing, standing there with a hurt look on his face. If this is hurting him too, then why is he doing it? What is going on here?

"So you're saying you never want to see me again after you leave." I put it out there and wait for him to confirm it.

He opens his mouth like he's about to say something but then doesn't. Instead, he rubs his hand over his chin, then up his face, over the thick stubble that's grown from three days of not shaving.

"Would you please just answer me?" I feel myself choking up and take a breath. "Kyle, please say something."

He looks down at the floor and says, "I can't."

"Can't what?"

"I can't have this discussion right now. I wasn't prepared to do this tonight."

"Do what? Break up with me?" Tears fall and I don't wipe them away. I want Kyle to see them, to see how much he's hurting me.

"Goddammit, Sage!" He storms to the side of the room, then stops, taking several deep breaths. His eyes lock on mine. "You knew this was going to happen. Why are you acting like this is news?"

"I didn't think if we fell in love that our agreement would still stand! It's not casual, Kyle. Our relationship has never been casual and you know that and have known it since the beginning, so for you to throw the whole casual agreement thing in my face is bullshit."

"Then I guess we should've talked sooner," he says with anger in his voice. "I thought the fact that we hadn't talked about it meant our agreement hadn't changed."

"Like that really needs to be stated? Why *wouldn't* it change?" I raise my voice. "We fell in love. People who are in love want to be together! They do whatever it takes to make that happen." I soften my tone. "I was willing to do whatever it takes, even if that meant working two jobs so I could afford to come see you. I was even considering moving to California after I graduated. I was willing to make sacrifices. Because I love you. But I guess...you don't feel the same way."

"You know I love you," he says, but he doesn't move closer. He doesn't try to reassure me with a hug or a kiss. He just stands where he is, several feet away from me, his arms at his sides. "Don't ever question that."

A humorless laugh escapes. "You love me but never want to see me again? Yeah, sorry, but if that's what you think love is, you're completely wrong." I look him in the eye. "Why don't you just be honest? This was just a summer fling to you. Nothing more." I walk to the kitchen and grab my purse and keys and hurry to the door. "Goodbye, Kyle."

He doesn't try to stop me. I go out to my car and when I look back, he isn't there. He didn't follow me. He didn't race out and try to get me to stay.

Because it's over. He's made that clear. Whatever we had together is over.

CHAPTER TWENTY-TWO

Kyle

A week has passed since Sage and I broke up but it seems like forever. I got so used to having her in my life that now I feel lost without her. She's all I think about, and at night, when she gets off work, I find myself waiting for her to come over. But then she doesn't and I spend the night missing her, wondering if she's okay.

I've had several angry phone calls from Nina. She doesn't even let me speak. She just yells at me until she's out of things to say and out of names to call me. I could hang up but instead I listen, silently agreeing with everything she's saying because it's all true. Sage deserves to be treated better than this. She deserves more than I can give her. So much more. She's a sweet, kind, good person who's been through hell the past year and now I just made it worse.

I don't know what I was thinking. I knew this wouldn't end well and yet I kept pursuing it. I let Sage think we could be together, knowing the whole time that we couldn't.

She loved me and trusted me and I let her down. And worst of all, I hurt her. I hurt the only woman I've ever loved.

There's a knock on the back door. Normally, that would spook me and make me race to get my gun. But now? My mind is too focused on Sage to even care who's at the door. This past week I haven't even been thinking about them finding me.

But I *have* thought about my brother. I worry about him every day. I need to get back there and get him away from my dad. I'm just not sure how yet. Every time I come up with a plan, I come up with a million reasons why it won't work.

I hear the back door open. "Kyle? You in here?"

It's Hank. I forgot it was Friday. He's here to mow the lawn.

"Yeah, I'm here." I walk into the kitchen and see him taking a beer from the fridge. I keep it stocked, just like he asked me to when we first met. I tried to pay him for the lawn work but beer is the only payment he'll accept.

His brows rise as he looks at me. "Guess the rumors were true."

"What rumors?"

He shuts the fridge door. "People in town said you've looked like shit ever since Sage and you broke up."

"Who told you that? I haven't even been in town, other than the gas station."

"Sheila works the register there. You know how she talks."

Sheila. I wasn't thinking about her, but he's right. She loves to spread gossip, and the other day when I went in to pay for my gas, she kept staring at me. I wasn't even thinking about why, but now it makes sense.

"I don't look so bad," I insist, but I know it's a lie. I haven't showered in two days and haven't shaved in over a week.

"You look like death warmed over." He sits at the kitchen table and takes his pocket knife out. It has a bottle opener attached to it, which he uses to flip the cap off his beer. "What's it been now? A week?"

"Not quite. Tonight will be a week." I don't want to talk about this but I can tell he's not going to give up until he says whatever it is he wants to say.

He nods, then takes a drink of his beer.

"What?"

He shrugs. "I'm trying to figure out the best way to say this."

"Just tell me so we can get this over with. I know the whole town thinks I broke her heart but as you can see," I point to myself, "I'm not doing so well myself. But it had to happen. We couldn't keep something going we knew was going to end."

He fiddles with the bottle cap, spinning it around on the table.

"You like stories?" He laughs. "What am I saying? Of course you do. You're a writer." He sets the bottle cap aside. "When I was a trial lawyer, I dealt with some bad people. Bastards who'd kill whoever pissed them off, even if that person was someone they claimed to love. I once met a guy who killed his wife because she never had dinner ready when he wanted it. Then there was a guy who killed his own kid because he thought he was stealing from him. Turns out he wasn't."

I'm completed focused on him, finding his story a little too coincidental. A guy killing his kid? Does he know something? Does he know about my dad? There's no way he could but hearing that story makes me even more worried for my brother. I need to get to him, and soon.

"One of these bastards decided I'd pissed him off," Hank says, "so he came after me."

"What'd he do?"

"Showed up at my house. He was out on bail. Showed up at my front door and my wife answered. Our youngest was just a toddler then and Lois was holding her. I asked who was at the door but she didn't answer. I went to the door and saw the bastard holding a gun on her and our daughter." Hank picks up the bottle cap and taps it lightly on the table, over and over again.

It still bothers him. He's still haunted by this story and I get the feeling he doesn't tell it often. So why is he telling it to me?

"I saw him there and lost my damn mind. I tackled the guy to the ground, which was stupid because he still had the gun which could've gone off at any time, hitting my wife or our daughter. Or me, but I didn't care about me. I cared about them, which is why I beat the guy into the ground until he finally passed out." He takes a breath. "After that day, I started thinking long and hard about the future. My goal was to be a judge and I was on that path, but it's a job that would put my family at risk. Criminals have friends so even if you lock them up, their buddies may come looking for revenge. I was scared to death another bastard would show up at my door. Try to kill my family. So..." He looks up at me. "I left them."

"You *what*? You left your family?"

"I walked out on them. Packed up a suitcase and left. Got myself a one-bedroom apartment on the other side of town."

"What'd your wife do?"

"She didn't speak to me. For over a month. Worst month of my life. But I was doing what I thought was best. I thought by going away I was protecting them."

"Did your wife try to divorce you?"

"No." He chuckles. "Worse."

"What do you mean?"

"She made me take a cold, hard look at myself and see what was really going on."

"Which was what?"

"I was being selfish. Moving out wasn't about them. It was about me. I was being a coward. I wasn't protecting them. I was protecting myself."

"I don't understand."

He sets the bottle cap down and looks at me. "If anything ever happened to them because of me, I didn't think I'd be able to go on. I'd be in too much pain. I'd blame myself every day. It'd be torture. I love them so much that imagining life without them was something I couldn't stand to even think about. So I removed the chance of that ever happening."

"By removing yourself."

"Yes. And when my wife forced me to acknowledge how selfish I was being, I went back to her. I moved back in the house."

"But weren't you still worried about your family?"

"Of course, but the truth is, criminals could go after my family whether I'm there or not. It's a risk for any of us who work in criminal justice. I wasn't thinking with my head. I was thinking with my heart, trying to avoid the pain I would feel if something ever happened to my family. Thank God my wife knocked some sense into me." He smiles. "I love that woman."

"It's a good story but why are you telling me this?"

"Because sometimes you need someone to point out when you're being stupid." He takes a drink of his beer.

"I'm not being stupid. I'm being realistic. Sage still has to graduate college, and when she's done I don't want her making decisions based on me. I don't even have a job. I'm trying to make this writing career work but if it doesn't, I don't know what I'll do for money or where I'll end up living."

He rubs his jaw, his eyes fixed on mine. "Try again."

"I don't know what that means. Try again with Sage?"

"No. Try another story because that one's full of shit."

"Sorry if you don't like it but it's the truth. Both Sage's future and mine are up in the air so it's not a good idea for either of us to commit to this relationship right now."

"I'm not talking about you and Sage. I'm talking about you."

He's making me nervous. His words and the way he's looking at me with that serious expression, his eyes locked on mine, it's almost like he knows something.

"What *about* me?"

He scoots his chair back and crosses his legs as he picks up his beer. "Where'd you get the money?"

"What money?" My heart lurches against my chest, beating out of control. What does he know? What the fuck does he know?

"I was down in the cellar last week to get some onions. Miller grows them every spring and stores them down there in a box. He lets me take what I want and Lois said we needed some so I went and picked out a few. While I was down there I noticed something I didn't recognize. A cloth sack. It was on the ground behind one of the shelves. It looked like it fell back there so I picked it up, and lo and behold, a stack of hundreds fell at my feet. Imagine my surprise."

Shit! He found the money. I thought I'd hid it where it'd never be found. I didn't think anyone went down there. There's a padlock on the cellar door. Hank must have a key. Fuck! Why didn't I just bury the money like I'd originally planned?

He continues. "I was even more surprised to find the bag was full of 'em. Stacks and stacks of hundred dollar bills." He leans back in his chair. "For a moment I thought maybe they belonged to Miller. I love him like a brother but he's a cheap bastard. Never spends a dime. But if he had that much cash laying around, he wouldn't put it in the cellar. He'd put it in coffee cans and bury it around the yard, then forget where he buried it, which is why I'd bet his money is in the bank. I could call and ask him just to be sure." He gets his phone out.

"No! Don't call him."

Hank slips his phone in his shirt pocket. "So where'd you get the money?"

"It's none of your damn business."

"It's a hundred thousand dollars. It sure as hell IS my business. The only people walking around with a hundred thousand dollars cash are criminals."

Shit, shit, shit! What do I do? What am I going to tell him?

"Maybe I'm from a wealthy family," I say, trying to sound cool. "You ever think of that? Maybe that hundred thousand is nothing to me."

"So you're a spoiled rich kid who decided to spend your summer in a run-down shack of a house in the middle of nowhere?"

"I wanted to see how the other half lives."

He nods. "Yes. Of course you did."

"Listen to me." I lean forward, slamming my hand on the table. "This is none of your damn business. I'm not your client. I'm not on trial. I haven't done anything wrong. So leave me the fuck alone!" I bolt up from my chair so fast it falls on the floor.

I'm furious. Furious at Hank for finding my money and furious at myself for not hiding it better.

"Calm down," he says, still seated. "I don't have the cops waiting outside. I haven't even told anyone this. Not even my wife."

Breathing hard, I say, "Why haven't you told anyone? You've known about this for a week and you don't say anything? Not even to me?"

"I was doing some research. Seeing if your story checked out. It doesn't, by the way. You're not a writer. There's no book. I looked up every publishing deal made within the past five years. Your name wasn't anywhere to be found."

"It's a small publisher."

"If you had an agent, like you said you did, the deal would be public, even if with a small publisher. And there are no writing samples online. No record of your participation in any writing classes or workshops. I doubt Kyle is even your name."

"Why the fuck are you doing this?" I pick up the chair and set it upright, slamming it down on the wood floor. "What are you trying to prove?"

"I'm trying to figure out who the hell you are. Why you paid Miller thousands of dollars to rent out this house for the summer. And yes, he told me how much you gave him, for both his house and his silence. He said you didn't want anyone knowing how much you paid. Why is that, Kyle? Because it would make them suspicious? Because it would make them question your story?"

"I don't have to answer your questions. We're not in a damn courtroom and I'm not going to be put on trial for something I didn't do. The money you found isn't stolen. It's mine. I wasn't lying when I said I'm from a wealthy family."

"How wealthy?"

"It doesn't matter."

"Why'd you leave?"

"I was tired of it. I was tired of the people, the lifestyle. It's all fake. I wanted to see what it's like to not be part of that world. I wanted something real." I look around. "This town? This place? This is real."

It's true, but I didn't know I needed to experience this until I got here and met Sage and got to live a life that wasn't filled with money and whatever money could buy. I didn't expect to like being here. It was just a hideout. A place I couldn't be found. But it turned out to feel like home. Until Sage left. Since then, it's felt like nothing at all. Sage is what made it feel like home.

"So you were a spoiled rich kid who needed a break?"

"Pretty much."

He huffs. "Try again."

"What the hell? I'm not lying. I'm rich."

"I get that, and I believe it, but the part about needing a break from your pampered lifestyle? I'm not buying it."

"Then what exactly am I doing here?"

"You're hiding out." He takes the last drink of his beer and sets his bottle down. "You're on the run. I just don't know why. I'm waiting for you to tell me. And if you don't then...well, I'm gonna have to share what I know with the police. Because if you're not running from danger, you're running because *you're* the danger. You either robbed someone or killed someone. And if either of those are true, you need to be locked up."

"If you really think I did something bad, you wouldn't have kept this to yourself this whole time."

"Which is why my theory leads me back to you being in trouble. Someone's after you. Someone dangerous. And if they find you they might..." He mindlessly taps the table a few times with his finger, "....kill you."

I gulp down some air and turn away from him. How the hell does he know this? He should've been a detective instead of a judge. He's good. He's damn good. And he can read people. He's reading me right now. He knows I'm panicking. He knows what he said about me is true.

So what happens now? He can't have me arrested. I haven't done anything.

"Why don't you sit down?" he says.

"Why?" I ask, my heart pounding, palms sweating.

"Let's figure this out."

I turn to him. "Figure *what* out?"

"How we're going to get you out of this." He sounds concerned for me. Not scared of me. Not threatened by me. But genuinely concerned. The type of concern my father should have for me but never has. "You can't run forever, kid. Now sit down."

I wish I could trust him. If I could, maybe he could help me. God knows I need it. I've been racking my brain trying to find a way to save both myself and my brother but can't find a solution in which at least one of us doesn't end up dead.

I sit down. "I'm not running."

He leans toward me, his arms on the table. "You want help or you want to keep living like this? Always worried they're going to find you?"

Dropping my head, I sigh. "Just leave it alone."

He sits back. "That bad, huh?"

If he only knew.

I remain silent as he gets up and goes to the fridge to get a beer.

"Gonna need another one of these," he says, sitting down again. He pops the cap off the bottle. "We could be here a while if you keep up this silent act."

"I have nothing to say."

He chuckles. "You wouldn't believe how many times I've heard that from my clients. But I'm a stubborn bastard. I can wait."

"You'll be waiting around for nothing. I'm not one of your clients. Even if I was hiding something, I wouldn't have to tell you."

"You don't have to do *anything*. But if you want out of this mess, you're going to need some help. And I'm the only one who's offered."

He takes a long sip of his beer, downing half the bottle at once. Then he sets the bottle down on the table and folds his arms over his chest.

"So what's it gonna be? Continue to hide? Live in a constant state of fear? Or end this shit and have a life again?"

It's tempting. It's so damn tempting to tell him the truth and see if he could help. But telling him puts me at risk. I like Hank, but can I trust him? I want to. At this point I could use any help he could give me, even if it were just suggestions of what steps to take next.

But what if he turned on me? What if I told him everything and he didn't believe me and handed me over to the police? What if he told my father I was here?

I need to make a decision. I tell him or I don't. If I tell him, I don't have to tell him everything. I could leave out some details.

He's staring at me, waiting for me to say something. After several long nerve-racking minutes, I make a decision.

I look him in the eye. "Let's say you were right. What could you do for me?"

"Depends on what you got yourself into."

"I saw something. Something I shouldn't have."

"And they found out."

"HE did. Not them. They were just hired to do the job."

"And who is HE?"

I take a breath. "My father."

CHAPTER TWENTY-THREE

Sage

It's Saturday night and I'm going out with Nina and Josh. Nina says I've been cooped up in the house too long, which is true. Ever since Kyle and I broke up, I've spent all my time in this house, feeling down and depressed and missing the idiot I fell in love with. The only time I leave here is when I go to work, and when I go there, I have to listen to Jesse say 'I told you so' about a million times.

It's been a horrible week so tonight I'm going to go out and try to have fun, or at the very least, drink until I can't feel the hurt anymore. Josh is picking me up and we're meeting Nina at the bar.

Josh and Nina are sort of dating now. I say 'sort of' because he says they are and she says they aren't. They bicker about it all the time. To them that's foreplay which is why they keep fighting about it. Josh spends every weekend at her apartment unless he has to work, like he did today. Since my house is on his way into town, he's picking me up.

The doorbell rings, a long drawn out ring because the doorbell is broken. It must be Josh but why is he here so early? He's not supposed to be here for another half hour.

"Just a minute," I yell as he knocks. I have a shirt on but no pants because I couldn't decide if I wanted to wear a skirt or jeans tonight. I grab some jeans and put them on, then run to the door.

"Why are you so early?" I ask, yanking the door open.

But it's not Josh at the door. It's Kyle.

"Hey," he says, in a deep quiet voice. "Can I come in?"

"What are you doing here?"

"I want to talk."

"We already did." I sound angry, but really I'm feeling hurt. Seeing him here at my door just reminds me of when he used to come over. When we used to make dinner then talk and hang out and fall asleep together. I miss that. I miss it so much.

"I need to say something."

"Unless you're coming here to say you've changed your mind, I—"

"I have," he says, his eyes meeting mine.

"Have *what*?"

"I've changed my mind. Last week when we talked I wasn't ready to commit to us being together because I didn't think it would work. But I've thought about it, and although I don't have all the answers right now, I need you to know that I don't want what we started to end. I love you and I want to keep seeing you."

"You said it wouldn't work."

"I know and I was wrong. Can I come inside?"

I let him in and we go to the living room and sit down.

"You hurt me," I say.

"I know." He's in the chair next to mine and reaches over to hold my hand. I let him, even though I probably shouldn't. I'm still so mad at him for what he did.

"How do you know I even want this anymore? You told me you loved me and then broke up with me."

"I didn't want to break up with you. I wanted to do just as you said and find a way to be together when we both leave here."

"Then why didn't you agree to it last week? Why didn't you at least agree it was an option?"

"I couldn't. Even now, I can't make you any promises. There are things I need to do, and until I do them, my life is kind of a mess. And I don't want you part of that mess."

"What mess? What are you talking about?"

"It doesn't matter. What matters is that I'm working on a solution. A solution that would ensure we could be together."

"Kyle, if you can't be honest with me then you need to leave. I'm not going to be with someone who keeps secrets from me."

"I get that, but I promise you, if you just give me some time to work this out, we could be together."

"Work *what* out? Tell me what's going on."

He sighs. "I can't." He turns to me. "But I will when it's over. I just need you to trust me."

I rip my hand from his and stand up. "Why would I trust you when you can't be honest with me? This can't work if you're hiding something from me."

"Sage, I—"

"Go." I point to the door. "I'm leaving soon and I don't have time for this. I have to get ready."

"I'm not going. I came here to talk to you. To get you back."

"I don't..." My voice cracks as tears trickle down my cheeks. "I don't want you back."

He steps up to me and puts his thumb on my cheek, wiping the tears. "You sure about that?"

I close my eyes and nod, more tears falling.

"What if I told you I love you more than I ever thought possible?" He puts his arm around my waist and pulls me closer. "What if I told you that since meeting you, the best parts of my day were waking up with you every morning and having you fall asleep in my arms every night?" He places a soft kiss on my lips. "What if I told you this past week without you has been one of the worst weeks of my life? Then, maybe, would you consider being with me again?"

I open my teary eyes. "Maybe."

"What can I do, Sage? What can I do to get you back?" He wipes more tears from my face. "What if I promised to work on my grilled cheese skills so you never have to make them again?"

I smile. "Wouldn't help. Grilled cheese sandwiches aren't really my thing."

"Then why do we have them all the time?"

"Because *you* love them. And I love you."

"You were only eating them because of me?"

"And because they're a cheap dinner."

"I'll buy you whatever you want. We don't have to eat grilled cheese." He shakes his head. "Shit, why you didn't tell me this before? Now I feel like an ass for making you eat something you didn't like."

"I didn't say I don't like them, just not all the time."

"That's it. No more grilled cheese. From now on, you make all dinner decisions. And I'll attempt to make whatever you want."

"You're acting like we're back together."

"We're not?" His face falls in disappointment. "But I thought—"

"I need you to do something for me."

"What is it?"

"I need you to go to New York with me next week. My mom bought us both a ticket. She doesn't know we broke up. She sold another painting last week and was so excited that I didn't want to tell her what happened with us. So she still doesn't know. And now I have these two tickets and I really want you to go. I want you to meet my mom."

He lets me go and turns around, rubbing his hand through his hair.

"What's wrong?"

"I can't go."

"Why?"

"I have to work. I'm so behind. Last week I wasn't able to write and my editor emailed and said I owe him three chapters by the end of next week."

"You have more than three chapters. You told me you've written five."

He turns to face me. "Sage, I want to go. I just...I just can't."

"We won't be gone long. It's only for a few days."

"It's not a good time. I really do have to work."

"Which you can do when we get back. This is really important to me, Kyle. I need you to go."

He pauses. "I'm sorry, but I can't."

"And you're blaming work, but that's not the real reason, is it?"

He says nothing, which is all the answer I need.

"You should leave," I say, not looking at him.

"Sage, I.." His head drops and he sighs.

"I can't keep doing this, Kyle. I can't be with you if you can't be truthful with me." I walk to the door. "You need to leave."

He remains where he's at, not saying anything.

There's a knock on the door and I open it and see Josh standing there.

"Hey, Sage. Ready to go?"

"Not quite."

Josh notices Kyle behind me. "What are you doing here?"

Nina told Josh that Kyle was just using me for a summer fling, which isn't true, but Josh believed her so now he pretty much hates Kyle.

"He was just leaving," I say to Josh.

"Good." Josh waits for him to go but he doesn't. "Your legs stop working or what?" he asks Kyle.

"I'm not done talking to Sage."

"We're done," I tell him. "In more ways than one."

"She told you to go," Josh says when Kyle doesn't move.

I look at Josh. "If Nina asked you to go to New York with her to meet her mom, would you go?"

"If her mom lived there, then yeah. Of course."

"I'll go," Kyle blurts out.

"You will?" I ask, surprised.

"Yes." He walks over and closes the door on Josh. "And if you're okay with it, I want to stay here tonight. I know you have plans with Nina so if you want to go I understand, but I've already gone over a week without you and I really don't want to have to go another night."

I smile. "You'll really go to New York? You won't change your mind?"

"If you want me to go, I'll go."

"Sage?" Josh tries to open the door but Kyle holds it shut.

"Tell me I can stay," he asks. "I miss you, Sage."

I smile even more. "I miss you too." I turn and talk to the door. "Josh, you can go. I'm staying here."

"With HIM?" he asks, sounding disgusted.

"Yeah. Tell Nina I'm sorry. We'll do it some other time." I hear him talking to himself as he walks away. I loop my arms around Kyle's neck. "You were saying?"

"I have nothing more to say." He lowers his mouth to mine. "Other than that I love you." He kisses me, his arms going around my waist, pulling me closer.

The feel of his warm body and deep penetrating kiss ignites an aching need that I haven't felt since he left.

"I want you," I whisper over his mouth.

He scoops me up and takes me to the bedroom.

"Does that mean you want me too?" I ask with a laugh.

"So damn much." He takes his shirt off, showing off that lean muscular chest of his.

The rest of our clothes go flying and we meet up in bed, with Kyle already suited up in a condom. His hand slips between my legs, circling, stroking, making my entire body tremble with anticipation. But I don't want to finish yet. Not this way.

I gently take his hand away and he kisses me as his body comes over mine. He pushes inside me then stills.

"I love you," he whispers by my ear. He slowly pulls out, then thrusts into me, hard and deep, filing my body with the sensations it's craved while he's been gone. The anticipation continues to build, my body begging for more but also wanting its release.

"Sage," he groans and I know he's close. I am too.

Moments later I get my release, and it's awesome. Better than any other time we've been together. He comes shortly after, and as our bodies come to rest, I feel a peace come over me. A peace that comes from knowing we're back together.

I love him. I love him so much. I didn't expect to find love for a very long time, and definitely not this summer, in this tiny town. But somehow, for some reason, we both ended up here and I have to believe it's because we were meant to find each other.

"Let's go out," Kyle says, his fingers lightly playing with my hair.

I snuggle closer to him. "But this feels so good. Why would we go out?"

"I don't mean go out to a bar. I mean, let's take a drive. Let's go back to my place and get my motorcycle and go."

"But it'll be dark soon."

"We have an hour of daylight left. We'll be back before dark." He turns on his side. "C'mon. You've never been on the bike with me."

I've never been on a motorcycle with anyone but I've always wanted to try it. My mom would kill me if she found out I went for a motorcycle ride. She hates motorcycles and told me I'm never to ride on one. But there's something really appealing about the idea of riding on a motorcycle with Kyle. Sorry, Mom, but I have to do this.

"Okay," I tell him, sitting up. "Let's go."

"Really?" He smiles. "I thought you'd say it was too dangerous."

"It IS dangerous but that's part of the appeal."

He pulls me back down to him and kisses me. "You like danger?"

"In small doses, yes."

He kisses me again. "I love you so much, Sage. How did this even happen?"

"How did *what* happen?"

"How did we find each other? How did we both end up here? I mean, I know how it happened. I just find it odd that two outsiders both end up in this tiny little town that probably hasn't had anyone new move in for fifty years, and yet we show up at the same time."

"I was just thinking the same thing. It's almost like we were meant to show up here when we did. Like we were meant to meet."

"Huh." He chews on his lip.

"What?" I laugh because he seems so deep in thought. It's like I lost him for a moment. "What are you thinking?"

"Nothing." He gives me a kiss. "Let's go."

We get dressed and go over to his house and get the motorcycle. We ride along the country roads, and at first I'm scared but I eventually relax and enjoy the ride. Nobody else is around. It's just Kyle and me on the open road and I love it. It's something I've never done, and I love that I'm experiencing it with Kyle.

When we're almost home, Kyle pulls over on the side of the road.

"What are you doing?" I ask as he helps me off the back of the bike.

"I want to show you something."

He grabs my hand and guides me through a path that has wheat fields on both sides. We end up in a clearing in front of what used to be a house. Now its roof is caved in and weeds are growing all around it.

"I'm not going in there," I tell Kyle.

He laughs. "I wouldn't let you. It's too dangerous. The thing's falling apart."

"Then where are we going?"

"Back here." He pulls on my hand and leads me to a giant oak tree that's behind the house.

"It's going to be dark soon. I don't want to be out here."

"We aren't staying long." He lets go of my hand and climbs up to the lowest branch of the tree. It's a big, wide branch that juts out over the lawn, which is now a field of weeds. He reaches down. "Give me your hand."

"I'm not going up there. I don't climb trees."

"Have you ever tried?"

"No."

"You should. It's awesome. Now hurry up. You're going to miss it."

"Miss what?"

"Would you stop asking a million questions and get up here?"

It's not very high up but I'm still not comfortable climbing a tree.

"What if I fall?"

"Then I'll catch you."

"You can't catch me from up there."

He sighs. "You were afraid of the motorcycle, right?"

"Yes." But I never told him that. He must've been able to tell.

"And you ended up loving it."

"Yeah."

"So give this a try. If you don't like it, you can climb back down. I'll help you."

"Okay, but if I break a leg, you're making dinner for the rest of the summer."

"Deal."

He holds his hand out. I take it and he pulls me up beside him.

"Look." He points straight ahead.

"Wow." I smile as I see it. "It's beautiful."

The sun is setting and looks absolutely stunning. It's like a painting, with the endless fields of wheat below, the country road off in the distance.

"I found this the other day. I needed to get out of the house so I got on the motorcycle and just drove. On my way back, I spotted this tree poking out of the fields. I went to check it out and sat up here for like an hour, just thinking about stuff. And then the sun started to set and I couldn't leave. It was so beautiful. I've seen a lot of sunsets, but this one here...it's different. Maybe it's because nobody else is around, but sitting here, watching it, made this calmness come over me. I've been coming here every night since."

He puts his arm around me. "I wanted to share it with you." I feel him kiss my head as he holds me closer. "I love it here because it makes me feel the same way I feel when I'm with you. You calm me, Sage, in a way no one else can. It's what drew me to you when we first met. I love that you make me feel that way. Nobody else ever has."

His words warm my heart and I'm happy he's opening up to me like this, but his comment has me wondering what he means.

"Why do you need that?"

"Need what?"

"Why do you crave the calmness?"

His arm stiffens around me. "I just do. Doesn't everyone?"

"I don't know. I never did until everything blew up with my dad. Before that, I was content in my life. I loved my college, my friends, where my life was headed. But then everything got turned upside down and I was surrounded by chaos. The peace I used to feel was gone. I just wondered if something like that happened to you. If there was something in your life that changed, that threw everything out of balance, created chaos where it wasn't before."

I feel his arm slowly relax and then he says, "I guess maybe my mom dying. She brought peace to the house. That feeling of calmness that welcomes you after a long day."

"Your mom died a while ago."

"Yeah, so you can see why I like this spot. And why I like being with you. It's been a long time since I've felt that calmness."

"So your dad..." I'm afraid to ask about his dad. He doesn't like talking about him. If I even bring him up, Kyle changes the subject.

"We should go," Kyle says.

Just as I predicted, he's avoiding the topic of his dad. I really want to know why but that'll have to wait for another day.

He jumps down from the tree and holds his arms out. "Go ahead."

"I can't jump. I'll knock you over."

"You think I'm that weak?" He laughs. "I'm insulted. Now hurry up."

I jump down and he catches me, then gives me a kiss. He holds my hand as we walk through the now-dark path that leads back to the road. Then we ride his motorcycle on the short trip back to my house.

I can't stop smiling. The motorcycle ride. The sunset. His promise that we'll be together after this summer. It all has me smiling so much I can't stop. He makes me so happy.

When I moved to this town, I was so depressed. I didn't think I would feel this happy for a very long time. But now I am. I really am.

I'm glad I gave the grouchy biker dude on the side of the road a chance. He turned out to be just what I needed.

CHAPTER TWENTY-FOUR

Kyle

"He's not there," Hank says as he comes into the house. He sits down on the couch and takes something from his jacket. I'm assuming it's notes about what he's found out, but it's not. It's something wrapped in plastic. He tosses it to me.

"What's this?" I ask, holding it up.

"Lois made cookies. She told me to bring you one. She worries you don't eat enough."

"That's sweet." I smile and set the cookie on the coffee table. "Tell her thanks."

I met Lois last week. She invited me over for dinner the day after I broke up with Sage. I didn't feel like going, given how depressed I was feeling, but Hank threatened to kick my ass if I didn't show up.

Lois loves to cook and made more food than I could possibly eat, especially since I had no appetite after losing Sage. I ate what I could and Lois sent the rest home for leftovers, including two pies that I've shared with Hank when he comes over.

The past week, Hank has been here every day. He pretends he's here to give me updates but he's really just checking in on me. He saw how much I was struggling without Sage, along with all my other problems, so he stops by every day after work to see how I'm doing. He's become a good friend. Someone I can confide in. And someone who might actually help me get out of this mess.

The fact that I found someone with the right connections for what I need astounds me when I think about it. It's like with Sage. I found the girl I love in the most unlikely place at a time when love was the absolute last thing on my mind. It doesn't even seem possible. And then I found Hank. Of course, I never would've known he could help me if he hadn't found that money and confronted me.

The day that happened we stayed at the kitchen table and talked for hours. I finally broke down and told him what was going on. I told him about that day. About the day that changed everything.

I remember it like it just happened. It was a Tuesday night and I'd come home from the gym and heard my dad out back by the pool talking to someone.

"You fucked up again," he said to the guy.

"No, Sir, I didn't. I made the delivery. I promise."

"Then where's my fucking money?" he yelled.

"It's coming." The guy's voice was hoarse and shaking. "They just didn't have it."

"You don't leave the goods without getting the fucking money! Any idiot knows that!"

"They had guns on me! What was I supposed to do?"

"You blow their fucking heads off, that's what."

I'd never heard my father curse that much. He always tried to act so refined, like the rich people he socialized with. Growing up in poverty, he'd always aspired to have wealth, so when he got it, he was determined to play the role of the refined gentleman and hide any signs that showed he didn't belong in that world.

Walking to the sliding glass door, I watched as they continued to argue. The wind blew and my eye caught sight of something just outside the screen door. There was an envelope on the ground and photos were falling out of it. I quietly slid open the door and picked up the envelope. Inside it were pictures of crates filled with guns. All kinds. Some looked like military-type guns, ones I'd only seen in movies.

The crates were familiar. Like the ones I'd seen at my father's import business. When I was a kid, he'd take me to the docks to watch the cargo ships pulling up to the shipyard. Then I'd watch as they unloaded the crates. I always wondered what was inside them. My father just said it was deliveries for his clients and left it at that.

Now I know that at least some of those crates were filled with weapons. Weapons that were not being legitimately sold but were being sold on the black market to people that shouldn't have them.

It explained why we were so filthy rich. The import business could be lucrative, but not THAT lucrative. My father had his own private jet. You don't buy a jet if you're just moderately wealthy.

As I looked at the photos that night, a shot rang out. When I looked up I saw the guy my father had been yelling at fall to the ground. My father shot him again, then got his phone out. I couldn't hear what he said but the call was short. He put his phone away, then casually tossed the gun in the pool.

He turned around and saw me and we both froze for a moment.

He stormed toward me. "What the fuck are you doing here?"

I couldn't move. Couldn't speak. I was too shocked.

"Answer me!" He shook my shoulders, then looked down and saw the photos in my hand. He yanked them from me. "What are you doing with these?"

"They were there." I pointed to the ground but my eyes were still on my father. The murderer. I knew he wasn't a good person but I had no idea he was capable of killing someone.

He tossed the photos aside and grabbed my shoulders, staring into my eyes. "You didn't see anything. You hear me?"

"You killed him," I said, searching my dad's face, hoping I'd see that maybe he was on something. That this wasn't him and that some pill he was taking made him do it. But I knew that wasn't true. He wasn't even nervous. He'd done this before, enough times that he didn't even care that a dead man was lying on his lawn.

"That's what happens when people fuck up and don't do what they're told." He grabbed my shirt and yanked on it until my face was right next to his. I could feel his hot breath as he spoke. "You don't keep your fucking mouth shut, you'll end up just like him."

"What?" I choked on the words. I couldn't believe what he'd said. Threatening to kill his own son? Had he lost his mind?

"You heard me. None of what you saw today is real. It never happened. Do you understand me?"

I nodded as best I could but his tight hold on the neckline of my shirt was making it difficult.

"Good boy," he said and then he slowly let me go. He smiled, but his eyes were dark and threatening. He didn't trust me to keep quiet. I knew he didn't. I could tell.

I hurried to my room and immediately started packing a bag. I didn't know where I was going. I only knew I had to get out of there. As I was packing, I heard a knock on my door. I shoved the duffle bag in my closet, hiding it.

When I opened the door, I saw my father standing there. He'd changed into a suit. He gave me a wide smile and said, "I'm attending a benefit at the opera house tonight. I need you to keep an eye on your brother. He'll be home soon."

"Okay," I answered a little too quickly.

He could tell I was on edge and patted me on the shoulder. "Jonathan, relax. There's no reason to be nervous. Today was just a regular day. Isn't that right?"

I quickly nodded. "Yes. A regular day."

"I expect you to be here when I get back."

"Of course I will. I have to watch Cain."

He smirked. "You're such a good son." And then he left.

Cain had been out with a friend but got home just after my father left for the opera house. As usual, Cain raced to find me so he could tell me all about lacrosse practice and whatever else had happened at school that day. He's a talkative kid. Always has been. I'm more of a listener, so I listened to him go on and on but didn't hear what he was saying. My mind was focused on how to get the hell out of there. I didn't trust my father.

I was right not to trust him because later that night, after Cain had gone to bed, I went down to my car to get my phone charger. The car was parked outside and when I went to open it, I felt something against the back of my head. I slowly turned around and saw two guys, both holding guns at me.

"Don't!" I said in a hushed voice, not wanting to wake up Cain. His bedroom faced the front of the house and his windows were open. "Please don't shoot. I have money. You can have my wallet." I went to reach for it but the one guy grabbed my arm, stopping me.

"We don't want your fucking money," he said. "We work for your father."

I suspected that but was hoping it wasn't true.

"My father told you to shoot me?" I asked, trying to hide the shakiness in my voice.

"Your father told us to keep you quiet," the other guy said. "By whatever means necessary."

"I already told him I wouldn't say anything."

"Then consider this a warning." The two guys smiled, then walked off into the dark cluster of trees that surrounded our property.

Back in the house, I went to my room and got the duffle bag I'd packed earlier, then went straight to the basement, to the storage room where we keep the junk we never use. Hidden behind one of the walls is a safe. There are safes hidden all over the house. About a year ago, I went down to the storage room and heard my dad mumbling to himself. He didn't see me so I stayed and listened and realized he was mumbling the code to the safe as he opened it. I used that code to unlock the safe that night. I took all the money that was in there, over a hundred thousand dollars. I shoved it in my duffle bag, then took off.

There was a bus stop a block from the house. I got on the bus and took it to Grand Central Station. Knowing there were cameras everywhere, I tried to hide under a baseball cap and a hoodie. I took the train as far as I could, then took a bus and then another bus until I ended up in Kansas.

As soon as I got off the bus a guy came up to me asking for money. He had a motorcycle so I asked him if I could buy it. He didn't want to sell it until I offered him way more than it was worth. It was a piece of shit bike but I needed a way to get around and it was my only option.

I drove it until I was out in the middle of nowhere. That's how I ended up here. I saw Old Man Miller sitting on his front porch and I approached him and asked if he'd rent me his house. I offered him a lot of cash for both the house and his silence and he took it, no questions asked. He said he'd always wanted to go to Florida and so he did.

"He took off for Boston," Hank says, bringing me back to the present. He takes a bite of a half-eaten cookie, then holds it up. "This was supposed to be yours, but don't worry. I got more in the car. She sent you a whole container of them."

"So they tracked my father to Boston? Do they know what he's doing there?"

"They suspect he's going to meet a new client. He probably wants to expand his territory." He finishes the cookie, then wipes his hands together to get rid of the crumbs. "He'd be better off sticking with New York. Going into a new city, he's going to upset the local dealers."

"He's going to get himself killed." I say it like I'm worried about him, but I shouldn't be. The asshole tried to have me murdered. I'm still trying to wrap my head around that. Part of me refuses to believe he would really do it. Before I found this out, my father was just a father. Not a good one, but still my father. A man I admired for rising out of poverty and becoming a successful businessman.

Now I know him as a murderer. A dealer of illegal weapons on the black market.

"Listen to me." Hank leans toward me and I meet his gaze. "He did this to himself. I know it's hard not to feel sorry for him or worry about him but he's a grown man and he got himself into this business. It's not your job to get him out. You can't save him, Kyle. And I hate to say this because I know it hurts you but...he chose this over you. You have to remember that in order to get through this. And to get through the trial."

He's referring to our end goal in all of this, which is to get my father arrested and charged and locked away. If we can get the people who work with him locked away too, then all the better, but if not, at least their ringleader will be gone and that will slow down or maybe even stop their activity.

It's up to the FBI to catch him. They're now on the case, thanks to Hank. Given his career in criminal justice, he has friends in the FBI. I wasn't willing to talk to them directly but I was able to provide them with information through an anonymous tip. Eventually, I'll have to come forward and tell them more, but I really don't know that much. They've been on the case only a few days and already know more than me.

"What else did they find out?" I ask.

"Don't know. That's all they'd tell me. And they only told me that so you didn't show up in Boston and run into him."

"I have no plans to be in Boston but I uh...I do have to go to New York next week."

He laughs. "Because you're in the mood to get killed? You got an odd sense of humor, kid."

"I'm serious. Sage is going out there next week to see her mom and she's making me go."

"You're going to have to tell her no. You're not going there."

"I have to. It was part of our agreement. She wouldn't take me back unless I agreed to go."

"The girl isn't going to break up with you if you don't go. She loves you."

"I told her I'd do this and I can't go back on my word. We're only going there for a few days. I'll make sure we stay close to her mom's apartment. My dad never goes to that part of town. There's no way we'd run into him. Hank, I have to do this. I made her a promise."

Hank shakes his head. "I'll see if my buddy at the FBI can keep track of him while you're there. I still think it's a bad idea but I understand. I've done plenty of stupid things for a woman."

We continue to talk and I tell him about being out with Sage last night and how I feel so much closer to her now that I can see a future with her. Once this thing is finally settled with my father I'll be able to live my life again. But it won't be in New York. I want to get far away from there. I might even go as far away as Hawaii if I could get Sage to agree to it. And Cain. I'll be taking him with me wherever I end up. Once my father is locked away, I'll ask for custody of Cain.

The plan is set in motion. Now I just wait for them to catch him. I don't know when that'll be but I hope it's soon. I want this to end. I want a life again.

CHAPTER TWENTY-FIVE

Sage

Tomorrow Kyle and I leave for New York. I can't wait to see my mom and for her to meet Kyle. She's got all these activities planned for us. Kyle's been to New York many times, but I've never been and I can't wait to see it.

"Hey." Jesse walks in looking more serious than usual. "Can I talk to you?"

He better not tell me I can't go tomorrow. If he does, I'm going anyway. The trip is planned and paid for and I'm not missing it so I can sit in this office doing paperwork.

"What is it?"

He closes the door. That's not a good sign. I look over at Helen's desk and see that she's not back from her break. She should've been back by now. Jesse must've told her to stay on break so he could talk to me.

As he sits down, I say, "If you're going to tell me I can't go on my trip tomorrow, I'm—"

"That's not it, although who you're going with is a problem."

"So this is about Kyle?" I roll my eyes. I'm so tired of Jesse being jealous of Kyle. "I thought we were done talking about this."

"I did, too, until I found out more about him."

"You've been spying on Kyle? You have nothing better to do with your time?"

"I haven't been spying on him. I got this information from my cousin, Travis."

"The one who lives in Kansas City?"

"Yeah. He was in town yesterday so we went to lunch and as we were leaving, we saw your boyfriend coming out of the grocery store."

"You better not have said anything to him."

"I didn't. I ignored him, but Travis kept looking at him. He said the guy looked familiar. He called just now to tell me he remembered where he'd seen him."

"Which was where?"

"At a town like two hours from here. There's nothing there other than a bar and a gas station."

Kyle didn't mention leaving town. It's not like I expect him to tell me everything but taking off for a two hour drive seems like something he might want to explain, especially since he's always saying he needs to stay home and write.

"When did he see him there?" I ask.

"Maybe a month ago? Could've been longer. He couldn't remember the exact day. He said he saw him go into the bar."

My gut is telling me this isn't good. That Kyle is trying to hide something. Something he doesn't want me knowing about. But I love Kyle and have to trust him. Maybe he was doing research for the book, but then why wouldn't he tell me?

"So he went in to get a drink," I say. "Big deal."

"He went during the day. The place is only open at night."

"Yeah? So? What are you saying?"

"Travis said the place is known for dealing."

"Dealing *what*? Drugs?" I suddenly feel anxious and a little sick. Kyle wouldn't do drugs, would he? I see him all the time and he never acts like he's on something.

"Drugs and...other stuff."

"Like what?"

"Guns. If you need to get a gun without people knowing, that's where you go."

"And how would Travis know this?"

"His dad got one there. He said they had all kinds, and if they don't have what you need they can usually find it for the right price."

"So your uncle is a criminal."

"He used to be. He's not now. He got the gun a few years ago. Tried to rob a convenience store and got caught."

"If it was that long ago, then how do you know this place is still selling guns?"

"Because my uncle knows people who still get them there. You can also get burner phones, knives, fake IDs. The place is basically a shop for people who are up to some bad shit. And your boyfriend was there. Travis saw him go in the building."

"That doesn't mean anything. Why was Travis even there?"

"He has a buddy nearby that he rides motorcycles with. They were meeting at a parking lot that's behind the bar. While he was waiting for his friend, he saw Kyle pull up and go inside. He didn't see him come out. His friend got there and they took off."

"Then you have no idea what Kyle was doing there. He could've just stopped there to use the bathroom."

"Dammit, Sage." He sits back. "When are you going to open your damn eyes and see that this guy isn't who you think he is? He didn't just happen to end up there. He went there looking for something. Drugs. A gun. Is that really the type of guy you want to be with?"

"Like you haven't done drugs?" I give him a blank stare.

"Yeah, I smoke pot now and then, but that's it. And I don't have to drive two hours to find it. You can get that shit anywhere. Kyle purposely went to that town to get something and I'm guessing it's a gun. The question is, why? He's hiding something, Sage. He's not who you think he is."

I get up. "I'm not listening to this. I know you hate Kyle but making up stories about him is wrong. Have you been spreading this story around town?"

"No." He stands up. "But I was gonna call up Josh and have him look into it."

"There's nothing to look into. Your stupid cousin saw Kyle go into a bar. That doesn't prove anything."

"It does, because nothing good happens at that bar. It's a front for bad shit."

"Then why don't you tell Josh about the bar? Have him get the cops who have jurisdiction in that town to look into it."

He rubs the back of his neck. "I'm not getting involved in that shit. I don't want people coming after me. I'm telling you this because I care about you, Sage. I always knew there was something not right with that guy and now I have proof."

"You don't have proof of anything. You're just making assumptions." I go to the door and open it. "You need to get back to work. And I need to go on break. Where's Helen? Have you seen her?"

"She had a dentist appointment. She won't be back for an hour."

"That's right. I forgot about that. But I still need to go on break."

He walks up to me. "Are you going home to him tonight? Even after what I told you?"

"What you told me doesn't matter. I love Kyle, and I know him a lot better than you."

"He was there, Sage. He was at that bar. I'm not making it up."

"But you have no idea what he was doing there." I motion to the door. "Go. You have customers waiting."

He shakes his head as he leaves. "Good luck on your trip. Hope you make it back."

He seriously thinks Kyle's going to do something to me? Like what? Kill me with the illegal gun he supposedly bought?

The rest of the afternoon I'm on edge, worrying if any of what Jesse said could be true, and if so, what it means. If Kyle really did go there to get a gun, what would he be using it for? Protection? Because he doesn't feel safe living out in the middle of nowhere? If that were true, then why not get one legally? Is there a reason he can't? Does he have some kind of criminal record?

In my heart, I don't believe he's done anything bad. Then again, I didn't think my dad would scam people out of their life savings.

When I get home, I shower and change clothes, then go over to Kyle's house.

"How was work?" he asks as he greets me at the door with a kiss.

"It was okay." I go inside and set my purse down in the kitchen. "What do you want for dinner?" I ask, opening the fridge.

He comes over to me. "What's going on?"

"What do you mean?" I search the fridge, which is nearly empty since we're going out of town.

"You're acting strange."

"No, I'm not." Or am I? I was trying not to, but I guess I can't hide it. What Jesse said is driving me crazy and I really want to ask Kyle about it.

"Hey." He closes the fridge and leads me to the table to sit down. "What's going on? Did something happen at work today?"

"Um...yeah, kind of." I just need to say it. Otherwise I won't be able to stop worrying and the trip I've been looking forward to for weeks will be ruined.

"What is it?"

"Jesse talked to me today."

"About what?"

"About..." I pause. "About you."

"What about me?"

"His cousin was in town yesterday and when they were out having lunch, they saw you and apparently his cousin recognized you."

Kyle sits up straighter, his shoulders stiffening. "Recognized me from where?"

"He said he saw you in some small town like two hours from here. It's not even really a town. Just a gas station and a bar. His cousin said he saw you go into the bar." I pause again, my stomach turning somersaults from my nerves. "Is it true? Were you there?"

"Yeah," he says casually, as if he has nothing to hide. "I was taking a drive on my motorcycle and I needed to stop, but the place wasn't open."

At least he's not lying. He admitted he was there and he admitted it was closed.

"Jesse's cousin said you went in."

"I did. I wanted something to drink. I didn't know it was closed until the guy running the place told me."

"But he still let you in?"

"Yeah. It was kind of strange."

"Strange how?"

"It's just strange that the place was even there. It was a ghost town. There was nothing there but some old abandoned buildings. I wondered how the place stayed in business."

"Jesse's cousin said they um...sell things." My heart is beating faster. I'm so afraid of what Kyle might tell me. I don't want him to be bad. I love him and don't want to find out he's been lying to me this whole time, pretending to be someone he's not. I can't handle that. After everything with my dad, I can't handle finding out that another person I trusted, a person I love, lied to me.

"He said they sell things other than liquor. Things like drugs and um...guns." There. I said it. I didn't directly accuse him of anything but I hinted at it.

My heart's beating out of my chest as I wait for his reaction.

"They *do* sell those things," he says. "But I didn't know that when I went there."

Given the even tone of his voice and his casual demeanor, I don't think he's lying. I really don't think he knew they sold that stuff.

A bad guy would know about places like that. An innocent man wouldn't.

I relax, my heart slowing back to normal. "So what happened?"

"I went in there and had a beer. I was dying of thirst. I'd been riding for two hours in the hot sun."

"How'd you know they sold drugs? Did the guy tell you?"

"Yeah, he asked if I wanted some."

"And what'd you say?"

"I told him no," he says, defensively. "Do you really think I'd do drugs?"

"It was just a question. Did he try to sell you anything else?"

"No. But as I was sitting there, I was starting to realize why the bar was out there in the middle of nowhere. It was a place where people could buy stuff without getting caught. I started to feel like I wasn't safe. Like if I walked out of there, I might run into trouble. That maybe I'd be followed. The guy had already hinted at what was going on there and if I acted clueless, he might think I was playing him."

"Playing him how?"

"He might think I was there to check out the place and tell the cops. Or maybe he'd think I WAS a cop. So I decided to play along and pretend I was there to get something other than a beer."

"But you didn't actually buy anything."

"Actually, I did. I bought a gun."

"What?" My heart's racing again. "Why would you buy a gun?"

"Because I don't feel safe living out here. If something ever happened it'd take a half hour before the cops even got here. Same with you. I got the gun to protect us both."

Is he telling the truth? It seems like he is and his answer actually makes sense. He had to make sure he'd get out of there safely. Pretending to be one of the bad guys was actually smart, if that's really what he was doing.

I'm so confused. I want to believe him but there's a hint of doubt nagging at me, telling me there's more to the story.

"You know I don't like guns," I say.

"Which is why I didn't tell you. It's locked away. You'll never even see it."

"Have you used a gun before?"

"Yeah. My dad and I used to shoot at the range when I was in high school. I'm not great at it but if I had to protect myself, I could." He puts his hand on mine. "I'm sorry I didn't tell you. I just worried you'd be mad that I bought it."

"I'm worried you're going to caught. You didn't buy it legally. You could get in trouble for that."

"Not if no one finds out. I'll never even use the thing unless I have to." He stands up and pulls on me to do the same. And then he hugs me. "Let's not talk about this. We're officially on vacation now. Tomorrow morning we'll get on a plane and a few hours later you'll get to see your mom."

"I'm really looking forward to that."

He pulls back. "Do you have everything packed?"

"Yeah, but I should probably check the flight time to make sure nothing's changed."

"Then go ahead and do that and I'll start dinner."

"We don't have anything. The fridge is cleared out."

He opens the cupboard and takes out the peanut butter. "PB&J?" He smiles. "Simple yet delicious. And something I know how to make."

I smile back. "Okay, but I want extra jelly on mine. And make it grape."

"Got it."

He's not acting strange or nervous so I don't think he's hiding anything. I think the story he told me is true. I hate that

I'm even questioning it but stupid Jesse has my head all messed up.

I'm not letting Jesse's suspicions ruin my trip. The rest of the night, I try to relax and focus on tomorrow. My mom already has a place picked for dinner. She told me about it last week. It's in her neighborhood and has a funny name, which I can't remember right now, but my mom always laughs when she says it.

***

The next day, as we're going through airport security, Kyle gets pulled aside by one of the security guys. The guy is holding Kyle's driver's license as the two of them talk. Then he gives it back and Kyle walks over to me.

"What's wrong?" I ask.

"Nothing." He puts his license back in his wallet.

"Why was he questioning you?"

"It was just a mix-up. He thought it was an expired license but he just read it wrong."

That's odd. The security people look at licenses all day. How could they misread it?

We get on the plane and I take a short nap so I'm rested when we arrive. My mom meets us at the airport. When I see her, I run up to her and give her a huge hug.

"Mom, I've missed you so much."

"I've missed you too honey."

I stand back and look at her. She seems different. She's lost some weight, probably from all the walking she does here in the city. And her hair is shorter, cut in a cute bob. "You look great, Mom! I love your hair!"

"I just got it cut. I wasn't sure about having it this short but I really like it." She sees Kyle approaching. "And you must be Kyle."

"Yes." He shakes her hand. "It's nice to meet you. Sage talks about you all the time."

My mom smiles at me. "She talks about you too."

"Should we go?" I ask, because people are filing past us, acting annoyed that we're blocking their path. "We can talk more when we get to your apartment."

Her apartment is across town and it takes almost an hour by cab to get there. It's on the second floor and tiny. So tiny that it feels almost claustrophobic. The kitchen is part of the living room, with the couch just a few feet away from the tiny stove and refrigerator. Everything is so small it reminds me of the dollhouse I had as a kid.

"What do you think?" my mom asks.

"It's nice," I say, trying to be positive. I wouldn't want to live here but she seems to like it and that's all that matters.

"I know it's small but I'm used to it now. And I don't spend much time here. I'm always at the studio." Her face lights up at the mention of her studio. "Let's grab lunch and then I'll take you over there."

We go to lunch at a place just down the street from where she lives. The place is so crowded that people are bumping into me as I sit at the table. Living in a small, quiet town, I'm not used to all these people and all the noise and activity. It doesn't seem to bother Kyle at all, but being from L.A., I'm sure he's used to crowds.

"So Kyle," my mom says, "tell me about your book."

He gives her a summary of the story and the two of them continue to talk. I don't interrupt because I really want them to get to know each other. I can see myself having a future with Kyle so having the two of them like each other is important to me.

Over the next couple days, my mom takes Kyle and me all over Manhattan, to tourist spots like the Statue of Liberty, but also to places that most tourists don't go, like small, almost hidden, art galleries.

There are so many artists here. My mom fits right in. It's like she's starting her life over again, going back to what she always wanted to do.

Seeing how happy she is makes me feel better about her staying here after the summer. She hasn't said that's what she's going to do yet but I'm going to tell her she should. I know it's what she wants. She just won't tell me. I think she's waiting for my approval, which she doesn't need. As long as she's happy, I'll go along with whatever she wants, even though I'll miss her terribly.

It's now our last night here and we go to dinner at a seafood place on the Upper West Side. It's really expensive so I'm surprised my mom picked it. She's making good money now, but still, this is a lot to spend on dinner.

"We're having a guest join us," she says as we're looking at the menu. "He'll be a few minutes late."

"A guest?" I look up from the menu. "Who is it?"

"A man who wants to commission me to do a painting."

My phone rings and I check it. Must be a wrong number. I don't recognize it.

"Why is he coming to dinner? Wouldn't it be better if you met with him without Kyle and me?"

"This was the only time he could meet. He's a very busy man. We don't have to talk business all night. I told him you and your boyfriend would be here and he was fine with that. He said it's always nice to meet an artist's family. He even offered to pay for dinner, which I told him he didn't need to, but he insisted."

My phone rings again. It's the same number that just called. It's a Kansas area code but nobody I know.

"What does he do for a living?" Kyle asks.

My mom doesn't answer. She must see whoever this man is because she's waving him over. I look back and see him walking toward us. He has dark hair and dark eyes and is wearing a black suit and tie. He looks rich, but I guess you have to be in order to commission artwork. I wonder how much he's paying her.

My mom stands up and smiles. "Mr. Bonacci."

Kyle backs his chair up so fast it falls to the ground. I go to pick it up but he's in my way so I just stand beside him.

Mr. Bonacci lets out a short laugh. "Well, what a surprise."

He's staring at Kyle and Kyle is staring back at him.

"Do you two know each other?" my mom asks.

"We do indeed," Mr. Bonacci says. "This is my son, Jonathan."

Wait—what? His son? He's obviously confused. He didn't even get Kyle's name right.

I look at Kyle to correct him but he doesn't. He doesn't say a word, his eyes locked on the man.

"Your son?" my mom asks. "Kyle is your son?"

"Yes," Mr. Bonnaci says. "And his name isn't Kyle. It's Jonathan."

What the hell is going on here? Is this man telling the truth? Kyle is his son? And his name isn't Kyle?

I look at Kyle to deny it but he's just standing there, not saying anything.

I think I'm going to be sick. Everyone warned me about him but I didn't listen. I trusted my instincts, which told me he was just a regular guy. But my instincts were wrong. He's a liar. He conned me into thinking he was someone else. But why?

What else don't I know about him? What is he hiding?

CHAPTER TWENTY-SIX

Kyle

What the hell is my father doing here? When I called Hank from the hotel last night he said my father was still in Boston.

Now that he's found me, I'll never get out of the city alive. He'll have his guys track me down and kill me.

"Jonathan and I have been estranged," my father says. "He ran off last May and I've been trying to find him, hoping to resolve our differences."

Sage is looking at me, completely confused. I have to tell her what's going on before my father has her believing some story that isn't true.

"Excuse us," I say, taking Sage's hand. "We need to leave for a moment."

"Are you kidding?" Sage yanks her hand back. "I'm not going anywhere with you! You lied to me! You told me your name was Kyle and that you were a writer from California!"

The waiter approaches us. "If you'd like to continue this, you'll need to step outside so as not to disturb our other patrons."

I lean down to Sage, lowering my voice. "I promise you I'll explain everything if you come with me." She eyes me suspiciously, like she thinks I'm dangerous, so I say, "We'll go to the lobby. We won't leave the building. I swear."

"Sage, why don't we sit down?" her mom says. "We'll get this all straightened out."

"Sage, please," I urge.

"We'll be right back," she says to her mom.

"Don't go too far," I hear my father say as we're leaving. "I wouldn't want to lose you again."

I glance back and see the sinister grin on his face.

That man is not the father I know. I never got along well with my dad. I knew Cain was his favorite son but I accepted that, thinking we just didn't click or something. I had no idea my father was capable of murder. I didn't know he could be that evil.

The restaurant is in a hotel. Sage and I go to the lobby and I lead her to a quiet spot down from the reception area. The place is crowded and there are security cameras everywhere so I know she'll feel safe here. It pains me that she thinks it's even possible I'd ever hurt her.

"You're not Kyle?" she asks, crossing her arms over her chest.

"No. My name is Jonathan and that man in there is my father."

"You said he lives in Sacramento! You said he sold insurance and—"

"Yeah, I lied. He lives here. And he doesn't sell insurance. He owns an import business."

"Why the hell would you—"

"Please, just let me finish."

I need to say this quickly. If we stay out here too long, my father will come looking for us. I'm sure he's already texted his guys to let them know I'm here.

I lower my voice. "My father tried to kill me."

"What?" Sage scrunches her face and tilts her head, which she does when something doesn't make sense. I know her so well. I've never known anyone as well as I know her.

"I know it sounds crazy but I promise you it's true. It's why I had to go on the run and hide out in a small town where nobody knew me. It's why I had to change my name and find a new identity."

"Why would your dad want to kill you?" She sounds skeptical. She doesn't believe me.

"Last May I saw something I shouldn't have. My dad did something. Something bad. And I found out he'd been doing other bad things. I can't tell you what they are. All I can tell you is that when my dad found out I knew the truth he told me to keep quiet but he didn't trust that I would. So he hired some guys to kill me. There were two of them. They held a gun to my head." I hear the nervousness in my voice just talking about that night.

"You're making this up." She uses a hushed tone but it's filled with anger. "You lied to me and now you're making up this story to cover your lies."

"Sage, I promise you, I'm not lying." I hold my hand out between us. "Look at this. Look at my hand shaking. That wouldn't be happening if I wasn't scared for my life."

She pauses a moment, that skeptical look still on her face, but my shaking hand and anxious voice must convince her that at least part of my story is true because she says, "If they held guns to your head, then how did you get away?"

"It was a warning. If I didn't keep quiet they'd be back, and next time they'd shoot me. I packed a bag that night and got the hell out of there. I left my car behind and took trains and buses until I reached Kansas City. I didn't plan to stop there. It was a last minute decision. I'd never been to Kansas and didn't know anyone there so I thought it'd be a good place to settle down for a month or two until I figured out how to go back without being killed."

"Is that when you got the motorcycle?"

"Yeah. I took some of my dad's money before I left. He stashes cash all over the house. I took as much as I could because I didn't know how long I'd be gone."

"If this is all true, why would you ever go back?"

"For Cain, my brother. He's 12. I don't want him in that house with my dad. I don't think my dad would hurt him but I never thought he'd hurt ME and look what happened. I don't want Cain accidentally seeing something and having the same thing happen to him that happened to me." I take a breath because I've been talking so fast. "I've been trying to find a way to get him out of there while also trying not to get killed. That's why I got the gun. In case they found me, I needed a weapon, and I couldn't get one legally."

"Why didn't you tell me this before? You know you can trust me. I would never tell anyone this."

"Maybe, or maybe you *would* in an attempt to try to help me. I know you, Sage, and I know what a big heart you have. You wouldn't be able to just stand by and do nothing. You'd try to do something, or tell someone, both of which could get me killed. Or *both* of us killed."

"Okay, I might've told someone but I would've told you before I did it."

"It doesn't matter. You know now and I'm asking you to stay out of it. There are other people involved. They've been trying to help."

"What other people?"

"Can I have your phone?" I hold my hand out and look around to make sure no one's coming for me. She hands me her phone and I see several missed calls from Hank. "Why didn't you answer this?"

"Because it was a wrong number."

"It wasn't a wrong number. It was Hank. He was trying to call you because he couldn't call me. He needed to warn me that my father had left Boston."

"Hank? You mean, Hank, the guy who mows your lawn?"

"Yeah." I call his number as I talk. "He found my money stash and I didn't want him reporting me to the police so I had to tell him what's going on."

"Why would he report you? How much do have?"

"A hundred thousand," I say as Hank's phone rings.

"Holy shit," I hear Sage mumble. "That's a lot of money."

"Kyle?" I hear Hank say.

"Yeah, it's me."

"I've been trying to call you. Your girlfriend wouldn't pick up."

"Yeah, she thought it was a wrong number. What the hell's going on?"

"He got away from us. They lost track of him and then all of a sudden he showed up in Manhattan. You're at her mom's place, right? You need to stay there until—"

"I'm at restaurant. With my father."

"What did you say?"

"My father is here at the restaurant. Sage's mom took us to this place for dinner and my father showed up. At our table."

"What the hell are you talking about?"

"He hired Sage's mom to make him a painting. He was here to talk about it. He didn't know I'd be here. He didn't know I was dating Sage."

"Shit! Where are you now?"

"In the hotel lobby that's connected to the restaurant. My father's in there with Sage's mom."

"Are you sure? He didn't leave, did he?"

"He couldn't have. The restaurant exits through the lobby. I would've seen him."

"Kyle." Sage nudges my arm.

I follow her gaze to the other side of the lobby and see my father coming out of the restaurant. He's walking toward us.

A chill shivers down me. "Shit."

"What is it?" Hank asks. "Do you see him?"

"Yeah. He's coming toward me."

"Run. Get the hell out of there."

"I can't." I look around. "There's nowhere to go. And if I ran, he'd track me down. Or his guys would."

"I'll get the police out there. Just stay where you are."

"No! Don't! The police would never believe my story. I can't prove it. My dad would tell them I made it all up."

My father makes his way through the groups of people in the lobby, slowly, methodically, like an animal approaching his prey. How did I go all these years and not notice he had this dark, evil side to him? Did he really hide it that well or did I just not pay attention?

"Go to your house," Hank says.

"What?"

"Just do it. Go there with your father."

"Then I'm on his turf. Isolated. He'll kill me for sure."

"It's not his turf. It was your house, too, until just recently. You know where he keeps his weapons, right?"

"Hank, I don't have time to talk about this. My dad is just a few feet away."

Our eyes have been locked this entire time, but my father looks away when some woman takes hold of his arm. She says something to him and smiles. He looks annoyed as he says something back.

Hank's been talking but I didn't hear what he said.

"Kyle?"

"Yeah, hurry up. My dad got stopped by a woman who seems to know him but he's trying to get rid of her." I watch as he pulls away from her and turns back to me, that evil grin on his face. "Shit, he's heading this way."

"Your brother's there, right? At the house?"

"I don't know. Probably. Why?"

"Use him as protection. Your father won't harm you if your brother is around."

"Why the hell would I even do this? What exactly am I supposed to do once I'm at the house?"

My father approaches Sage and me. "You two have been out here for quite awhile." He looks at Sage. "Your mother would like you to join her. Go ahead. I'd like to have a word with my son."

Without saying goodbye to Hank, I end the call and give the phone back to Sage.

"Kyle and I are done talking," she says to my dad. "We were just heading back in."

"I understand that, but I'd still like to have a word with him." He smirks at me. "And his name is Jonathan, not Kyle. I'm sorry he's deceived you for so long." He nods toward the restaurant. "Go join your mother. We'll be in there shortly."

"Go ahead," I tell her. I can tell she doesn't want to, but she can't be part of this.

Once she's gone, my father grabs my arm and yanks me back a few feet to the hallway that leads to the restrooms.

"So *Kyle*," he says, emphasizing my fake name, "I hear you've been living in Kansas."

"What else did she tell you?" I need to find out how much he knows. I hope Sage's mom didn't tell him much.

"That apparently you're a writer." He chuckles. "You made up quite a tale, didn't you?"

"I learned how to lie from the best," I say through gritted teeth. I yank my arm free. "So what's your plan? Are your men waiting outside to kill me?"

"I don't know what you're talking about. In fact, I don't even know why you ran."

"Your men held fucking guns to my head," I say in a hushed tone. "You're going to pretend you weren't responsible for that?"

He looks around. "You're clearly confused. I would never harm my own son."

"You would if you thought I was going to rat you out to the cops. Destroy your little side business."

"Let's go home and discuss this."

"There's nothing to discuss. I'm leaving." I turn to walk away but he grabs my arm and pulls me back.

"We're going home." He looks around to make sure no one is watching us, then slowly lifts his suit jacket, showing me the gun.

I'm not surprised he has one but it still sends a chill through me. I try to relax and act like it doesn't bother me.

"You just said you're not going to kill me," I say, glaring at him.

He smirks. "I need to talk to you, Kyle. That's all this is about. Now let's go."

"We're in the middle of dinner. If we leave now, Sage and her mom will want to know why."

"I'll tell them we need to talk. I'm sure they'll be okay with that." He gets his phone out and texts someone. I'm assuming it's Sage's mom. Moments later, a text comes back and he smiles. "She said she understands and that we'll discuss the painting later."

"I need to talk to Sage. She's going to wonder what's going on."

"You didn't tell her?" he asks, his brows raised. "I find that hard to believe."

"I've lied to her this whole time. Why would I stop now?"

He can't find out Sage knows the truth. If he does, he'll go after her.

"So you're not in love with the girl," he comments.

"No," I lie. "She was just something to pass the time."

He grins. "Like father like son."

Since my mom died, my dad's been with countless women. Honestly, I think he was with other women even when my mom was alive. I think that's why they slept in different rooms. My mom said it was because my dad snored but I think that was just an excuse.

"My car's in the garage," he says. "Let's go."

If I go with him I could be heading to my death. But at this point I can't escape him. If I tried, he'd have his men track me down and kill me. I'm better off going with him, having it just be him and me.

"Where are we going?" I ask as he drives through the city.

"To the house."

"Why? What are we doing there?" I try to hide the anxiousness I'm feeling and pretend we're just having a conversation, but in my head, all I can see is an image of him holding a gun to my head the minute we arrive at the house. Or maybe he'll have one of his men there waiting to do it so he doesn't have to deal with the mess.

"We're going to talk and figure out what to do."

"About what?"

He glances at me. "Are we really still playing this game?"

"Why are you doing this? I would've kept quiet. I never would've said a word."

"A promise I've heard one too many times."

"What does that mean? Someone reported you?"

"She would've but wasn't able to."

"Who's *she*? Who are you talking about?"

"We'll talk when we get home."

He's quiet the rest of the drive and I'm left wondering who it was that found out about him and what he did to her. I'm sure he killed her but when? How long ago did this happen? Even all these months later, I'm still trying to wrap my mind around the fact that my own father is capable of murder.

As we pull up to the house, adrenaline courses through me, my fight-or-flight instinct kicking in, telling me to run. As he pulls in the garage, I try my door handle but it's locked. He shuts off the car, then closes the garage door before finally unlocking my door.

I get out but still feel trapped. He's got me here alone, with no witnesses to see what he's about to do. I can't let him do this. My life is not ending this way.

"After you," he says, holding open the door to the house. We go into the hallway that's just off the kitchen.

"I'm going to use the bathroom," I say, heading toward it.

"Later," he barks, grabbing my arm and shoving me forward. I could try one of my martial arts moves on him but he's been trained in it for a lot longer than me so would probably end up taking me down.

He brings me to the living room and pushes me down on the couch, then keeps his eyes on me as he goes to the bar cart and pours himself a drink.

"Where's Cain?" I ask.

"At a friend's house." He finishes off whatever he just poured himself, then refills his glass. "He misses you. Asks about you all the time."

Cain's just a kid but he's smart. He knows it was me calling him the past few months. He'd say my name and wait for me to respond. When I didn't, he'd say he was okay and then wait for me to hang up. He knew I was calling to check on him, and the fact that I just listened and didn't say anything told him I didn't want to be found. He was smart enough not to tell Dad that I'd called. He may not know why, but he knows the reason I left somehow involves our dad.

"What did you tell him?" I ask. "When he asked where I went, what did you tell him?"

"That you were struggling with some issues and had to leave."

"What issues?"

"Substance abuse. I told him your drinking had gotten out of hand."

I huff. "You told him I'm in rehab? Is that what you told other people too?"

"I had to tell them *something*." He finishes his drink and sets the glass down. "They weren't surprised. You have a history of being out of control."

He's referring to the time I got arrested for public intox. I was 21 and it was right after my birthday. It wasn't a big deal but he made it seem like I'd committed a crime. He took my car away for three months.

"I wasn't out of control," I say, but then realize it's a waste of time to argue about this. It doesn't matter. I don't care what he told people. The only thing I care about right now is what he's going to do to me. I'm also wondering what else he's done.

Now that it's just the two of us alone in a room, I wonder if he'd tell me the truth.

"Who was she?" I ask.

"Who?"

"You mentioned a woman earlier. You said she knew too much. What did you do to her?"

He casually walks to the other side of the room. "I didn't do anything. It was an unfortunate accident."

"That's a lie. You made it look like an accident to cover up what you did."

He stops and turns to me, his brow furrowed. "You know?"

"Know what?"

He stares at me, crossing his arms over his chest. "Is that why you ran? Because you knew I'd follow through on my threat?"

"What are you talking about?"

"You knew what I did to her, so you knew I'd do the same to you."

"I don't—"

"It wasn't the same. Her actions were intentional. You just stumbled into something you shouldn't have seen."

I still have no idea what he's talking about, but curious if he'll tell me more, I pretend that I do.

"What was she going to do?" I ask. "Did she tell you?"

"She had a friend at the FBI." He huffs and shakes his head. "She called him a friend but I knew what he was. I followed them to his house more than once. I had a suspicion it was going on. She'd done it before and I knew the signs."

So this woman was cheating on him. But my father was cheating on my mother with this woman so he shouldn't have gotten upset over it. Cheaters attract cheaters. He should've known this woman wouldn't stay faithful to him.

"If she'd cheated on you before, then why did you stay with her?"

"Because of you," he says as though that should be obvious.

"Me? What do I have to do with this?"

He chuckles. "You don't know?"

"Know what?"

He returns to the drink cart and fills his glass again. "I thought that's why you left. I assumed you found out."

"Found out *what*? I left because you tried to kill me."

"That was a warning. If you'd kept quiet, you would've been fine."

"I DID keep quiet," I lie. "I haven't told anyone. Now tell me what you were saying. What do you think I knew?"

He swirls his drink in his glass. "When she cheated the first time, she became pregnant. She swore it was mine so I took her back, not wanting to break up our family."

He's trying to tell me something but I'm not sure what.

And then it hits me and everything suddenly makes sense. Why I've never connected with him. Why he loves Cain but not me. Why he's willing to kill me.

"It was Mom," I say. "The woman you're talking about is Mom."

"My beloved wife," he says, gripping his glass.

"I'm not your son."

"No." He sets his glass down and pulls out his gun. "Which is what makes this so much easier."

CHAPTER TWENTY-SEVEN

Kyle

"Dad," I say, trying to muster up any drop of fatherly instinct he has for me. He can't completely hate me. He raised me. He did at least a few father-son activities with me over the years. It's his hatred of my mother and what she did that's fueling his rage right now. "I didn't do anything wrong. Like you said, I stumbled into something I shouldn't have. I promise I won't tell anyone what I saw or what I heard. I'll go away. I'll never come back."

"It's not that simple. You're like your mother. You can't be trusted to keep quiet."

"I have nothing to tell anyone. I don't even know what it is you're doing. I saw stuff but I don't know what it means." I slowly get up.

"Don't move." He steps closer, his gun aimed at me.

"Even if I knew what you were up to and wanted to tell someone, it's not like I could prove anything. I'm not a threat, Dad. You don't need to do this."

"Maybe I want to." He sneers. "Maybe I'm sick of looking at HIM whenever I look at you."

"Then I'll go away like I said. You'll never have to see me again."

I'm trying to think of a way out of this but my mind keeps going back to what he said about my mom and how she died. She was allergic to shellfish. So allergic that even a small amount could be fatal if she didn't get a shot of epinephrine right away. The night she died, she was with my dad at a party at someone's house. She accidentally ate something that had remnants of shellfish either on it or in it. She went into anaphylactic shock. Her epinephrine pen jammed and her extra one wasn't in her purse. She died on the way to the hospital.

He did something to that pen and made sure she didn't have an extra. He obviously put something in her food that night. And because he's a greedy bastard, he sued the people who hosted the party as well as the caterer, and won. The asshole killed my mom and made millions off her death.

"Dad?" I hear Cain's voice and whip around to see him coming down the stairs.

"Cain, what are you doing here?" my father yells.

"I got home early. What's going on?"

"Go to your room! Now!"

Cain remains on the stairs, looking confused. He's wearing track pants and a t-shirt and looks taller than when I saw him last. He also looks older. I wasn't gone that long. How did he change so much in just a few months?

"Why do you have a gun?" he asks, sounding scared as he continues down the stairs.

"I said go to your room!" my father yells even louder. "Right now!"

"No," Cain quietly says. He comes up beside me and stops. "You can't hurt my brother. I won't let you."

He's such a good kid. He always has been. He has a huge heart.

"He's not your brother," my dad sputters. "Now get upstairs! And don't come down until I tell you to!"

"What are you going to do now?" I ask my father, putting my arm around Cain. "Kill us *both*? Are you going to kill your own son? Your ONLY son?"

Cain looks up at me. "What do you mean? You're not my brother?"

I squeeze his shoulder. "I'll always be your brother. That'll never change."

We both look back at our father.

"Get away from him," he says to Cain.

"No," Cain says defiantly. He usually doesn't stand up to our father. I'm the only one who ever does that.

"Then you'll be seeing something you don't want to see." My father aims the gun at my chest. "You sure you don't want to leave, Cain?"

He's challenging him but Cain remains at my side. He's shaking. He's so scared.

I don't want him seeing this. Knowing I'm not my father's real son, I have no doubt he'll pull the trigger and I don't want Cain to have that memory.

"Go upstairs," I tell him, letting him go.

"I'm not letting him hurt you."

"He won't," I assure him. "Dad and I were just talking and things got out of hand. He's just angry. We'll talk it out."

Cain pauses, then says to our father, "I won't let you hurt him." He steps in front of me, in front of the gun.

"Cain, stop it!" I grab him and pull him back. I try to push him to the side but he keeps fighting me. Then he turns and grabs hold of me in a hug position, his arms so tight that I can't get them loose.

"Listen to your brother," my father says. "This is between him and me."

Cain's quietly crying now. "No. Please don't hurt him."

My heart aches for Cain. He's only 12. He shouldn't be seeing this. He shouldn't be trying to protect me from the man who raised us. This is so wrong.

Cain lets me go and storms up to our father, his body just inches from the gun. "Put it down!"

"Cain, stop!" I come up behind him but he shoves me back. Hard. Harder than he's ever done.

He's up to something. He has a plan. A plan I'm sure I wouldn't agree with if I knew what it was, but one I can't stop. Cain is stubborn like me. If he's determined to do something, he'll find a way to do it.

"Back away," my father says to Cain. "You're going to get hurt."

"Put it down." Cain sets his eyes on our father. I remain just behind him, afraid if I move, one, or both of us, will get shot.

"Cain, just go to your room," I tell him.

"If I go, he'll shoot you. I'm not leaving." I notice his foot make a slight twitch. His hands fist and release. He swallows. He's about to do something. Something we're probably both going to regret.

I'm about to grab him when he suddenly swings his leg out and slams it into the side of our father's knee so hard that his knee buckles and he drops the gun.

"Shit!" He goes to grab the gun as Cain charges him, putting all his weight into it.

As my father falls to the ground, Cain tackling him, I quickly grab the gun.

"Get off me!" my father yells at Cain.

"Cain, get up," I say.

Cain looks back and sees me holding the gun. He slowly stands up. "I did what you taught me."

"I know, buddy. Now back away."

Last year Cain was being bullied by a kid at school so I taught him a few self-defense moves, one of which was that kick to the side of the knee move. It worked on the bully but I'm surprised it worked on our dad, given that Cain is so much smaller than him.

"Go call for help," I tell Cain as he steps back. "Call nine one one." I hold the gun directly over my father. "Tell him Dad's been shot."

"You wouldn't do it," my father says, slowly standing up. His suit and shirt are wrinkled, a look I've never seen on him. He's always so meticulous about his appearance, probably so nobody would ever guess he has this dark, seedy side. That's his true self. The man in the tailored suit is just a role he plays, just like the role of grieving widower and doting father, roles he never played very convincingly. Even right after my mom died, he didn't seem that sad. At her funeral, he didn't shed a tear. Now I know why.

He killed my mom. And Cain's mom. He took our mother away and made us think it was an accident.

"An eye for an eye," I say, aiming the gun at him. "You killed our—" I stop because I don't want Cain to know the truth about our mom. Knowing what really happened would be too much for him.

My father glances at Cain. "Your brother is playing you. He's not the man you think he is."

I keep my eyes on my father. "You can say whatever you want. He won't believe you. He knows you're a liar. Cain, call the police. Right now."

"My phone's upstairs."

"Then go get it. Hurry up."

"If you call them, he's dead," my father says.

Cain looks at him confused. "You can't hurt him. He has the gun."

"Don't listen to him, Cain. Just go upstairs and call the police."

"I have people who will kill him," my father says. "You call the police, they'll take me away but your brother won't live to testify against me. I have people who will get to him first. He won't live if you make that call."

"He's lying, Cain. Just go."

I know that sick bastard is telling the truth. He'll send people after me. He'll try to get me killed. But if Cain knows that, he won't call. He'll try to protect me.

"Remember Jerry?" my father says to Cain. "And Paul?"

Cain nods repeatedly. The poor kid looks scared to death.

"They work for me. If I tell them to hurt your brother, they will. So if you call the police right now, you'll be responsible for your brother's death. You don't want to do that, do you?"

Fuck. I can't believe he's doing this. Using my little brother to save himself. It's not going to work. I'll shoot the bastard if I have to. I didn't want to, but he's backed me into a corner.

"Get the phone and I'll make the call," I tell Cain.

He looks at our father. "I...I can't. He'll do something."

My father grins. "Good boy." He reaches for Cain and I shoot. I aimed for the ground just to startle him and get him away from Cain but instead I hit his foot.

"Fuck!" He stumbles back, then grabs hold of the back of a chair, trying to regain his balance. He lifts his foot and stares at it like he can't believe what just happened. "What the fuck did you do?"

"Touch him again and I'll shoot higher," I say, my hand trembling. I just shot my father. I know it was just his foot, but still. I've never shot anyone before and it's a strange feeling.

He leans against the side of the chair and reaches his hand out. "Give me the gun."

"And have you shoot me?" I aim at his chest. "Don't move or I swear I'll shoot again."

"So how exactly does this end?" he asks in a smart-ass tone. He still thinks he's in charge, even with a gun pointed at him. "If you kill me, my men will come after you. You don't shoot me but turn me in? My men will still come after you."

"Not if they've already been caught."

His brows furrow. "Meaning what?"

"I wrote it all down."

"Wrote WHAT down?" He cringes from the pain in his foot, which is oddly satisfying to me. I feel no regrets about shooting him. He's lucky I didn't aim higher.

"I wrote down what I knew about you and your little side business. I may not know everything but I know the men you brought to the house and met with privately in your office. I overheard the phone calls. Saw the packages they left you. Saw the men who held a gun to my head. I wrote down as much detail as I could, and anything I saw or overheard that seemed strange? I wrote that down too."

"So you kept a diary," he says, mocking me. "Good for you."

"It IS good because I gave it to someone before I left."

His eyes narrow. "You said you hadn't told anyone."

"Yeah. About that. I lied."

"It doesn't matter. You have no proof of anything. It's your word against mine."

"And if you're dead, then it's just *my* word. And Cain's."

I grip the gun. I want to do it. I want to shoot him and end this. But I don't know if I can.

I hear Cain's shaky breaths from behind me. He's scared. Afraid of what I might do. After witnessing this, he knows his father is evil, but seeing him get shot? Or killed? It's too much. I can't do that to him.

"I knew you were too much of a coward," my father says. "You couldn't shoot that gun if your life depended on it. That's proof you're not my son. I'm not even your real father and you still can't shoot me."

"You're wrong." I set my eyes on his.

"And yet you haven't pulled the trigger."

"Don't!" Cain says from behind me. "Don't do it! Please don't!"

Ignoring Cain, I say to my father, "I'm not wrong. If I wanted to pull the trigger I could. But I don't want to, and that doesn't make me a coward. The coward is the person who shoots someone to get rid of their problems."

"You really don't understand how the world works, do you?" he asks.

I step closer to him, the gun still aimed at his chest. "Your world is not mine. Never was. I always knew there was something not right with you. Now I know why Mom never liked you."

"Your mother was a whore," he spits out. "She deserved what happened to her."

His words kick whatever self-control I had straight out the window. I cock the gun, holding it steady as I prepare to shoot.

"Kyle, put the gun down," someone says from behind me.

I glance back and see a dark shadow in the hallway. I can't tell who it is but the voice sounds familiar.

"Hank?" I ask, but there's no way it could be him.

"Put the gun down." He steps out from the hall into the light of the living room. It IS Hank.

My father whips his head toward Hank. "Do something!" he yells, putting on the helpless victim act. "The boy's trying to kill me! Call for help! Hurry!"

Hank ignores him, his eyes on me. "You can relax, Kyle. It's gonna be okay."

"What are you doing here?" I ask Hank, keeping the gun on my father.

"You think I'd let you come here alone?" He walks over to me. "If something happened to you, who would I have a beer with on Fridays?"

"Who the hell is this man?" my father demands.

Ignoring my father, I say to Hank, "You've been here this whole time? In New York?"

He shrugs. "It wasn't so bad. Got to see a show. Take in the sights."

"Why didn't you tell me?"

"Didn't want you to worry. You had enough to worry about." Hank turns to Cain, who's behind me. "You all right?"

I hear Cain softly say, "Yeah."

"I'm Hank. Everything's going to be okay now." Hank's deep smooth voice is soothing and consoling. Cain's shaky breaths are already sounding more steady.

"Kyle, put the gun down before someone gets hurt," Hank says.

"Not until I see him in handcuffs."

Just then, the door flies opens and five cops walk in, all with guns in their hands. They storm up to my father and read him his rights.

"What's happening?" I ask as Hank takes the gun from me.

"After you called me from the hotel, I alerted my contacts and told them what was going on. They've been tracking the men you described to us. Your father's workers. Just this morning they caught them doing a deal and arrested them. They talked to get a lesser sentence. Told us everything we needed to know." He leans close to my ear so Cain can't hear. "Your father's going to be going away for a long time."

I nod and give him a look that we'll talk later. Cain is my priority now. I pull him into my side. "You sure you're okay?"

He nods, but still looks scared to death.

I lean down to his level. "Whatever happens, I'll take care of you. I won't leave you again. I promise."

He nods and then hugs me, even tighter than before. "I missed you."

"I missed you too, buddy."

"He's lying," my father yells. I look over and see him being handcuffed. "My SON is the criminal, not me! He's the one who ran off and changed his identity!"

Cain and I watch as they take our father away. He's fighting them as they do, yelling that he's going to sue them for harassment and false arrest.

"Where's Sage?" I ask Hank.

"In the car, about a mile from here. She wanted to come with me but I wouldn't let her."

"Are you sure she's safe?"

"She's with Josh."

"Josh? Like Kansas City Josh?"

"I thought it'd be best to bring someone along and he was the most logical choice."

"The guy hates me."

"He did before he realized what was going on. After I told him, he offered to help with whatever we needed." Hank gets his phone out and sends a text. "I told them it's safe. They'll be here in a minute."

"What's gonna happen now?" Cain asks me. "Is Dad coming back?"

"I'm not sure. But whatever happens, you're going to be okay. I'll be here. I'm not leaving you. I promise."

A few minutes later, there's a knock on the door. Hank answers and Sage comes running in.

"Kyle, are you okay?" she asks, hugging me.

"Yeah, I'm fine. They took him away."

"I was so scared. I thought..." She doesn't finish the thought as her eyes do a quick check of me to make sure I'm not hurt.

"Who's Kyle?" Cain asks.

"That's what she calls me," I say. "This is Sage. Sage, this is my brother, Cain."

"His name's Jonathan," Cain says to Sage, sounding annoyed that she didn't use my real name.

She smiles and holds out her hand to him. "Hi Cain, it's good to finally meet you."

He doesn't shake her hand. "Who are you?"

"I'm dating your brother."

"She's your girlfriend?" he asks me.

"Yeah." I put my arm around her. "We met while I was away. She lives in Kansas, where I've been living."

"You live together?" he asks.

I look at Sage. "No. Not yet."

She smiles at me. "Maybe someday."

"If she lives with you, and Dad doesn't come back, where am I going to live?"

"You'll live with us," I say. "I told you, I'm not leaving you, even if I have to drag your butt to Kansas."

Josh walks in. "I checked the perimeter. Everything looks good."

"Hey, Josh," I say. "Thanks for coming."

"No problem." He pats Hank on the back. "I couldn't let the old man come here alone."

"Who you calling old?" he says to Josh. "I beat you in basketball just last week."

"He did?" I ask.

"Long story," Josh says. He looks at Cain. "You Kyle's brother?"

"His name's Jonathan," Cain says, sounding annoyed again.

"I'm Josh. Kyle—I mean, Jonathan—and I are friends."

Friends. I never would've called us friends in the past. Acquaintances, maybe, but even that would be a stretch. But having Josh come all the way out here to help me? That definitely makes him a friend. Not many people would do that.

"You like sports?" Josh asks Cain.

"Yeah."

"You play any?"

His eyes light up. "I play lacrosse at school."

The kid loves lacrosse. It's his favorite thing to do. He could talk about it for hours.

"Cain," I say, getting his attention. "Go pack a bag. We're getting out of here."

"Where are we going?"

"We're going to stay at a hotel tonight."

"Why can't we stay here?"

There's so much I need to explain to him but it's all stuff I don't want him to know. I may have to make something up. I'll figure it out later. For now, I just need us both to be safe, and until I know they've caught all the people who work for our father, I won't feel safe.

"C'mon," Josh says to Cain. "I'll help you pack."

I nod at Cain to go with him.

As they walk up the stairs, Josh says to him, "I don't know much about lacrosse. Why don't you tell me about it?"

Cain starts talking, his voice getting excited. It's good Josh asked him about lacrosse. It'll get his mind off what happened.

"Josh is good with kids," Sage says. "He runs a youth basketball team. Some of the kids are around Cain's age."

"I didn't know he did that."

"He's been doing it for years," Hank says. "I'm going to keep watch outside. Call if you need me."

"We will," Sage says. "Thanks."

When he's gone, Sage hugs me tighter than she ever has. "I was so scared for you."

"I was scared for you too. I told my father I didn't tell you anything but I don't think he believed me."

"So what are we going to do now?"

"We're going to pack up our stuff and go home."

She looks up at me. "But *this* is your home. Aren't you coming back here?"

"Only to testify against my father. I'm not living here again. This is my old life. I have a new one now."

"In Kansas?"

"Until you graduate, yeah. After that, who knows?"

"So this isn't ending after the summer?" she asks hesitantly.

"I already told you it wasn't."

"But that was Kyle. This is Jonathan."

"Call me whatever name you want. I'm still not letting you go after the summer. We'll get a place close to your college. We could move there now. We don't have to wait. I have plenty of money and I don't have to hide out anymore."

She doesn't say anything. She's thinking something but I can't tell what. Is she still upset that I lied to her? Does she think she can't trust me?

I hope she doesn't tell me she wants time apart to think about things. Because that could lead to us breaking up, and I can't let that happen. She's what's been keeping me going all summer. She's been my hope, my inspiration. Seeing her smile every day, despite the hell her father put her through, has helped me believe I could get through my own personal hell. And I did. I have. Now I'm ready to move forward with the woman I love.

But her silence is making me think she may not want that.

CHAPTER TWENTY-EIGHT

Sage

"You don't want to live with me," Kyle says, sounding disappointed.

He made that assumption because I haven't responded. It's not that I don't want to live with him. I'm just trying to think through everything that's happened today. Just hours ago, I found out Kyle wasn't really Kyle, a writer from California, but Jonathan, who is actually from New York. I don't even know if he's really a writer.

"Is it because of Cain?" he asks. "Because I swear he won't cause any problems. He's a great kid. He'll need time to adjust to the move but—"

"It's not about Cain. I just..." She pauses.

"What?"

"It's all so much to take in. All this time I thought you were just a regular guy but it turns out you had this whole secret life I never knew about. I think I just need some time to process that."

"Sage, I know it's a lot, finding all this out, and I understand if you need time to feel like you can trust me again, but I need you to know I never wanted to lie to you. I just couldn't bring you into this. It was too dangerous."

"Is it still? I mean, what exactly was your dad involved in?"

"He was selling weapons on the black market. Guns, and I don't know what else. I don't know all the details but I know that's how he was making most of his money. His business, the legal one, is an import business. He brings in products from overseas and sells them. He makes good money but not enough to afford this house and his lifestyle."

"I'm sorry, Kyle." She rubs my arm.

"About what?"

"About your dad. You already lost your mom and now you find this out about your dad. And he tried to hurt you. I can't even imagine how that feels. My father stole from me and lied to me but he'd never physically hurt me."

"He wasn't my dad."

"What?"

"My mom had an affair. My dad just told me. It's a long story and I don't want to talk about it right now. I need to accept it first. We're both finding out stuff today and it's a lot to take in."

She nods. "So um...what exactly do you do? I assume you're not a writer?"

"No. I don't really do much of anything. I know that sounds bad but the past couple years I've been trying to figure out what it is I want to do."

"And you never went to college?"

"Actually, I did. I told you I didn't so you wouldn't try to look me up under my fake name to see if I really went there. I only went for three years. I never graduated. I dropped out before my senior year. That's when my mom died. After that I kind of lost my motivation to do anything."

"What'd you study in college?"

"Business, but it really didn't interest me. I just had to pick a degree."

"You could always go back."

"I guess, but I don't know what I'd go back for." He chuckles. "The funny thing is...I did kind of like writing."

"You were actually writing a book? You didn't make that up?"

"I didn't write a book, but I did write a few pages of what happened when I first got to town last May. I wanted to remember it so I wrote it like I was writing a story. The first scene was you driving up beside me on the road."

"Really?" I smile. "Are you sure you want to remember that? We fought that day."

"Only because I was being an ass. But you were sweet. And kind." He leans down and kisses me. "And the most beautiful girl I'd ever seen." He looks in my eyes. "I never want to forget that day. Or any of the days that followed. You made me have faith in people again. You were the light in some very dark days. You helped me get through this, Sage. You didn't know it at the time but you were the only thing keeping me going." He kisses my forehead and brings me into his arms. "I love you, Sage."

"I love you, too."

"I hope you can forgive me for not telling you the truth. If you need time, I understand, but I really don't want to wait to be with you. If you were willing, I'd do as I said before and get us an apartment next to your school. And if you'd let me, I'd pay for you to finish your last semester. You could go back in September. You wouldn't have to wait."

I pull away from him. "Would you go with me?"

"What do you mean?"

"To college. I'm sure you could get admitted. You could finish your last year there."

"I don't really care about finishing. I don't even know what I want to do."

"It's better than sitting around thinking about it. If you take some classes, maybe you'll figure out what you're interested in." I smile. "And going to college together might be fun, although you'll have a lot of girls flirting with you. You'd be the hottest guy on campus."

"It won't matter because I already have someone."

"Would you do it? If you agree to it, I'll let you loan me the money so I can go back in September."

"It's not a loan. I'm giving you the money. I have plenty."

"It's a loan," I say sternly. "I'm paying you back. So will you go or not?"

"I'll think about it. Although the odds would improve if the beautiful woman I'm in love with would agree to share an apartment with me and my sweet, adorable, yet sometimes annoying brother."

"I'll think about it," I say in the same casual tone he used when he said it to me.

"I'm ready." Cain comes bounding down the stairs with Josh close behind. Cain drops his duffle bag next to Kyle and looks up at him. "What about school? Where am I gonna go if we move?"

"We'll figure it out. We've got some time." Kyle musses his hair. "I've missed you, kid."

"Then don't leave again," he says like he's angry.

"I won't. You're stuck with me now." He picks up Cain's duffle bag.

Those two are so sweet together. Just watching them interact, I can see how much Kyle loves his little brother and how much Cain looks up to him. I'd never do anything to separate those two. If I decide to live with Kyle, Cain will definitely be there with us. He's a part of our lives now.

"Car's out front," Josh says. "But we may not have enough room for everyone."

"I've got my rental out back," Hank says as he walks in.

"You should take one of Dad's," Cain says to Kyle. "He's not going to be using them."

"You're right," Kyle says. "Let's take the SUV." He pauses a moment. "You know what? We're going to skip the plane and drive back to Kansas. I'm sick of driving that piece of crap truck. I could use a new vehicle."

"You sure that's okay?" I ask. "It's not yours. You don't want to get in trouble."

"I'll get it transferred to his name." Hank winks at me. "Just because I'm retired doesn't mean I've forgot how the laws work."

"Thanks again for everything you've done," Kyle says to him.

"We still have a lot to do but it'll work out. It always does."

"We'll see you back at the hotel," Josh says to Kyle.

"Yeah, okay."

Josh and Hank head off in their rental cars and Kyle, Cain, and I take the SUV. It's a luxury SUV with soft leather seats and every possible upgrade.

And that house? Wow. It was gorgeous. What a huge change for Kyle to have to leave that and go live in what must've seemed like a shack in comparison. Miller's house is old and small and needs a lot of repairs.

It takes us almost an hour to get back to the city. When we're almost at the hotel, I check the back seat and see that Cain is asleep, his head falling to the side. I look over at Kyle, whose staring out at the road, deep in thought, probably wondering how the hell his life took such an odd and unexpected turn. Living in Kansas? Raising his little brother? His dad headed to prison?

Maybe that's why Kyle and I had such a strong connection when we first met. We both had our lives uprooted and turned upside down from forces outside our control. And the uncertainty and apprehension that resulted from that brought us together, bonded us to each other, made us fall in love.

We've both been through hell, but if we can get through that, we can get through anything.

CHAPTER TWENTY-NINE

Three months later

Sage

"What's for dinner?" Cain asks as he comes into the kitchen. He grabs a chocolate milk from the fridge and shakes the bottle to mix it up.

Kyle and I just got done putting groceries away. It's nice not to have to scrimp on food anymore. I can go to the store and buy whatever I want. Sometimes I feel guilty letting Kyle pay for groceries and all our other bills but when I tell him that, he says we're a couple now and his money is mine. He's always been generous like that, even when we weren't a couple.

"I don't know," Kyle says to his brother. "What are you making us?"

"I can't make dinner. I have homework." Cain takes off for his bedroom.

"Lame excuse!" Kyle yells after him.

I laugh. "What do you think he'd make us?"

"Probably bowls of cereal with marshmallows on top."

"And chocolate milk," I add.

"The kid does love chocolate milk. As soon as we buy it, it's gone."

"I know." I bite my lip. "Although I might've had a bottle or two myself."

"You're the one drinking all the milk?" He pulls me down on his lap and tickles me.

"I'm sorry," I say, laughing. "I'll never do it again."

He stops tickling me and kisses me. "I'll buy you all the chocolate milk you want. And anything else you want."

I sigh. "I wish I had my own money so you wouldn't have to pay for everything."

"Hey, don't start. It's *our* money, not mine. And you're not getting a job. You're going to finish school first."

"You can't tell me what to do," I tease.

"No, but I can kiss you until you break down and agree with me." He does just that, kissing me until I forget all about money and jobs and who's paying for what.

My phone rings and I get off Kyle's lap to answer it. It's my mom.

"Hey, Mom, what's up?"

My mom decided to stay in New York but she moved out of her friend's place and got her own apartment. It's super tiny but she's not there much. She's always in the studio, which she rents out with other artists. She's living her dream. I'm so happy for her.

I'm happy for me too. I'm back in school and so is Kyle, but he's not in college. He's taking some writing classes taught online by some guy who's written like thirty novels. So far, Kyle likes the classes and since they're online, he's able to be home with Cain after school and take him wherever he needs to go.

Cain just turned 13 so he's officially entered his teen years but he hasn't hit a rebellious stage yet. He's a really good kid. He keeps his room clean and does his homework, and for the most part he listens when you tell him to do something. He likes his new school but he's still having a rough time accepting the fact that his dad is a criminal.

Given all the evidence against him, there's a good chance Cain's dad will be convicted and sentenced to many years in prison. That's hard for a kid Cain's age to deal with. It's hard for anyone to find out their father wasn't the person you thought he was. I know that first-hand. I've told Cain my story in hopes that it would bring us closer and it has. Cain feels like a brother to me now. My sometimes annoying, but usually sweet little brother.

"I have some news," my mom says.

"You sold another painting?" I ask. She's selling paintings so fast she can't keep up with the demand.

"Actually, this is about something else." I hear the seriousness in her voice and get concerned.

"What is it?"

"It's about your father."

My chest immediately tightens. I take a breath, trying to remain calm as I prepare for whatever she's about to tell me. I pull out a chair and sit down across from Kyle at the kitchen table.

"What about him?" I ask.

"They found him."

I'm relieved but also worried. I don't want to deal with this again. Being in the news. Being harassed for what he did. I thought it was over. I was finally living a normal life.

"Did they arrest him? Is he back in town?"

Kyle realizes what we're talking about and reaches over for my hand, concern on his face.

"No," my mom says. "He um..." She sighs. "I'm sorry, honey. I hate telling you this."

"Telling me what?"

"Your father...he wasn't alive when they found him. They don't know exactly what happened. They found him on the beach. It happened sometime last week. He'd been living in an apartment in a remote area of Mexico. The police think he'd been drinking and went into the ocean for a swim and drown. I'm sorry, honey. I wish I didn't have to tell you this."

Part of me is shocked but the other part of me isn't. My dad was careless and a risk taker. But I didn't think he'd die. Not yet.

"Honey, say something," my mom says. "How are you feeling?"

"I'm not really, um...I'm not really sure."

"Despite what he did, he was still your father so I know it's hard to hear that he's gone."

"It is, but I'd kind of already accepted he was never coming back. So, in a way, it's like he already died."

Kyle squeezes my hand, mouthing the words, *I'm sorry.*

I nod. "Can I call you later, Mom?"

"Of course. But before you go, I need to tell you something else."

"Go ahead."

"They found some of the money. They think they'll find more if they keep looking. They'll be paying back the people he stole from, as many as they can. That means we'll probably be getting at least some of our money back. But since I've been doing well selling my paintings, I'm going to take whatever money comes back to me and give it to the people he stole from. He spent a lot of the money he took so the authorities will never recover all of it. I want my portion to go to whoever needs to be paid back. Unless you want me to give it to you."

"No. Absolutely not. It's your money and you should decide what to do with it. And I agree with what you're doing. Those people deserve to get their money back. Some of those people gave him everything they had."

"I knew you'd understand. I love you, honey."

"I love you too."

"And tell Kyle I'll be sending him a check to reimburse him for your tuition. The painting I sold last night at the gallery should cover it."

"Really? Mom, that's great. That's a lot of money."

"It was a large painting, but yes, I was shocked when it sold for that much."

"I want to hear all about it. Can I call you tomorrow?"

"Of course. But if you're struggling with the news about your dad, please call me, even if it's the middle of the night."

"I will. Bye, Mom." I end the call.

"Something happened to your dad?"

"Yeah," I say, still shocked by the news. "He's gone. They found his body on a beach in Mexico."

"Come here." Kyle motions me to come over and when I do, he sets me on his lap and hugs me. "I'm sorry."

I let myself cry, because even though he wasn't a great person, he was still my dad and it's sad knowing he's gone and never coming back.

I tell Kyle what happened and how whatever money is found will be returned and how my mom isn't taking her share so that more people can get their money back.

"I'm giving mine back too," I say. "I want to make sure everyone in town gets their money back."

I'm referring to the town we used to live in. Those people weren't always nice to me but that doesn't mean they don't deserve to get back what my dad took from them. What he did was wrong and I want to make it right. That's my memorial to him. My tribute. To fix the damage he caused. To right his wrongs.

"Oh, and you'll be getting your money too," I say. "For my tuition. My mom said on the phone just now that she's sending you a check."

"I'm not cashing it."

"That was our agreement."

"That was *your* agreement, not mine."

"I don't want you paying for college."

"It's one semester. Big deal. And besides, I owe you for all those grilled cheese sandwiches you made me last summer. That alone is worth more than a semester of college tuition."

"And rent? Groceries? And everything else you pay for? It's too much, Kyle."

His expression turns serious. "No amount of money could ever repay you for what you've done for me. You've given me a life again, Sage. Hope for the future. You can't put a price on that."

"I love you," I say, hugging him. "I'm so glad I stopped when I saw you on the side of the road."

"Yeah, about that." He gently pushes me back to look at me. "Don't ever do that again."

"But look what happened because I did."

"Yeah, but it doesn't always turn out this way. Don't you watch horror movies? You never stop for a guy walking on the side of the road. You could get killed."

"You *did* kinda look like a serial killer."

"Then why'd you stop?"

"Because you were also really hot." I smile. "And serial killers aren't usually hot."

He sighs. "Please just promise me you won't do that again. I know you have a huge heart and want to help everyone, but maybe find a different way to help. Like maybe help homeless puppies or little kids who are lost."

I sit up. "Ooh! Can we get a puppy? I've always wanted a dog."

He chuckles. "If that's what it takes to keep you from stopping for guys wandering along the side of the road, then yeah. We can get a dog. Cain would love that. He loves dogs."

Cain and Kyle, my new family. And soon we'll add a dog.

My life has changed so much the past few months and it all started when I stopped to help some sweaty, ornery, not-at-all friendly guy walking his motorcycle along a dusty road.

Kyle's right. I probably shouldn't have stopped, but I had a feeling about him. A feeling that he needed help, and not just with his broken down motorcycle. I had a feeling he needed help in whatever he was struggling with, and at the time, I needed help too.

We ended up helping each other, and along the way, we fell in love.

www.ingramcontent.com/pod-product-compliance
Lightning Source LLC
La Vergne TN
LVHW091028080826
845145LV00002B/394

* 9 7 8 1 9 4 2 7 8 1 1 0 3 *